HIGHLAND CHIEFTAIN

Bethoc gave herself over to Callum's kiss. She hated to admit it, but it was why she had come. She had missed the feel of being in his arms, of the sheer delight she got from kissing him. It was a delight that lingered in her thoughts long after she left his side.

By the time he pulled away she could barely catch her breath and she rested her head against his chest. It pleased her to hear his heart pound and his breathing was also harsh, as if he too was having difficulty.

Callum rubbed her back and Bethoc smiled. It was nice to just lie curled up beside him and be soothed. She did not really need soothing but enjoyed it too much to move. . . .

HIGHLAND CHIEFTAIN

HANNAH HOWELL

ZEBRA BOOKS
KENSINGTON PUBLISHING CORP.

http://www.kensingtonbooks.com

ZEBRA BOOKS are published by

Kensington Publishing Corp.
119 West 40th Street
New York, NY 10018

All Kensington titles, imprints and distributed lines are available at special quantity discounts for bulk purchases for sales promotion, premiums, fund-raising, educational or institutional use.

Special book excerpts or customized printings can also be created to fit specific needs. For details, write or phone the office of the Kensington Sales Manager. Attn.: Sales Department. Kensington Publishing Corp., 119 West 40th Street, New York, NY 10018. Phone: 1-800-221-2647.

Zebra and the Z logo Reg. U.S. Pat. & TM Off.

First Printing: October 2016
ISBN-13: 978-1-4201-3505-3
ISBN-10: 1-4201-3505-8

eISBN-13: 978-1-4201-3506-0
eISBN-10: 1-4201-3506-6

10 9 8 7 6 5 4 3 2 1

Printed in the United States of America

Chapter One

He needed to get his head above the water. Callum struggled upward, every movement sending pain ripping through his body. His lungs were ready to burst by the time he succeeded. Despite the pain dogging him, he took a moment to catch his breath and look around.

The shore appeared to be miles away, although Callum knew that was not true, was just an illusion. He could vaguely recall the men tossing him in. Ignoring his screams, they had taken him by his arms and legs and swung him a few times before letting his body go. Callum knew he was not far from the shore but the pain throbbing in his leg told him it would be a long, hard haul to get there. The water did not ease the pain at all.

Gritting his teeth, he attempted to swim back to the shore. Pain tore through his leg and he bit back a scream, hissing out curses between his clenched teeth. He turned onto his back and let his wounded leg just hang. His arms were not in much better shape but they were not broken and he used them to propel himself along. Very slowly. Then his foot touched the ground, agony tore through his leg, and he floundered. Callum gave out a shaky curse when he settled again. The pain really was too much. He did not think he would reach the shore any longer.

"Sweet *Jesu*," he muttered, lying in the water with a useless leg dangling beneath him.

Just a few more strokes, he told himself. Just a few more and he could collapse on solid ground and think about his next move. Each move he made would have brought a scream if he had not clamped his mouth shut. He did not know what had been done to his leg, aside from breaking it, but he was now determined to have a look. After that, once he was fully recovered from his injuries, he would make the bastards who had done this to him pay dearly.

The moment his hands could reach the bottom without his head going beneath the water, Callum turned and used them to pull himself up onto the bank. He gave up when he was half the way out of the water, his arms folding and dropping him to the ground. A soft grunt escaped him when the side of his face hit a rock but he did not, could not, move. Callum thought about checking his leg to see how bad it was but he was exhausted. He closed his eyes and, even as he wondered where he was, he passed out.

Bethoc Matheson winced and cursed as she walked along, every bruise her father had given her protesting her movements. She suspected that bringing little Margaret was not helping her but the girl needed some time away from the brutality of her father, from the pall of unhappiness that hung over the house. The man grew worse every day. Bethoc dreamed of leaving but there was the problem about where she should go.

She supposed she could hunt down her real father

but had no idea of how to do that. Her mother had given her a name as she had lain dying after birthing little Margaret but the name meant nothing to Bethoc. Nor could she ask anyone since her father's demands and the care of the children kept her tied to the house. These short trips to her cave were all she could allow herself. Even now she felt some guilt about that for the boys were left on their own. She did worry about what could happen if their father came home before she did, but she needed to get away for just a little while. The walls of the house had begun to close in on her, her fears and worries growing too big for her to handle.

"Enough," she muttered as she started up a small hill that led to her hidden cave. "Ye need to cease fretting."

Later. She would think about it all later. What her mother had told her weighed on her, however, and as Margaret grew, requiring less constant care, the need to think grew stronger. Having to call a man Father when he was not also became a problem. She had a feeling he knew and often wondered if that was why he was so brutal, but that thought did not hold. He was brutal to all of them. She even had to protect Margaret and there was no doubt that Margaret was his.

In truth, she began to believe that Margaret was the only one who was. She had six brothers, aged sixteen down to six, yet only one of them looked anything like her father. Yet, if they were not his, how had they come to be with him? She could not recall her mother carrying any of them but knew the shapeless, ragged gown her mother always wore would have hidden it from her. It was possible her mother had borne each of them at night with only their father to help. Yet, after having aided her mother in the birth of

Margaret, Bethoc doubted that. Surely her mother would have said something if the boys were not hers?

Bethoc abruptly stopped, unable to take another step as her mind was flooded by ideas, each one more bizarre than the first. Each one impossible to prove unless her father suddenly felt a need to confess. Yet she could not shake the sudden suspicion that the man she called Father had stolen those babies and brought them to her mother to care for. But why?

Six hard workers, six boys instead of the useless girls he always accused her mother of having. Bethoc stared out over the water. How would her father know her mother could only bear girls? Had there been others and, if so, where were they? Then Bethoc heard her mother's last words as clearly as if the woman stood at her side. "Watch over Margaret. Never leave her. Promise me."

She clasped one sturdy little leg that was dangling at her side. Her mother had been so insistent, so fierce in her demand that Bethoc had sworn to do as asked. As she struggled with these new, terrifying thoughts, she caught sight of something at the water's edge. She squinted as she tried to bring it into clear view and a plump little arm stuck out from beside her head, finger pointing.

"Mon," Margaret said. "Mon."

Releasing Margaret's leg, Bethoc cautiously began to go down to the riverbank. *Mon* was one of the three words Margaret could say and the closer she got to the riverbank, the more certain she was that Margaret was right. The only doubt she had was whether the man was alive or dead.

It was not easy with a child strapped to her back and a bag of supplies at her side, but Bethoc hitched up her skirts, crouched down, and slowly pulled the man the rest of the way out of the water. He groaned when she turned him onto his back and she breathed a sigh of relief. Using one of Margaret's changing cloths while silently praying the child would not need it, she lightly bathed the dirt from his face. Bethoc found herself staring at a very handsome man. An instant later he opened his eyes and stared back. Those eyes were washed out, pain stealing the color from them, but she could still see a strong hint of green.

She also smelled no taint on him. She was not sure what his smell was but it was pleasant and she relaxed. It was a silly thing to be able to do, smell some unknown scent on a person, but it had served her well over the years so she just accepted it. She still wondered why her father had recoiled from it though.

"Who are ye?" he asked.

"Bethoc Matheson. And ye?"

"Sir Callum MacMillan of Whytemont. There were some men . . ." he began as he quickly looked around. Worried that he had drawn her into his trouble.

"No one is here, sir. Just me and Margaret."

"Margaret?"

"Mon! Mon!"

Bethoc sighed and patted her sister's leg. "Aye, Margaret, 'tis a mon."

"Ah, a bonnie wee lass. Greetings, wee Margaret."

Bethoc sought to remain steady as Margaret bounced on her back. "Can ye be moved, sir?"

Callum struggled up until he was seated and slowly shook his head. "Leg is broken. Left one."

She looked at his leg and silently cursed. It was bent wrong, not terribly but enough to prove his words. She cautiously moved to his side and studied it. There was no bone peeking through and she was grateful for that, but she would need to set it and bind it somehow before she could even think of moving him.

Standing up, she looked around and then moved toward a fallen tree, digging a knife out of her bag. Boards would have been better but sturdy sticks would suit for the short distance she had to move him. Picking two thick branches, she cut off the twigs and branches before returning to his side.

"This will hurt, I fear," she said as she braced herself to do what needed to be done.

"I ken it. It cannae be helped. Do ye have anything I can bite on?"

Bethoc took the band of leather from her wrist, the only thing her mother had given her. It was thick and the designs etched on it were simply something she had found attractive. "Will this do?"

Callum studied the Celtic runes on the leather band. "My teeth will no doubt ruin this."

"No more than Margaret's did." She pointed out the marks her sister had left on it. "Her teeth were coming in and I had nothing but this to give her."

"I will try nay to bite through it," he said as he turned it and placed the barest part in his mouth then nodded at her to begin.

She ran her hand over his leg until she found the exact place it had broken; to her relief it felt to be a clear, simple break. She tore three strips of cloth from her petticoat, set them by her side, and reached for his leg. The deep moan he gave as she worked to straighten his leg nearly made her stop, but she closed her ears to his sounds of pain. The bone had to be put back together to heal. She then wrapped the leg tightly to hold the now aligned bone in place better.

Once she had the sticks tied on either side of his leg, she sat back and took a deep breath before looking at him. He was pale and sweating but still conscious. Bethoc was astonished by his stamina as he was a lean man, his muscles clear to see but not bulky. Setting his leg had caused a lot of pain, excruciating pain, yet he clung to consciousness. After a few deep, slow breaths, he appeared more at ease. She hoped it was because most of the pain had now passed.

He looked at his leg and then gave her a smile. "A fine job, Mistress Matheson."

"I thank ye. Now, I fear there is more trouble ahead." She rubbed her hands on her thighs. "I need to get ye somewhere ye can rest and regain your strength in safety."

Callum tensed, not sure he could trust her. "Why would I need to be safe?"

"Sir, I ken weel the marks of a beating nor do I believe ye hurled yourself into the water. A mon who wants to die doesnae struggle as hard as ye obviously did to get to shore. Someone tossed ye in there. Someone broke your leg ere they did so, which means they planned on ye drowning." She lightly touched the marks on his wrists and ankles made by the men holding his struggling body. "Ye dinnae to tell me the why of it, but I *ken* I need to leave ye somewhere safe. That means a wee cave just up the hillside." Bethoc pointed up the hill that ran down to the edge of the water.

Staring where she pointed, Callum grimaced. His leg throbbed with pain and he seriously doubted he could make it even partway up that hill with only one leg. The lass had been a great help but he doubted she could carry him.

"My horse," he said, and looked at her. "Did ye see my horse?"

"Nay, sir, I didnae. Mayhap the ones who did this

took the beast. A good horse would be tempting to steal. It could bring them a good price."

"They wouldnae be able to hold him. Stormcloud is a hard mount to hold on to."

"Stormcloud? A fanciful name."

"It suits him in both look and temperament. Unless they were verra alert, the horse would get away from them, and they didnae strike me as being verra quick-witted. Brutish, aye, and good at what they do, but nay more."

"I shall look for him but first we must get ye to the cave."

"Ah, weel, I was thinking that would be where my horse might be of help."

Bethoc thought a moment on having a look for his horse. She could see nothing in the area, not even the shadow of an animal. She looked back at Sir Callum and sighed.

"I cannae leave ye here as I search, sir. I doubt those who attacked ye will return but one can ne'er be certain and ye are unable to defend yourself. I think it best if we get to somewhere safe first. Aye?"

Callum hated to agree, dreading what needed to be done, but what she said made too much sense to argue with it. "Aye," he agreed, and almost smiled over how sulky he sounded.

"I will find ye a stick to help ye walk. Ye will nay be able to set that foot down just yet." She grimaced. "Probably nay for quite some time."

He watched as she returned to the fallen tree. She was not a big woman but he had no doubt she was strong. She moved easily with a child on her back and whatever was in the pack she carried. What puzzled him was that she spoke well yet her clothes were those of a poor crofter, neat but subtly ragged, signs of many patches easy to see.

The other thing that puzzled him was why she was helping him at all. Most women, especially with a child to watch out for, would have fled, not wishing to risk getting caught in the middle of any trouble. She had stepped right up, dragged him out of the water, and tended his wound. Yet she had to have considered the possibility that his attackers might return. A small raven-haired woman would be no obstacle to them.

Callum used the time she was distracted to indulge in a close inspection of his rescuer. It was not easy to judge her figure when she had a child on her back but he could see that she had a small waist. The way her skirts were bunched up made it impossible to judge the curve of her hips but it did reveal strong, well-shaped legs. He smiled, thinking that few women would see that as a compliment.

It was her face that fascinated him, however. There was gentleness there, a calm that soothed him, and something that reminded him of someone else. Callum puzzled over that for a moment then decided he was too tired and in too much pain to care. He fought the urge to close his eyes and give in to his weariness, to gain some respite from his pain through sleep. She needed him to remain aware for a while longer, he thought, even as he closed his eyes.

Bethoc finally found a thick branch that had a fork at the top. She took the small axe she had brought with her to collect firewood out of her bag and removed the branch from the dying trunk. As she walked back to Sir Callum she hoped it would be the right height. She also wished she had a blanket at hand so she could make a litter for him. Dragging that up to the cave would be a chore, but a lot easier than helping a barely upright, hobbling man.

Once back at his side, she tested the length of the stick, needing to take off only a small bit at the bottom. The man looked to be asleep and she hated to wake him but knew she had to get him hidden away as soon as possible. Kneeling by his side, she gently shook him until his eyes opened.

"We have to try and get to the cave now," she said.

Callum wanted to say no, to just leave him to sleep, but knew she was right. It was not safe to stay out in the open. He did not really think the men would return but he could not be absolutely sure. Careful not to put any weight on his broken leg, he took the stick from her and settled it under his arm. It was awkward, but he suspected it would still work.

"'Tis nay such a long walk to the cave, sir," she said, "but I fear it is nay a smooth one, either."

"Then we had best get started."

"Margaret, sit up," she ordered her sister, and then put his arm around her shoulders plus her arm around his waist. "I will try to pick the smoothest parts of the trail."

"Just pick the quickest," he replied, and gave her a brief smile before adjusting the stick beneath his arm.

"All I ask," she said as they began to move toward the hill, "is that ye tell me if ye think ye are going to stumble for I will be walking close to the edge of the path and could fall."

He made a sound of agreement that was more of a grunt and she knew even the current easy pace they did was paining him. The cave opening was only partway up the hill but she knew it was going to be a long, slow climb for him. Bethoc held him as tightly as she dared, trying to give him as much support as possible, as they began their way up the rocky path to the cave. The fact that she only reached his armpit made that a difficult chore.

It felt as if hours had passed before she got him to the cave. Every step had to be taken carefully and progress was slow. A few times he had nearly stumbled and, although he had warned her as she had asked him to, her heart had leapt into her throat. She could all too easily see herself tumbling down the rocky hillside, a fall that could easily prove fatal.

Carefully propping him up against the rocks at the mouth of the cave, she removed the brush she used to hide the entrance. Not only did it keep her father from finding her hiding place but, she prayed, it also kept her safe from men like those who had beaten Sir Callum. Bethoc helped him inside and settled him on the pallet she had made of old blankets and leaves. The moment she was certain he was simply recovering from the journey, she hurried to pull the brush back into place.

Kneeling by his side, she quickly checked his leg to be certain the bracing sticks and bandages were still in place. Bethoc wished she knew more about broken bones. She had little idea how long he would need to heal. He could be trapped here for weeks. She did not know if she would be able to hide helping him for that long.

"Do ye wish for some food and drink?" she asked as she brushed his hair from his sweaty face, forcing that worry from her mind for she had no choice.

"I suspicion I will soon but dinnae trouble yourself."

"T'would be nay trouble at all." She set down the pack and began to pull out some food, a little surprised at how much she had packed.

Callum almost smiled. "I begin to think ye have one of everything in that pack."

Bethoc felt herself blush and avoided his eyes. She always kept the pack ready, stuffed with all she would need if she could ever make herself desert the others and flee the house. "I try to be prepared." She did not wish him to know that he was hiding in her special secret place, her private haven, if only because he might ask why she felt the need for one.

"Sensible." He struggled to sit up and felt her wrap her arm around him to help.

She carefully set a small plate of bread and cheese on his lap and then poured him a tankard of cider. Sitting back on her heels she watched him eat. His clothes were drying out but they would never return to the obviously fine attire they had once been. Bethoc had to wonder exactly why such a gentleman would be riding around the countryside on his own. Most of the ones of his ilk avoided this area or had a strong, well-trained guard with them. Thieves abounded in the area and the river was frequently used for smuggling. A fine-looking gentleman on what she suspected had been a very fine horse would be too great a temptation to let ride away.

As soon as he was done, she took the plate and tankard, cleaned them off with a rag, and stuck them back in her pack. She turned to help him lie down again, trying not to breathe in his scent too much for it made her stomach clench and she was not sure why. Fighting a blush, she briskly told him where the chamber pot was and then where he could find a little more food and drink if he wanted.

"I need to return home now," she said as she idly straightened her skirts and tried not to resent the loss of the quiet respite she had planned on. She got too few of them. "I will do what I can to find your horse."

"If he gets loose, he will come back here so I wouldnae trouble yourself o'er it too much."

"That would be helpful. Sleep, sir. That is the best of medicines. No salve or potion can do better. I will try verra hard to return on the morrow."

Callum was about to ask her why she was even coming to this place, why she did not just take him to her home, when he realized she was already headed out the opening. He cursed softly and stared up at the stone ceiling. There had been nothing to give him for the pain but he decided that was probably for the best. He was crippled and alone. It would not do to be unconscious as well. He was easy game with his leg broken and saw no point in making himself even easier game by being unconscious.

Why had she not offered to take him to her home? he wondered again. His eyes widened as he suddenly recalled the bruises he had seen. He had assumed they had come from wrestling his body out of the water but now he was not so sure. Now that he was no longer consumed by his own pain and worry about his attackers, he could see the bruises for what they were—the marks of a fist, the injuries of man's hard grip, and the signs of abuse. Bethoc did not take him to her home because someone there was hurting her.

He pushed aside the anger that always filled him with when he recognized such abuse. As Payton was fond of telling him, he could not save the whole world and had to learn to be satisfied with his small part of it. But since she had been so kind to help him, he could not help but worry about her. It was a fruitless exercise though, he thought crossly.

If nothing else, he was in no condition to do anything about it. Nor had she asked him to, although that was no deterrent his rage would heed. When he recovered enough to move around, however, he would find out who had put those bruises on her and why she felt the need to have a hideaway. Then he would see to it that the one who hurt her paid for every bruise on her fair skin.

Chapter Two

Bethoc felt her steps slow as she approached her home. It angered her that her father made her afraid of a place that should have brought her comfort and safety. For as long as she could recall, he had been the darkness in her life, stealing all the joy, and it had gotten worse as she had gotten older. The few glimpses of a good man there had been became less and less seen, buried beneath the bitterness and anger. It was true that he was harder on the boys if they did not do as he said but, with her and even little Margaret, it appeared that his rages had no reason.

She frowned as she neared the door and young Magnus came running up to her. "What is wrong?" she asked quietly.

"He is angry, verra angry, but then he gets all happy again. 'Tis verra odd. I dinnae like it," Magnus said firmly. "And he has a new boy with him, one who doesnae say much."

"A lad? Why does he have a lad with him?"

"Took him, I be thinking. Like he took me."

She opened her mouth, then closed it again, stunned

by what he had said. It was true that she had wondered about it but, to her shame, had never asked. Instead, she had pushed the thought away, not wanting to know where her brothers had come from. Nay, she thought, fighting to be honest with herself, she had been afraid to ask, afraid to know, and, mostly, afraid of asking questions that could anger her father.

That moment of truth brought tears to her eyes but she blinked them away. Now was not the time to bemoan her own cowardice. Bethoc looked at Magnus, noticing how closely he watched her with his dark brown eyes, a color that neither her mother nor father had. That made her even more certain of what a coward she had become.

"And like Bean and Colin," she murmured and Magnus nodded, breaking her heart. "And Liam and Georgie and Gavin." He nodded again, still watching her closely. "Are they all waiting inside?"

"Aye, and being verra quiet. Quiet is good now." He bit his lip. "Some food would be as weel, I think."

Bethoc nodded. "I think ye are right. I had nay realized it had grown so late. Come along then," she said as she took him by the hand. "I had best get on with it."

He smiled briefly and nodded his agreement. Her father's tempers settled some when his belly was full. The moment she stepped into the cottage she felt his glare on her but ignored it as well as she could while she let go of Magnus and removed Margaret from the sling. She set her bag over by her bed, handed Margaret over to Bean, and turned her attention to the making of a stew.

When he stood up, she tensed but fought to keep all of her attention on the preparations of the meal. The man she still called Father was not tall, barely six inches above her own meager height of five foot two and he had gone soft. It could be seen in his expanding belly. Yet he was more than strong enough to do her harm. She had not fully recovered from his last show of temper.

"Where have ye been, lass?" he demanded.

"I was just on a walk, getting some fresh air," she replied.

"Went to see a mon, did ye?"

"Nay. I have seen no mon. Just walked. Checked a few bushes for signs of berries but 'tis too early yet. May put some net over a few to keep the birds away so there will be some ripe ones to harvest." The spoon she held flew from her hand when her father suddenly grabbed her and jerked her around to face him.

"Who is he? Who is the mon ye met?"

This was not good, she thought as she struggled to hide the fear threatening to swamp her. He was furious. She knew he had no idea where she had been or with whom so she did not understand his insistence that she had been meeting with a man. How could she argue with a suspicion he had simply plucked from the air? Bethoc was about to reply when he slapped her. She placed her hand over the spot and stared at him, not sure what to do or say to escape his fury.

"I met no mon, Father. I ken no mon save for the few ye have brought home now and then."

"Tell me who he is!"

"Father, I . . ."

He struck her again and she fell to her knees, dazed. She knew she needed to get up, that she was helpless, yet could not hold that thought in her head long enough to act on it. That last blow had come too close to sending her into unconsciousness. Then he kicked her and she cried out in pain. Before he could kick her again, she was suddenly surrounded by dirty feet. Blinking to clear her vision, she saw that the boys had surrounded her and she feared for them.

"Get out of my way, brats," their father growled. "She has been out with a mon. Rutting like a whore just like her mam."

Bethoc made a noise, a denial she hastily smothered as she struggled to sit up.

"With Margaret along?" asked Bean. "Ye think she could be rutting with a mon with a bairn strapped to her back?"

Bean's words appeared to stun her father as much as they did Bethoc. Not only was Bean ridiculing the man's opinion but he did so in a tone that made it no secret. Fear for him gave her the strength to struggle to her feet.

"Ye watch how ye speak to me, boy."

"We need her to make the food," said Colin, and there was only a hint of scorn in his voice. "She needs to get back to cooking."

Her father grunted but his gaze was narrowed as he studied the boys. She had the feeling he was suddenly thinking too much on how they were growing. Both Bean and Colin would soon tower over him and they were visibly stronger. Bethoc accepted the sad fact that she was going to have to try to plot a safe escape for them as well and probably very soon.

She got to her feet and brushed her skirts clean before returning to the stew. Her face hurt, the skin tightening as the swelling began. She badly wanted to place a cold cloth on it but did not dare. Long ago she had learned that making a fuss over any injury he had inflicted just inspired him to make more and lately the beatings had gotten more vicious. He seemed to take it as some insult that one would actually acknowledge the injury he had done you. One of her back teeth felt loose and she prayed she would not lose it.

As Bethoc served the stew she studied the boys. They watched both her father and her. Their gaze on their father was wary, the one they cast her way now and then was watchful. She knew they were looking for some serious injuries and so she made an effort to hide the many aches and pains she was suffering from. It was not easy although she was accustomed to doing so. Her ribs ached with every move she made but she was as certain as she could be that they were not broken.

The boys watched her father so carefully she feared for them. They were making themselves a threat. He did not appear to notice it yet, but he would. He had already taken note of their size. It would soon matter a lot. He would notice and then there would be trouble, the kind that could get one of them killed. She would have to talk to them soon, let them know she was aware of the truth as well.

She quickly sat down next to Margaret. As she helped her sister eat, she studied the new boy her father had obtained. He was small, perhaps four or five years of age, maybe younger. Big brown eyes, wild, curly reddish hair, and clean, he did not look like a street child. Innocent though he appeared, his presence made Bethoc nervous. This was not some filthy street child he had dragged home. She braced herself to ask who the boy was, knowing that her father did not appreciate questions.

"Who is the lad?" she asked, feeling her stomach knot with fear and hating herself for that.

"An orphan lad," her father replied and she knew he lied.

"His name?" she asked tentatively, hoping that by keeping her voice soft and respectful she would not raise his ire.

"Why do ye want to ken it? What does it matter?"

"Nothing. I but thought it would be convenient."

"It be Cathan. Just Cathan. That be all ye need to ken. He will stay with us now."

Bethoc recognized the little speech. It was the same one he had given with each brother. She could recall it now. Why had she never questioned it? It was plausible except that her father was not a man who did good deeds like taking in orphaned children. They were always boys, too. Boys who were immediately put to work in the fields. Only Bean and Colin had been babies when they had appeared in her life and he had said each one was her brother. Ignorant of such things as childbearing, she had never questioned it.

Suddenly she could barely swallow the stew she was trying to eat to keep herself from asking more questions. She had so many and each one would be a spark to set off her father's temper. A part of her was deeply ashamed that she had never been curious about where the boys came from, her child's mind consumed with the need to avoid her father's fists. Yet, as she had grown older, she should have pressed for answers, should have found the courage to do so. She was one and twenty now yet, instead of demanding answers, she filled her mouth with food she did not want just to avoid asking any questions that might anger the man. Her own cowardice appalled her.

Hiding the fact that she had not finished her meal, Bethoc collected everyone's empty bowl. She listened to the talk of what had been done in the fields today as she cleaned up. Nothing had gone wrong so her father's mood was good as the boys climbed the stairs to the loft where they slept. To her relief, her father then took himself off to the tavern even though it meant there was a good chance he could return drunk. His drinking had also grown worse lately and she suspected it was one of the things that made his temper so uncertain.

As soon as she put Margaret to bed, she moved to the large wooden chest in the corner of the room. The scent of lavender wafted up to her as she began to go through all the clothes stored there to find a small nightshirt. Little Cathan had nothing and she was sure the boys had not thought to give him anything. She finally found one that she suspected would fit, closed the chest, and headed up to the loft.

Bethoc sighed when she found young Cathan huddled under a blanket on a pallet near the wall. She would have to see to a rope-strung cot for him. He stared at her wide-eyed when she sat down near his bed and held out the nightshirt.

"Has Callum come for me?" he asked.

For a moment she could not speak, she was so stunned. How did this child know Sir Callum? "Sir Callum MacMillan?" she asked as she helped him sit up.

Cathan nodded as she took off his shoes, a little surprised that he had kept them on. "Aye. Sir Callum, a great knight and a laird. He saved me from the bad men."

She tugged off his shirt and winced at the bruises on his little body. "Bad men who did this?"

He frowned and touched a bruise over his ribs. "I wouldnae be quiet. I kept yelling for Callum but they were beating him and then threw him in the river." He looked at her with eyes awash in tears. "He is dead, aye?"

"Och, nay. Nay." She slipped on his nightshirt and gently hugged him. "I found him but it must stay a secret. Do ye understand?"

Cathan nodded. "So when will he come to get me?"

"I dinnae ken." She urged him to lie back down and tucked him in. "He needs to heal. He was badly injured."

"But the bad men might take me again."

"Who are these bad men, child?"

"The ones who want me. My papa had some things they wanted but they are mine now."

"What things?"

"Land and coin." He puffed up his skinny chest. "I am a laird, ye ken, and they want all that." Then he looked close to tears. "My *maman* took me to Callum and asked him to help us."

"And your papa?"

"He died but I dinnae want to 'member how, but it was when the bad men came and all the trouble started. *Maman* and I had to hide but we could see. We could see," he added in a whisper, and shivered.

She brushed his red curls off his forehead. "I am sorry, lad."

"Will Callum come for me?" he asked as his eyes started to close. "He has to come for me. *Maman* says he is our champion."

"I am sure he will as soon as he is weel."

Bethoc sat beside him until he was asleep. She did not know what to do. Her father had put them all at risk. The men little Cathan feared could well come after her father. If they came to this house, all of them would be in danger, and these men had shown no hesitation to kill to get what they wanted. She could not believe he would be so foolish. He had to have not known what trouble followed the boy although she could not feel confident about that. Her father often thought himself invincible because of his cleverness.

What had she got herself in the middle of? The minute she thought that, she sighed. All she had done was help someone in trouble and she could not see herself doing anything differently. She could not have left him to drown, or to just lie on the shore unable to move. A soft noise at her side pulled her from her thoughts and she turned to see Bean and Colin flanking her.

"Ye ken this Callum he asks for," said Bean as he sat down.

For a moment she thought about lying, then grimaced. They had closely heard what was said. They were also at risk. It was only fair that she let them know. If nothing else, they should be prepared for the possible arrival of bad men.

"I ken who he is, aye," Bethoc said quietly.

"How? And how do ye ken he is hurt?" Colin asked.

"Because I found him. He was barely on the riverbank, half in the water, half out. And his leg was broken. He had also been severely beaten before being tossed in the river to drown."

Cathan had also been beaten, she thought. If those men came to the house looking for Cathan she did not want to think what they might do to her boys. How could her father have put them all in such danger? She was certain he had some grand scheme to make money but he was ignoring the danger he risked, a risk they now all shared.

"Are ye going to take the laddie to him?" Bean asked.

"Nay yet. It wouldnae do to suddenly have him go missing. Yet he must go soon. I think these men he speaks of would be a great deal of trouble for us." She idly tucked the covers more firmly around the sleeping child. "They were harsh in their handling of him, leaving bruises, and appear to be after some inheritance he has come into. They nearly killed a mon over it. They have already killed his father and frightened his mother into running off. What will they do to us? Nay, I need to be verra careful in what I do next."

"Dinnae forget us," said Colin. "We can help."

"I dinnae wish to tangle ye up in this problem," Bethoc said.

"I think we are tangled up in it now. Father brought the lad here and I think he kenned he wasnae one like us, alone or with no one who would care much if he went missing. Men after the lad dinnae ken that, do they? They may see us and think we are part of it all or ken more than we do. Seems to me they would be seeing us as a means to make Da do what they want."

She wanted to tell him he was wrong but feared he was not. Colin was too clever not to have seen the risk this boy brought with him. Bethoc was reeling from the truths she had learned about her father in the last day. She was having difficulty thinking of any plan, any clear direction to take.

"I wish I had the courage to just demand some answers from the mon," she muttered, and was surprised when Bean patted her on the back.

"Best thing is to speak as little as possible and ne'er ask questions," he said. "'Tis how we all deal with the mon. I think ye need to talk to that fellow Callum. It would help to ken who the men are and how badly they want the boy. If they were willing to kill the mon with him, I suspicion they want the boy verra badly indeed."

"True." She sighed and stood up. "I need to get some sleep and shouldnae leave Margaret alone any longer. It would be best if I sleep on it, decide what to do on the morrow." She looked at Bean and Colin. "And I thank ye for standing for me at supper."

"Time he ceased beating on you," Bean said. "Does it too often and has gotten fierce in the doing of it. Kicking ye like that. He could have broken something."

She was rather surprised that he had not, but simply patted both boys on the shoulder and went down the stairs. Leaving a small lamp lit for her father, she got ready for bed. She had a tiny alcove and needed to share it with her sister. Slipping in as gently as she could so as not to wake her sister, she tucked the child up against her. Then she reached out to unhook the material that hung over the opening and let it fall, enclosing them both in darkness.

Bed was a hiding place. It was just not very secure. Her father had yanked her out of it before. When he was out she would sleep but she always woke when he came back, snapping into full alertness at the sound of the door opening. Then she would lie still, listening as he moved around the room. Just lately he had taken to stopping right outside her alcove and standing there for several minutes. She could feel his stare and it terrified her.

Bethoc had the sick feeling her father was slowly ceasing to think of her as a daughter, one he had openly said was not his, and think of her only as a woman. She feared the night he would take that final step in his thoughts. Tonight, however, his steps indicated he was well into his cups as he came into the house and stumbled his way to his bed. She doubted he had even bothered to take off his clothes. For a long time, there was no sound of movement and then she heard him start to snore.

Little by little she allowed her muscles to relax, surprised at how tense she had grown. He had left the light on. That, too, was becoming common even though it was both wasteful and dangerous. She sighed and, after a moment, slipped out of bed to put out the light.

The man had not even turned his covers down or removed his shoes. He looked as if he had just collapsed on the bed, falling asleep even as he fell. The smell of ale and sweat coming from him was powerful. Even if he had not turned down the covers she was going to have to wash all the linen just to be rid of that smell.

Drink had aged him, she realized. Drink and anger. The lines on his face were many and deep. Bethoc had to wonder what had happened to make him see the world through such a dark veil of disappointment. He always felt cheated somehow, that he was deserving of something greater and had been denied it by fate. She shook her head, snuffed the light, and crawled back into bed. There was nothing to be done to change the man now.

Margaret cuddled up against her, taking her braid and pressing it against her face. Bethoc smiled and patted her back. The children were why she was still at home. Without them, she was sure she would have run after the first beating or when her mother had died for that was when Kerr Matheson's temper had grown out of control. It had become the kind of anger that ignited without warning or even reason.

And why was she still calling him her father? she asked herself crossly. He was not. She knew it for a fact now. Her mother had told her the name of the man who had sired her. It was, perhaps, past time she went looking for the man. Fate could not be so unkind to give her a real father as bad as the one she had now. He might not want anything to do with her, but he could bestir himself enough to find her a safe place—her, Margaret, and the lads.

With that decided, she fought to clear her mind when the drape hiding her bed was thrust aside. She felt panic swell then ebb as she saw, faintly, the shapes of two boys. A moment later, her eyes adjusted to the faint light in the house and she saw Colin holding the hand of a silently weeping Cathan.

"What is wrong?" she asked, and reached for the child who threw himself against her and clung tightly.

"He wouldnae cease weeping." Colin sighed and rubbed his eyes. "It was keeping us all awake."

"What ails ye, Cathan? Do ye hurt?" she asked softly when she realized Colin had spoken in a whisper.

"I am afraid."

"Of what?"

"Everything."

"Ah, poor lad. Do ye want to stay with me and Margaret?"

He nodded and Colin sighed with relief. "Then I will leave him with ye. Good sleep, Bethoc."

The moment he left, Bethoc settled down again. Since she could not hug both children, she curled around Margaret and let Cathan curl up against her back. She was touched when he slipped his arm around her waist and grabbed hold of her hand. If he had told the truth, he had lost too much and been tossed around too often in the last few months.

"It will be fine, Cathan," she whispered.

"Will ye take me to Callum?"

"What I will do is speak with him about ye. Nothing can be done until he heals, ye ken, so ye must be patient. Patient and silent."

"I willnae say anything. I swear."

She prayed that the vow of a small child was one she could put her trust in.

Chapter Three

Callum opened his eyes and fought to catch his breath. Then he realized he was not in the water, not fighting to get to the surface and precious air, and began to calm down. Slowly, he studied his surroundings as his mind cleared and more memories of the day before returned. He attempted to get up and pain shot through his leg. It was then that he remembered everything. The beating, the river, losing Cathan, and the girl who came to his aid. And, most important, his broken and useless leg.

He braced himself and cautiously pushed his body into a seated position. After studying his leg for a moment, he tightened the ties on the sticks bracing his leg. Then he looked around for something to use as a walking stick only to find the one she had cut for him leaning against the cave wall within easy reach. His little savior had thought of everything.

Except how difficult it was going to be to get up from the floor, he mused. Muttering a curse, he inched himself backward until his back was against the wall and he could use it to help pull himself up. The hardest thing to do was to keep all weight off the foot on his broken leg. Taking a deep breath, he grabbed hold of the walking stick and began to move. Once he had relieved himself, he slowly hobbled around the cave. It was a good size and surprisingly well equipped. This cave was being made into a place to live. His rescuer must be planning to leave her home. He wondered if it was because of whoever put those bruises on her.

Finally back at his pallet he began the slow, awkward process of sitting down, which was a bit more painful. A broken leg was a serious problem for him. It ended his search for Cathan and it meant he was stuck in this cave for a long time. He could not even be sure his friends would find him and he was deeply worried about little Cathan. Instinct told him the boy's kinsmen took him in not because they loved him but because they wanted his inheritance. That greed put the child in danger just as it had killed his father. He looked at his bandaged leg and sighed, because he knew he was useless to the child now and would be for a while.

Shifting so that he could sit with his back against the stone, he tried to make plans. There were too many indefinites for that to be a useful exercise, however. After several minutes of useless thinking in circles, his mind centered on the woman who had saved him.

Bethoc Matheson was not hard to think about. She was a pretty little thing. Slim yet curvaceous, long, curly black hair, and wide blue-green eyes. What she also brought was a twinge of recognition yet he was not sure why. He wanted to think on it more as he closed his eyes, feeling tired. Weariness dogged him and he decided he might as well give in to it. If nothing else, a lot of rest was good for healing and he was eager to heal so he could find Cathan and get home.

* * *

It was late and Bethoc cursed as she slipped out of the house, Margaret strapped to her back as always. Her father had been ill in the morning and she had been forced to wait on him hand and foot. It had taken every ounce of willpower she had not to say a word about how his illness was caused by his own drinking. She knew he would have recovered enough to beat her senseless for the remark. He saw any criticism as a lack of respect.

Now it was the middle of the afternoon and he was finally gone. She would only have a short time to visit with Sir Callum before she had to return to make the night's meal. Walking briskly but not so fast she exhausted herself, she hurried toward the cave.

She was almost there when something stopped her. Off to her right was a horse. It was saddled and had saddle packs yet there appeared to be no one around him. Bethoc walked toward the animal, watching closely for any sign that he had an owner nearby. No one appeared and she began to think she had found Sir Callum's horse.

As she reached the animal's side, it looked at her. "Easy, lad. I think I ken where your owner is," she said and she was all too aware of its size and the possible threat.

The horse tossed its head and danced to the side. She continued to speak calmly as she reached for its dangling reins, silently praying it would not think to bite her. Once she grasped them, the animal stilled and she dared to stroke its nose. It was a big, strong, mottled-gray gelding and she knew it would win any argument but the longer she stood gently patting him, talking soothingly, the more it calmed down.

She decided that, even though she did not know if it was Sir Callum's horse, it was obviously lost or cast

aside, so she would take it to the man. When his leg
healed enough to move about more, he would have
need of a horse. This one would do as well as his own.
It took two tugs on the reins before the animal began
to follow her, but once it began it offered no further
resistance.

When she reached the opening of the cave, she released the animal, praying it would stay. To her astonishment, the horse was intent on barging its way
through the brush she was trying to move. She
grabbed its reins the moment she got the brush out of
the way and struggled to pull its head down so it could
get through the opening.

"Sir Callum," she called as she struggled to pull the
animal through the doorway even as it tried to pull free
and race inside.

"Ye found him," Callum said as he blinked awake
from a light doze and was shocked to see Stormcloud.
"Stormcloud, go easy. Easy now, boy."

"He was just standing around. I think he may have
been wandering about the place where he last saw ye
when he got free of the men. Weel, if the men e'en
tried to take him." She went over to where he sat and
set down the basket she had brought with her. "I have
something for ye to eat and drink."

"Thank ye," he said as he watched her lay out cheese,
bread, and cold meat. "Will this nay be missed?"

"Och, nay. One thing we appear to have enough of
is food. We are verra fortunate."

"Aye. So what shall we do with this beast?" he asked,
pushing the horse's face away from his food.

"I fear he will need to be kept here. I dinnae think
we can leave him outside. If there are men looking for
you, the horse could lead them right to you."

"True and I am in nay condition to fight them." He

scowled at his leg. "I willnae be much use for a good long time."

"Nay, a month, or three. We but need to keep ye hidden until then. Or"—she frowned—"until ye can stand putting some weight on that foot. When ye can do that without much pain, ye can do more."

"And when will that happen?"

"I dinnae ken. Six weeks, two months? I fear I havenae had much to do with broken limbs though I learned how to tend them. Colin broke his arm once and we managed but it wasnae a bad break." She combed her fingers through her hair. "I just dinnae ken. I wish I had more knowledge but I dinnae."

"Ye have done a fine job, lass." Cautiously, he reached out a hand to take hold of hers and gently squeezed. "And I heal fast. T'will be fine."

She was startled by how good that gentle hold felt and, disconcerted by that, she stood up, reached for the horse's reins, and pulled him away from Callum. "I will settle him in the rear of the cave. Get this saddle and all off him and wipe him down."

Callum swore as he watched her work. He hated being helpless. What he did notice, however, was how efficiently she worked all the while keeping a close eye on the little girl. Bethoc was obviously accustomed to work, to watching out for the young ones in her family.

She set the girl down and stepped out of the cave to collect some grass and flowers for the horse. Leaving a small pile of flowers next to Margaret, she dropped the rest in front of Stormcloud. Setting a shovel against the wall, she walked back to him.

"Ye need to be careful, nay do anything too quickly," she said as she sat down in front of him.

"I ken it. I will be verra careful and cautious," he promised. "I dinnae wish to slow the healing in any way."

She nodded. "Good. That is good. Now, I need to ken what happened to ye. I mean, I ken ye were beaten and tossed aside, near drowned, but naught much else. Why were ye here? Why did they want to kill ye?"

"Weel, pour me some cider, if ye would be so kind, and I will tell ye what I can recall. I fear some of it may nay be as clear as ye, or I, would like for I was knocked in the head a lot. Aye, and nearly drowning didnae help. Thank ye," he said as he accepted a tankard of cider and had a drink.

Taking a drink gave him some time to order his thoughts. Callum was not sure he should mention the boy. She may have saved his life but he knew nothing about her. He could not be sure he could trust her with such knowledge. It could also bring a lot of trouble to her door.

"There were five of them," he said. "They caught up with me in the clearing down at the base of the trail. I tried to fight them off, even made some progress, but there was a mon I didnae see who swatted me from behind. Once down, weel, it wasnae pretty. They finally broke my leg and tossed me into the river to drown. I dinnae ken what was worse, their laughter or how they grabbed my wounded leg to toss me into the water." Callum shook his head. "I lost consciousness for a wee while but woke in time to claw my way to the surface. They were gone so I made my way to shore where ye found me."

"So, they didnae wait to make certain ye were dead?" she asked softly.

"Nay. None too clever of them, was it? I believe they assumed they had succeeded."

"But what did they want? Your money? Your horse?"

Callum sighed, knowing he was going to have to tell her one of the things he had thought to keep a secret.

"Ye could say they wanted my horse and what it was carrying. A boy. A wee lad I was helping."

Her eyes wide, Bethoc said, "Cathan."

"How did ye ken that?" he asked, afraid he had just made a terrible mistake.

Bethoc was a little surprised by how his voice had gone hard and cold, but decided to ignore it. "Cathan, who is about four, with big brown eyes?"

"Aye, how do ye ken who he is?"

"Because my father has him. Nay!" She grabbed him by the arm when he tried to get to his feet. "He willnae be hurt, nay badly," she added softly, and winced at the look he gave her. "My father takes lads and uses them to care for his crops and animals. He has been doing it for years. With Cathan there are now seven. He must have taken the boy from the men though I cannae see how. Or why."

"He just takes them?"

"I dinnae ken how he obtains them," she replied, frustration tainting her words. "The boys are all too young when they arrive for them to ken either. At least, none has ever said anything about how they came to be there, only that my father had taken them. I only just fully realized it all, ne'er e'en asked how they got there for fear of my father's anger. I have never given it a thought, e'en though I called them all Brother. It shames me to think of how witless I was."

"Ye would have been naught but a child yourself," Callum said quietly.

"In the beginning, but nay always. Yet I still said naught." She sighed and shook her head. "When I was older I should have questioned."

"And what would ye have accomplished?"

She frowned at him. "Weel, I would have kenned the

truth." And been heartily beaten for it but she decided that was not something to tell this man.

"But what would ye have done with it? Sent the lads home? They say they dinnae e'en ken if they have one. Would ye go through the whole village asking people if they had lost a boy?"

"He cannae just snatch up a bairn as he pleases and put them to work for him. 'Tis nay right."

Callum smiled faintly, thinking her quite striking in her outrage. "I ken it and he will, or should be, punished for what he has done."

"I dinnae see how," she said. "If they are naught but boys tossed on the streets, who will care? Aye, he took them but all would say he gave them a home and work. Under his harsh fist. Another thing I did naught about."

Guilt, Callum thought as he fought the urge to stroke her hair. He recognized guilt. He had suffered it often enough. If only for Cathan's sake, he needed to give her some confidence and strength to keep on doing exactly what she had been doing. She had cared for those boys and, he had no doubt, shielded them from her father. He needed to revive that strength.

"Your father beats ye, aye, lass?" he asked quietly. "Ye have the bruises and swelling that comes from some hard slapping. Does it to the boys, too, aye?"

"Aye." Bethoc tried to show the humiliation she felt over confessing that.

He took a deep breath to still his anger and then took a risk, reaching forward to take her hands in his. "Bethoc, look at me," he said quietly, and waited until she did. "Ye are a wee lass. I suspicion ye have lived under the mon's fists all your life and learned as a child that the best way was the quiet way. Dinnae say anything that might make him angry. Dinnae do anything that might stir his temper. Aye?"

Bethoc did not want to admit it. Yet, as she stared into his green eyes, she saw understanding. Glancing down at their joined hands, she finally nodded.

"'Tis nay an excuse though," she muttered.

"Och, 'tis and the best of ones. Children learn the lesson quickly and weel. They learn to be quiet in speech and movement, to do what is ordered quickly, and e'en when to hide. And they often learn to hide verra weel. Dinnae fault yourself for it."

She looked at him. "Ye seem to ken a lot about such things."

He smiled fleetingly. "A bit. I have seen a lot in my time. Now, how many lads has your father got?"

"He is nay my father." She was shocked that she had said that but then realized she had wanted it known.

"Nay your father? Did he take ye as weel?"

"Nay. He married my mother but he is nay my father. She was already carrying me when they wed. I have wondered on that, once I kenned he wasnae my father, for t'was a strange thing for him to do. But when my mother was dying, after she had Margaret, she told me the truth. She made me swear to watch over Margaret and never leave her. She was verra adamant about that." She glanced toward where the little girl sat watching the horse.

"And ye havenae, have ye?"

"Nay, and when I thought on it, weel"—she shrugged—"it gave me some verra dark ideas as to why she would ask that."

He nodded, easily imagining the thoughts she had. "Do ye ken who your father is?"

"What difference does it make? I will find him when 'tis time."

"I may ken who he is."

Bethoc sighed. "She met him at court. They were both rather young, but sixteen. She said he was all any lass could wish for." She rolled her eyes. "But then he had to leave. Had to return home. He gave her a letter in which he put how to find him if she got with child but she lost it. *Maman* was a good woman, verra sweet and all, but I dinnae think she was particularly quick of wit. She remembered his name though. Brett Murray." She saw the shock on his face and prayed it was because he knew the man and not because the man was notorious.

"*Jesu,*" he breathed. "Are ye certain?"

"Aye, she was verra certain too and I heard her correctly. Brett Murray. Ye would think him an angel come to earth if ye had heard her." Bethoc softly cursed. "I fear he may have been her dream."

"Her dream?"

"Exactly. When things are nay as ye wish them to be, ye dream of what ye wish ye could have. I think she dreamed of him."

"Weel, I dinnae ken what he was like when he was young but he is a knight now and newly wed."

"Ah, then mayhap I should leave him be."

"Nay. Murrays are good folk and want to ken about offspring, those begot within and without marriage." He shook his head. "Ye have told me now and I couldnae possibly keep it a secret from him."

"Ye ken him weel then."

"He is the brother of my foster father, Sir Payton Murray." He looked toward where Margaret sat idly holding up flowers for Stormcloud to munch on. "He could be of great help."

"I am nay looking for his help."

The stiffness in her body matched her tone and he inwardly grimaced. He had been reluctant to tell her much; not at all sure he could trust her. What he had told her was more than enough but he was beginning to feel guilty about holding back. Her response to the idea of gaining any aid from her true father made him feel even more guilty.

"Then dinnae ask," he said, "although I suspicion he will offer when he kens what ye are dealing with."

"Oh. He wouldnae like my da, aye?"

"Aye. No Murray would allow such treatment of women and children."

That sounded impossible to Bethoc but she said nothing. She had rather thought that what she lived with was not unusual, perhaps only a bit harsher than was normal and that harshness had grown as the drinking had gotten worse. The few men she had seen in her life were all much akin to her father: rough and loud with a quickly roused temper and a love of drink.

"I must think on it all," she said as Margaret hurried over to them. "It is nay just me that I must consider."

"Mon," said Margaret, and toddled over to Callum who tensed as she drew near his wounded leg.

"Nay, Margaret," Bethoc said, and caught the child. She pulled her close and pointed at the bandages on Callum's leg. "He has an ouch there. See?" The little girl nodded. "So if ye wish to say hello, go to the other side. Dinnae go near the ouch. Dinnae touch it. Do ye understand?"

"Aye." When Margaret wriggled free of Bethoc's hold she walked a wide circle around Callum to come up on his wounded side. "Nay ouch."

Callum laughed. "Verra true. There is nay ouch

there." He was startled when she straddled his good leg and carefully sat down.

Bethoc was shocked. Margaret had shown no hesitation in approaching the man. She had never shown such easiness around men.

"What is it?" asked Callum when he saw the way Bethoc was staring at the child who was chattering incomprehensibly about the flower she held.

"She has ne'er done such as this. 'Tis as if she has kenned ye forever."

He shrugged. "The bairns tend to like me."

"She has e'en started to be shy around Colin and Bean and they are but sixteen and fourteen. I am trying to make her see there is no need, nay with them."

"Because of your father?"

"Aye."

"Children can often sense that sort of darkness in a mon."

"Colin and Bean would ne'er hurt her."

"Which is why she is only shy around them and nay afraid." Callum sighed. "'Tis how I kenned I could trust Payton. Moira, a wee lass who was one of us, had no fear at all of the mon. None."

"And ye needed to ken that."

"Oh, aye, I needed that." He laughed when Margaret held the flower against his nose and then he took a deep sniff. "Verra nice. Verra pretty."

Bethoc watched them for a little while, her sister babbling away, and Callum patiently responding. He had a way with children. There was a kindness in him she could not ignore but she knew she had to, should not place too much worth on it. She hated to end it but she had to get back home. Fortunately, Margaret only protested a little when she picked her up.

"I am nay sure when I can return, which is why I

brought ye so much food," she said as she settled Margaret on her back. "My father noticed I was gone last time. He accused me of meeting with a mon."

"Weel, ye are," Callum said, and returned her brief smile.

"Nay as he thinks. I will return before ye have need of more food, even if it is only to dash in and leave some. Rest, Sir Callum."

"'Tis about all I do," he grumbled.

"Because 'tis the best medicine."

Then she was gone and Callum sighed as he leaned against the wall. It was going to be a very long few weeks. He worried about Cathan but knew he could do nothing about the boy, and all his instincts told him the boy was in good hands. Despite her father's tendency to hit, the boy was still safer where he was than trapped in a cave with a crippled man.

He glared down at his leg. Despite what Bethoc said, he was sure he would be useless for a few months at least. It was a wretched time for such an injury. Callum shut his eyes and sighed. He would have to put his faith in Bethoc. She was the only thing that kept him alive. Since he did not think that was much to count on, he also prayed his friends would find him soon. He was going to need their help.

Chapter Four

"Where is the food?" demanded her father as he marched into the house followed by the boys.

"Near to ready," said Bethoc as she turned to the meat on the spit.

"Damn weel should be," he grumbled as he moved to clean up, all the boys waiting patiently as he used the water first.

A flash of anger went through her but she forced it down. He had no right to complain about the meals, the timing or the quality. That made no difference to him, however. Criticizing was what he did best.

Bethoc looked at the boys. They all wore the tight, blank expressions she knew hid strong emotions. Cathan looked as if he fought tears but she saw no visible bruises on him and suspected the boy was just not accustomed to such constant tension and alarm. Her father needed to be more careful, however. He was losing his workforce but she doubted he took much notice.

By the time everyone was seated, and after her father had taken his share first, they began to eat. Bethoc was wondering how he could not sense the anger the boys were holding in. She could and could barely eat because of it. Something had happened and she wished she had the freedom, and courage, to just demand to know what was wrong.

Kerr Matheson was pushing too hard, she thought. The boys had never been so unified in their anger. She was going to need to have a talk with them, she decided. They were still too young, too weak, to go up against the man. Bethoc did not even want to think of what would be the result of such a confrontation. They were also too young to just leave and face the world.

There was no talk over dinner and that was different. It could be because he had been in the fields with the boys but she suspected it was because the boys were intent on being silent. Her stomach was tied up in knots as she waited for something to happen, for the confrontation that was so obviously brewing. She prayed her father was not in the mood for a fight. He ended that hope with his next words.

"Are ye going to sulk for the whole night?" Kerr asked, his attention still on his food.

"Ye destroyed weeks of work," Colin burst out.

"Ye shouldnae have wasted precious time on planting berry bushes."

"Food is ne'er a waste of time."

She could not fully stop herself from jumping when her father lunged across the table and grabbed Colin by the front of his shirt. It was immediately followed by a hard slap to the boy's face. Bethoc could see Colin clenching his fists repeatedly as their father threw himself back into his seat.

"Ye best watch what ye say, boy. Show some respect."

"To what? Ye throwing a fit and ripping out weeks of work? For nay reason at all!"

Bethoc whispered a protest but no one paid her any

heed as her father rose from his seat, grabbed Colin, and dragged him across the table. The way the man set on the boy alarmed her. Colin got in a few good blows but one good punch to the head ended his fight. It did not stop her father, though. She raced to the man, grabbed him by the shoulders, and tried to pull him off Colin.

"I told ye to ne'er dig there. Ye wouldnae listen. Ye ne'er listen. Dinnae dig there!"

The boys ran to help her. Finally her father stood up. He shook himself, grabbed his cloak and hat, and walked out. Bethoc looked down at Colin and had to choke back a sob. He was a mess. Her father had never beaten Colin like this before. Instructing the boys to move him onto Kerr's bed, she rushed to get what she would need to treat his wounds.

By the time she had bathed and bandaged his injuries, Colin was awake. "Why? Ye ken how he is. Why goad him? Why let him see how ye feel?"

"We worked so hard on those bushes but ne'er once neglected our other work. I couldnae see the harm." He winced as he tried to move. "The mon took one look and went mad. Ripped the whole lot up, screaming at us the whole time."

"That makes no sense."

"Nay, it doesnae, does it. He has ne'er cared what we plant, ne'er done more than look and grunt. But, though he never gave us any compliment, he didnae complain, either." Colin struggled to get up and Bethoc helped him, the other boys staying close by him once he was on his feet.

"Ye should go to bed, Colin," she advised as, with Bean's help, he started out the door.

"Nay, he is hiding something and I mean to find out what." There was a mutter of agreement from the other boys and Bethoc quickly picked up Margaret and followed them.

It was a short walk to the field the boys worked but Colin was pale and sweating when they reached the place. It was a small field, not one they used for their crops that went to market, but mostly for a kitchen garden. She looked at the bushes tossed carelessly in a pile as if readied for burning. It was a waste and she could not understand Kerr Matheson's actions. Then, as she thought back on what she had wondered about her mother and why the woman had never had any other children until Margaret, she felt a chill. Suddenly she was terrified of what they might find.

Colin was settled against a tree as she sat beside him while the boys dug around. She felt her stomach tighten with every shovelful of dirt tossed to the side. Colin was right. Kerr was hiding something and they did have a right to know. She just feared it was going to be bad.

"Bethoc, what do ye think we will find?" Colin asked.

"I dinnae ken," she replied.

"Och, aye, ye do. Ye are like a cat sitting on a wasp waiting for the sting."

"Babies," she whispered. "I was thinking the other day how odd it was that my mother had no bairns for near to twenty years."

"*Jesu.*" He ignored Bethoc's muttered scold for his language. "'Tis a possibility. Lassies, I would wager. He ne'er had a use for lassies."

"Aye, 'tis what I thought."

"The bastard. I ne'er saw it. Ne'er saw your mother with child or birthing one until this little wretch." He tickled Margaret's foot.

"Hey, Colin, I found something," called Liam, his freckled face pale with alarm.

"What is it?" asked Colin.

"Something wrapped in a rotting blanket."

Colin clasped Bethoc's hand when she made a small sound of distress. "Put it aside and keep digging." He looked at Bethoc. "We have to ken, Bethoc."

"And when we ken what do we do about it?"

"That I dinnae ken. I am just certain *we* need to ken what he has done. For our own sake. For our own safety. We have to ken what he is capable of."

By the time the boys were finished they had found four little bodies. Bethoc wept silently as she looked at each one. No wonder her mother had become more and more lost in her dreams. She had lost so much. It was why she had made Bethoc promise to never leave Margaret. She knew at least some of these babies had been killed. Knew it without a doubt yet there was nothing she could do about it. All her father had to do was swear they were born dead. She had no power, neither did the boys, and all they had was bones.

Once the babies were reburied next to her mother's grave, they all moved silently back into the house. After Colin was helped into his bed, Bethoc had the strong urge to go see Callum. She did not know why, only that she had a need to be with him, mayhap even to speak of the bairns. It was still light enough but it had been three days since she had seen him. It was an urge she really did not understand but she decided to give in to it.

Before she thought on it too much, she packed up Margaret and a basket full of food and set out. It would not be long before the sun began to sink in the sky but she felt she had time enough. She paused to study the berry bushes near the bottom of the hill. They were nearing ripeness so she set down her basket and pulled some netting out of her bag to drape each bush in the hope of saving at least some berries from the birds. It was just as she was about to pick up her basket and head to the path leading to the cave that she knew she was no longer alone.

Afraid, she turned to survey the clearing. Her heart leapt with fear as she saw five men ride into the clearing. They had already seen her and were heading straight for her. She waited, for every instinct told her that running would be a mistake.

The man in the lead stopped and studied her for a moment before speaking. "Mistress, we are searching for someone. A mon. Our friend became separated from us and we are trying to find him, fearing he may be hurt."

It was well said, but Bethoc did not believe a word of it. "I have seen no one."

"No one?"

"Nay, no one." She took a step back when he dismounted for his smell was bad and not from his unwashed state. "I came here to try and protect the berries that are so near to ripening." She waved toward the bushes.

"What is in the bag?"

His voice, she noticed, was getting colder and harder. "Weel, it held the nets I needed and now all it holds are the things Margaret may need," she replied, finding it very easy to lie to him and trying hard not to glance to where she had set the basket of food just behind one of the bushes while she had arranged the nets. "'Tis Margaret's bag."

He reached for the bag but Margaret's hand grabbed it first. Once declared hers, the child would never let it go. To her surprise Margaret screeched. The man jerked back, releasing the bag as he stared at Margaret. A peek at her sister revealed Margaret's sweet face pressed into a fierce scowl, her bottom lip pushed out. Bethoc had to bite the inside of her cheek to keep herself from laughing.

"Make her let go of the bag," he ordered.

Worried they might do something to Margaret, she reached for the bag handles. Margaret clutched the bag as close as she could and growled. It was hard not to laugh. She struggled with Margaret until the men waiting on their horses started laughing.

"Och, leave it with the brat." The man glared at Bethoc. "Ye are certain ye havenae seen any mon wandering about?" Bethoc shook her head. "Fine," he grumbled as he remounted and scowled at Margaret. "Little brat. *Jesu*," he yelled when Margaret screeched at him.

Bethoc watched them leave then glanced back at Margaret. "Weel done, my clever lass," she said, and kissed her on the forehead.

Margaret bounced and Bethoc fought to keep her balance. She fought with the child for a moment to loosen the bag from her little hands. Then she had a good look around and saw no one, nor did she hear their horses. Deciding she needed to move quickly, she grabbed her basket, hurried up the path, and moved just enough brush to slip into the cave, yanking the brush back in place.

"Greetings, Mistress Matheson," Callum said, biting back a smile, but he quickly grew serious when he saw her face more clearly. There was the hint of fear there. "Is anything wrong?"

She unhooked Margaret and set her down then kissed her on the forehead again. "Smart lass." She looked at Callum and felt something inside her ease a little. "I believe I just met your attackers." A shiver went through her even though the men had not threatened her.

He sat up quickly. "Are ye all right?"

"Oh, aye. They asked about ye. Said they were looking for a lost friend and feared he may have been hurt. Wanted to look in my bag."

Margaret walked over to Callum, bent over a little, and shoved her forehead close to his mouth, pointing at it. "What is this?" he asked.

"Ah, I think she expects ye to say 'smart lass' and kiss her forehead." She laughed when he did so and Margaret walked away looking very pleased with herself only to grab the bag and drag it with her when she went to sit and watch the horse.

"Why did I just do that?" he asked.

"Because when he tried to grab the bag, she would nay let him have it. Screeched at him. Held on tight, too. Ye see, I called it Margaret's bag. No one was going to get hold of it after that." Bethoc sat down next to him and began to unpack the food. "It wasnae until he tried to get the bag that I feared I might have put Margaret in danger but they really were nay interested in us once I couldnae tell them anything about ye."

"That was it? Ye said it was hers?"

"All it needed. If Margaret hears ye say something is hers, she grabs it and 'tis verra, verra hard to get it back. She is a wee bit possessive about what is hers. I think I shall have to do something about that. 'Tis nay a good thing but it was useful this time."

Callum could not help it, he started to laugh. "Defeated by a two-year-old?"

"I suspicion a lot of people have been," said Bethoc, smiling faintly.

He laughed even harder. "Och aye."

It was a few minutes before he could calm down. "Did they nay ask about the food?"

"Nay, I had put the basket down behind a bush for I

needed to cover the bushes with netting and it was getting in the way. It was nicely out of sight. But it does mean they are still lurking about the place. That cannae be safe for ye."

"I am as safe here as I would be anywhere. Dinnae worry on it."

"There are five of them and none of them have a broken leg."

"True but they have to find the cave."

"I ken it. I will be sure to hide my trail when I leave."

He put his arm around her and tugged her close, kissing her forehead. She blushed but also smiled. "Are ye going to call me 'smart lass' now?"

"And so ye are." He tipped her face up to his. "Ye also worry far too much about what happens to everyone but ye." Keeping an eye out for any sign of rejection, he gave in to the temptation he had fought for days and kissed her.

Bethoc felt the warmth of his mouth on hers flood her body. She wrapped her arms around his neck and held on tightly. Although she had gained a tiny bit of knowledge about kisses, she had never known they could make one feel so warm and needy. When he nudged his tongue into her mouth, she was startled but that surprise lasted only a moment. The feel of his tongue stroking inside her mouth caused a delicious tightening in her belly. Her heart pounded and she had the urge to crawl up in his lap, to get as close to him as she could possibly get.

She also smelled cinnamon. It was a heady smell that filled her lungs and warmed her. She realized it came from his desire and that was a heady knowledge. When he left her, his mouth moving to her neck, she sighed for that smell began to fade.

"That was, mayhap, nay the smartest thing I have

done," he said as he lifted his head to look at her, catching a look of embarrassment suddenly sweep over her. "Because," he said quickly, "I have a broken leg." He was relieved when she suddenly looked confused.

"I am nay touching it," she murmured.

"Lass, kissing leads to more and I am in no state to do anything more." He grinned when she blushed.

Bethoc pulled away from him. "I ne'er, I mean I wasnae expecting . . ." She shut up when he gave her a quick hard kiss.

"I rather suspicioned that. I was but referring to me and what I was feeling."

She was not entirely sure what he meant but did not want to say so. It would also explain his scent. What occurred between men and women was a bit of a mystery to her. She knew of desire but not of what it entailed or what was done about it. It was enough to know the ending of the kiss was nothing to do with her, or, worse, how she kissed. She rather hoped she did well enough that he would wish to do it again soon.

"I had best leave as it must be near sunset by now." She stood up and brushed down her skirts. "'Tis nay a good idea to be caught out after dark when ye are near the river."

"I have heard a few things at night. Feared it was the men who had attacked me but the sounds never left the river."

"Aye, smugglers most like." She shrugged. "I am nay sure what some of them are doing but I suspicion most of it is illegal."

"True enough. Mayhap e'en some poaching. Be careful, Bethoc, and nay just because it would be awkward if I didnae have your help any longer." He grabbed her hand and kissed it.

Bethoc was just wondering what he would do if she

flung herself in his arms and asked for another kiss when Margaret suddenly ran up to him and stuck out her hand. Laughing when she gave it a little shake, Callum gently kissed the child's hand. As she picked up Margaret Bethoc shook her head.

"Weel, are ye nay the little flirt," she said as she put Margaret in the sling and settled her on her back.

Callum dragged himself to his feet and followed them to the opening. He leaned against the rock and watched them as they left, then did a quick survey of the area before ducking back inside and putting the covering over the opening. He hated the fact that he could not escort her home. He suspected soon he could manage such a walk, slowly, but his leg would ensure he could offer little help if an attack came. The only thing that would be served was his pride.

Moving back to his pallet, he grimaced. Sitting and doing nothing was beginning to drive him mad. He was going to have to think of something to keep himself busy. Glancing at his rough, unadorned walking stick, he smiled. No need for a man not to decorate the tools he used. He pulled out a knife from his pocket, grabbed the stick, and began to work.

Bethoc slipped into the house and breathed a sigh of relief. Kerr was not at home. She was not sure where he was or what he was doing except drinking when he spent so much time in the village, but life was easier with his absence. Putting away the basket, and her cloak, she went looking for Margaret who had only just been set down. She found the little girl sitting beneath the tree with Cathan. She went and sat down with them.

"Are ye done for the day then, Cathan?" Bethoc asked.

"Aye," he muttered.

"Ouch," said Margaret, and grabbed his hand, ignoring his attempts to get it free as she showed it to Bethoc.

"'Tis all right. Colin tended it."

Seeing the bandage and smelling the herbal scent of the cream she put on such injuries, she had to nod. He had done well, which told her he watched every time she tended their injuries. She took Cathan's hand in hers and carefully examined the whole thing before letting go.

"Aye, he did a verra fine job as weel. I will change the bandage after we sup."

"I dinnae ken why he made me come sit here. I can still work with this hand."

Bethoc looked at the hand he held up and winced as it was filthy. "Nay, ye cannae and that is that."

Cathan looked at his hand and frowned. "It is nay hurt so I can."

"It is dirty. If ye get any dirt on your hurt hand it could be bad."

"Why?"

"I really dinnae ken but I do ken that clean is better. Mayhap ye can come in, wash that hand, and give me some help with the meal."

He did not look very happy about it, but he followed her inside along with Margaret. She started another stew using the meat left from the other night. Soon, as she fell into the rhythm of preparing the meal, her thoughts began to wander.

Thinking of Callum brought a flush to her cheeks. She knew she should not allow him to kiss her but she also knew she could not wait for him to do so again. He was a handsome fellow and there was a kindness in him that was hard to resist. So hard, she knew she would be slipping back there as soon as she could.

She wondered if this was what her mother had felt. If so, it was rather easy to see how she could have become lost in dreams as her real life had worsened. Bethoc just wished the woman had had the strength to recall that there were children around her that needed help. She knew she never would, never could, forget.

The boys sat at the table once they had washed up. Her father had arrived and was sullenly drinking ale. Bethoc always got tense when she saw him drinking as she could never be sure what might stir his anger then. The boys watched him carefully as they waited for their meal. It was evident that they understood the danger that came with Kerr drinking.

It occurred to Bethoc that this was how all their mealtimes went. There were times when it was better but they grew fewer and fewer as time slipped by. She wondered what it would be like to simply sit and have a meal filled with talk, laughter, and good companionship. It would be wondrous, she thought. Perhaps, if she was very fortunate, she would have that.

If she married, she thought, and suddenly frowned. She was more than old enough to be married yet her father had never made an effort to match her up with anyone. While she was pleased he had not done so with the friends he occasionally brought round, it was curious. It could have brought him some money as some men were more than ready to pay for a young wife. It was odd that her father, who was always on the hunt for a way to get money without working for it, would not think to use his own daughter. She doubted she would make him rich but she was sure she would add a fair number of coins to his purse.

Shaking away such thoughts, she began to serve the

food. As she sat down to eat and help young Margaret eat her food, she wondered about asking her father why he had not seen to her marriage. Just as quickly she decided not to say a word. Now that she had met Callum, even if he was not the man for her, she could not envision marrying anyone her father picked out. It was better if he never had a thought about it, she decided, and shook away the faint image of Callum that still lingered in her mind.

Chapter Five

"I will watch Margaret for ye if ye are eager to get out," said Colin as he stepped up beside her in the doorway.

Bethoc turned from watching Kerr disappear down the road and looked at Colin. He was badly bruised, even after a week of healing, but the swelling had gone down a bit. It would be a long time before he completely healed and she was still concerned about the bad bruise on his temple. It was also a wonder that nothing had been broken.

It had been a very long week since she had seen Callum and she truly missed him. She had not been able to do more than hastily deliver some food to him and then hurry back home. It seemed odd to her that she should be feeling such a need to see the man. He was very handsome with his dark red hair and green eyes, and grew more so as each bruise faded away. But all they had done was talk some as she had tended to his injuries. Even that kiss was but one time. It seemed hardly enough to cause her such a need to go and see him.

"Nay, Colin, I cannae leave Margaret," she said, not able to hide all her reluctance. "I promised my mother

I would ne'er leave her." At times that promise felt like a chain around her neck but then she would feel guilty for having such a thought for she adored Margaret.

"And we ken why now, didnae we? He got rid of them. Probably brought her one of us to make up for it. But I doubt she meant for ye to keep her attached to your side as ye do."

"Odd though it is, I believe she did."

"Ye want to go and see your mon."

"Colin! I dinnae have a mon."

He laughed. "Och, aye, ye do, though I dinnae ken why ye are keeping him in a cave."

She gaped at him. "What cave?" she asked weakly.

"Do ye really think we would let ye just wander off all the time? Nay. We followed. After the first time it was always just me or Bean. Did think we might have to do something when those men approached you." He grinned. "But our wee Margaret put on a fine show, didnae she. I wouldnae have wanted to touch a child who could screech like that either. Sounded possessed."

"Aye, she did weel. Ye have always kenned where I have gone?"

"Always."

She slowly sat down in the doorway. A moment later, Colin sat down beside her. Bethoc did not know what to say or do. The cave had been her secret place for so long. It had been what she loved about it, the fact that it was her place and no one knew where she was. She had been slowly making it more comfortable, more livable. She did not know what she should do now that she realized it had not been much of a secret at all. And what should she do about Callum? He needed to be hidden. It was alarming to know that he was not.

"Does Kerr ken?" she asked quietly, suspecting her father could make money by telling the men where

Callum was and that would be too sore a temptation for him to resist.

"Nay. Why would we e'er tell him?" Colin shook his head. "Ye dinnae need to look so afraid. We would ne'er let him find out. And I dinnae think *he* believes any of us go anywhere. If we had somewhere to go the whole lot of us could have left by now. I think he believes his fists are enough to hold us. Fool. 'Tis just that we have naught else and whether we like to admit it or nay, we are all too young to be just out on the street. Hard to get a bed or food. Also ye are easy prey for any mon who wants to beat on something or the like."

Bethoc thought about that for a moment and nodded. Kerr felt he had them all cowed, that they would never leave because they were afraid of what he would do once he caught them again. He believed they had built their own cages and kept them filled with a bed and just enough food to make them stay. It was also a trap she had no idea of how to escape.

She sighed as Margaret toddled up and sat on her lap. The little girl handed her a brush and then sat up very straight. Bethoc decided she had just been given a chore.

"Fix," said Margaret.

"Demanding wee thing, arenae ye?" teased Colin as he tickled her and she squealed with laughter. "Ye should be talking by now, pet. Ye dinnae think she is a wee bit . . ."

Brushing Margaret's wild curls, ones so much like their mother's or her own, Bethoc said before he could finish his sentence, "Nay. I think wee Margaret just doesnae say a word until she is sure she can say it exactly as she hears it and ye can understand her, until she has it just right. And I was told that children raised in a house like this quickly learn the value of being verra, verra quiet. That could be part of it."

Colin nodded. "Aye. Wish I had remembered that lesson the other night. I was just too angry to think. Even as the words leapt from my mouth, I was telling myself to hush." He laughed bitterly. "Truly wish I had listened to that voice."

"I have a bad feeling he actually could have killed you. He has ne'er done ye like that before."

"He was trying and, aye, he wasnae quite sane. 'Tis because he feared what we might find. Found it anyway though, didnae we." He shook his head. "We buried the bairns next to Mother and then wrote on a stone and set it over the grave. He saw the stone, too. Now he kens we found them. If he hadnae lost his mind, we ne'er would have. Put the bushes back in as weel. Some are a wee bit sad, but I think they will recover. Then ye willnae have to walk all over the countryside to get some berries."

She thought of what the boys had painstakingly etched into the stone. *Four angels laid to rest with their mother at last. May she hold them in her arms forever.* It brought tears to her eyes, even though she scolded herself for being so sentimental. Despite Kerr Matheson's brutality, her boys were growing up to be good men. She prayed she could soon find them something better than being Kerr's workers or something he could punch when the anger in him got too much to hold in. They deserved a much better life than that.

"Thank ye, although I ne'er minded. I was so afraid when he saw that stone, too, but he hasnae done a thing," she said in wonder.

"Dinnae think he will," Colin replied. "He needs us to work his fields. Needs ye to cook and clean. Knock the life out of any of us now and he loses his whole kingdom.

I dinnae think he worries about any of us at the moment. What I want to ken is, what is he watching for?"

"What do ye mean?"

"I have followed him into the village."

"How do I keep missing all this sneaking about ye are doing?"

"Because I am verra good at it?" He grinned, then said seriously, "He stays to the shadows and is always looking around. E'en when he goes into the tavern. He sits in a shadowy corner, drinks, and watches everyone."

"Ye went into the tavern?"

"Aye, they dinnae pay attention. Da didnae either. Too busy watching his own back."

"It sounds as if he fears some trouble is headed his way."

Colin grunted softly. "A lot of it, I am thinking. Nay sure he kens how to escape it either. He asked me yester eve if me and the lads had a good place to hide. I said, 'Aye,' even as I tried to think of a way to nay tell him where it is or then wondered if I should. He didnae e'en ask. Just told me, 'Run for it when the trouble comes.' Then he left. Didnae give me a chance to ask what he was talking about."

"He ne'er asked me that," Bethoc said, and realized she was not surprised that Kerr gave no thought to the safety of his daughters.

"I ken it. Was getting madder and madder about that but now ye ken. Ye and Margaret will run with us. Ye may as weel. We mean to go to your cave and hide."

"Huh. Silly of me to think I had a wondrous secret place to go to."

He laughed, stood up, and picked up Margaret with barely a wince, which she saw as a good sign. "Go. I will keep her with me and ne'er let her out of my sight. Go on now. Your mon probably needs some food by now."

"He is nay my mon!" she said but Colin just laughed.

Bethoc stood for a whole minute before she gave up trying to resist the urge to run to the cave. It was clear to see that whatever shyness Margaret had suffered from had vanished and the child was happy to be with Colin. She went and gathered up some food, putting as much as she could spare into the basket and bag in case she could not get out of the house again for a while. With a last look to make sure everyone was where they were supposed to be, she headed out. This time she kept a close eye out for any sign of the men looking for Callum. She was especially careful as she entered the clearing.

Deciding it was all clear she hurried up the path to the cave. As she moved the brush, she frowned. Someone else had moved it. A tickle of fear entered her heart and she hurried inside. Callum sat on his pallet and smiled at her.

"Ah, ye are here," she said, then blushed and turned to put the brush back in place.

"Aye. Where did ye think I might be?" he asked, still smiling.

She went over and sat down in front of him. "For a moment, I feared someone had found ye. I saw that the brush had been moved."

"Ah. Nay. I emptied the slop buckets and cleaned up after Stormcloud."

"I have brought ye more food. I am sorry I havenae been here much. Colin was"—she hesitated—"ill."

He grasped her hands, stopping her fussing about with the food. "Tell me what happened. That time ye did run in before, I could sense something had happened, but ye gave me no time to ask. What has happened, Bethoc?"

"My mother had more babies," she burst out, and then took a few steadying breaths. "Four over the years. The boys were planting some bushes and Kerr went mad. Truly mad. He tore them all up, screaming all the while, and when Colin complained, he beat him. If we hadnae all pulled him off I fear he would have killed Colin. I have ne'er seen him so maddened."

"Over bushes?"

She suddenly stood up, tearing her hands free, and began to pace. "It wasnae the bushes. It was where they were digging. I always wondered how my mother could go so long without having a child. Grieved for her, thinking she may have nay carried some to birth, mayhap e'en because Kerr hit her and that brought on her loss. But, nay, she had babies. She had four and they were all buried in the area where the boys had planted the bushes. That is why Kerr went so mad o'er the planting of them. He was terrified of what they may have dug up. And then, after he left, Colin wanted to see what was buried there."

"What made Colin think there was something buried out there?"

"Because Kerr wasnae sane when he attacked Colin. There truly was a madness to it, and he said something about ne'er digging there. He also seemed intent on killing Colin, which he has ne'er done before. In truth, Colin ne'er usually got more than a hard slap because he cannae always watch his tongue.

"Colin said there had to be something there that he didnae want them to find. So, after Kerr left, Colin wanted to see what was buried there e'en though he could barely stand. They propped him up against a tree out in the garden. The other boys then dug up all around the area and they found the four wee bodies." She took a deep breath but it did nothing to stem the flow of tears.

"Come here, lass," Callum said, and held out his hand.

Bethoc looked at that hand and she knew she ought not to take it even as she put her hand in his. He tugged her down next to him, on the side of his good leg. When he put his arm around her shoulders, she slumped against him. It was weak, she thought, but it was good to have the sympathy. Being held so close to him was enough to ease some of the ache in her heart.

"Four bodies?" he asked, giving in to temptation and resting his cheek against her hair.

"Aye. My sisters."

"Ye are certain they are all girls?"

"Kerr wouldnae kill a boy. E'en Colin said that. Aye, they are all girls. And, save for one, I think they were all born alive. One was too small. It could have died simply because it was born too early. But it explains why my mother insisted I stay with her when she labored with Margaret. She clung to my hand. She knew. He knew too. He hung about until he kenned I was going nowhere and then left. He was angry, too. Mother was pleased."

"So, no midwife."

"Nay. He ne'er allowed one. Said women were made to have bairns. They didnae need any help."

"I am sorry, Bethoc. Sorry that ye can ne'er be certain, either."

She nodded. The uncertainty over how the babies had died would probably always trouble her. Each had stolen a piece of her mother's heart and mind. All she could do was pray that, if they had been born alive, Kerr had killed them before burying them.

"Ye realize ye dinnae call him Father any longer."

Her eyes widened in surprise and she looked up at him. She knew she had constantly told herself she should stop calling him Father. Yet she was not sure exactly when she had stopped. At some time even the habit of it had just stopped. He had simply become Kerr in her mind, and her heart. The few times she spoke to him she did not call him by any name at all.

"Aye, I suppose I have. Sad, isnae it."

"Aye"—he brushed a kiss over her temple—"but ye have made the family he didnae give you. Ye have been the mother to all those lads dragged off the streets."

"Nay a verra good one," she muttered. "They still got hit."

"What did I say about this guilt ye wish to carry?" He tilted her face up to his and kissed the tip of her nose.

"That I am a wee lass who couldnae stop him," she said, and grimaced. "I ken it. I do and ye are right in all ye say. Yet I cannae stop thinking that I should have been able to do something about it all. It just doesnae seem right that one mon can hold so many others with just the power of his fists."

"It wasnae just that. He got the lads when they were little. May weel have gotten them off the street. What did they have? With him they had a place to sleep and food to eat. A powerful temptation. All they had to do was avoid his fists."

"And as Colin said, they had nowhere to go anyway," she murmured.

"Aye, so why leave. And, they had you."

"Oh, I dinnae think they thought on that much."

He decided not to argue with her about that. She could not see how she had become a mother to them all. Instead he turned her in his arms so that he could kiss her more thoroughly.

Bethoc gave herself over to his kiss. She hated to admit it, but it was why she had come. She had missed the feel of being in his arms, of the sheer delight she got from kissing him. It was a delight that lingered in her thoughts long after she left his side. By the time he pulled away she could barely catch her breath and she rested her head against his chest. It pleased her to hear his heart pound and his breathing was also harsh, as if he too was having difficulty.

Callum rubbed her back and Bethoc smiled. It was nice to just lie curled up beside him and be soothed. She did not really need soothing but enjoyed it too much to move. Finally, however, she had to sit up, for time was passing and she did not want to get home after Kerr had returned. The man asked too many questions when she did.

"I have to go," she said as she climbed off the pallet.

"'Tis still light."

"I ken it but if I come in after Kerr has come home he pesters with questions I cannae answer. He has already accused me of slipping away to meet with a mon. I dinnae trust him to keep ignoring that now."

"Nay." He dragged himself up off the pallet. "It would be best if ye dinnae get in any trouble o'er this. What have ye told him?"

"That I am keeping a close watch on some berry bushes so that I might harvest some of the berries before the birds do."

"Clever." He gave her a quick kiss.

"That may be but I dinnae think he will believe it for verra long." She grimaced. "And I am nay the best of liars."

"No shame in that, just rather inconvenient at times."

She laughed. "Oh, aye. Verra inconvenient."

He leaned against the inside of the cave opening as

she moved some of the shrubs, enjoying how she looked. When she stood up and picked up her basket, he grasped her by the hand and pulled her up against him. She felt right there, in his arms.

"Ye would run off without giving me a kiss?" he teased. "Coldhearted woman."

Bethoc laughed softly and gave him a kiss before slipping free of his hold and hurrying off down the path. She always felt so much lighter and happier after she had spent time with him. It was something that should probably bother her but she would not let it. One day soon he would have to leave and return to being a laird, a man far above her touch. For now, she intended to thoroughly enjoy what she could share with him.

By the time her home came into view she lost a lot of that happiness. Bethoc felt a weight settle over her and sighed. It was not what one should feel when coming home. She straightened her shoulders and went forward. There was no other choice.

To her relief, her father was not home. Colin played quietly in the corner with a happily babbling Margaret. She hurried over to give the little girl a hug.

"Are the boys still working?" she asked Colin.

"Aye, and I should be helping them." He frowned toward the door but made no move to join the others.

"Soon, Colin. Ye didnae have anything broken that I could find but it was bad. Everything was bruised and that takes time to heal."

"I ken it. Do ye e'er think there has to be something better than this?"

"All the time," she answered as she hurried over to start their supper. "It is out there. Some day we will be free to seek it. But I dinnae think t'will be all that much different from what we do now, just in a different place with different people."

When he just murmured in reply, she turned her attention to what she needed to have to make a meal. She did believe they would have something better. Some days it was all that kept her going. It just seemed that they had to have something better than working themselves into exhaustion only to watch Kerr Matheson drink and gamble the earnings from their labor away.

Briefly she considered asking Callum but hesitated to do so. She had the feeling he would offer her something out of charity and that was not what she sought. She and the boys could work. They needed to have something they could work at, something that would put the profit in their hands instead of Kerr's.

As she worked she thought over how to put the question to the man. He had been out in the world in a way none of them ever had so she was sure he would know better what their chances would be of getting, perhaps, a small farm they could work. Bethoc got lost in the thought of it and only partly took note of her father's arrival.

"Hey! Are ye e'er going to put that on the table?" Kerr yelled.

"Of course, I was just making certain t'was done." She placed the pot on the table and watched him spoon out a large serving for himself as the boys sat and waited.

And that was why her mother got lost in her dreams so often, she thought. It was what she had to do to escape a deeply selfish, angry man and the ugliness in her life. It was an effort to bring herself back but Bethoc did, and breathed a sigh of relief. It was not a happy place she returned to but she knew she had to be here. The boys needed her to stand for them, to be here in body and in spirit. Someday, she mused as she doled out a share of what was left to all the others, this man will rule us no longer.

Chapter Six

"Why are we back here?"

Uven frowned at Simon. "Because this is where he disappeared."

"I ken it but we have already been here, several times."

"True but the fact that it has been a month of hunting and we have found naught makes me think he ne'er left this place." Uven frowned as he stared at the river and searched the bank carefully. "We have ne'er found a body, no horse, no word of him at all. Havenae found any sign of the boy, either. 'Tis as if they were all just swept away."

Simon ran his hand through his hair. "Weel, people have gone missing before."

"True but there was almost always something one could find e'en if ye ne'er found the person. Just something that let ye ken the person had been in that spot at some time." He looked around. "Where did Robbie go?"

"Said he saw something odd up on the hill," Simon answered and Uven looked up the hill to where Robbie stood staring at some dying bushes. "There he is, studying the area round those bushes it appears. Wonder what he has found?"

A few moments later, Robbie rode back down the hill and faced them. "We need to have a look up there. I am thinking there is a cave and, if I am judging it aright, someone has been up to it recently."

"A cave? That would be a fine place to hide if one was injured." Uven dismounted and took his mount's reins in hand. "I think we should walk up to it. Secure the horses at the base."

"It is a narrow path, true enough," said Robbie as he also dismounted. "Uneven, too. So watch your step."

By the time they reached the brush hiding the entrance, it was easy to see what it was. Uven cautiously moved the covering as Robbie and Simon stood beside him with swords at the ready. Then he drew his own sword and stepped inside, needing a moment to see clearly in the dim light. Callum sat next to the wall grinning at him.

"Took ye long enough," said Callum, laughing as his friends marched over to clap him on the shoulder. "Heard Robbie sniffing around and almost called out but decided I should wait in case ye were fleeing someone."

"Had no one chasing us. Didnae ken what we would find," said Simon.

"Ah, aye, they broke my leg, the bastards, but, weel, I am healing now."

"If we are to stay here for a while, I think we best move the horses," said Uven.

"I will do it," said Robbie, and strode out of the cave.

"How did ye find the cave?" asked Callum.

"It wasnae hard once we followed the path. The brush set there is good when ye see it from afar but nay perfect up close."

"That willnae please Bethoc," said Callum quietly.

"Ah, a lass." Uven rolled his eyes. "Why am I nay surprised?"

"'Tis nay what ye think," protested Callum. "And cease talking like I am a young Payton when we both ken I am not, nay e'en near to being so. She pulled me from the water, dragged me up here and I wasnae in a state to help much, and has worked to fix my leg."

Uven studied his leg. "Did a good job with what was at hand. Can ye move at all?"

"A little. I begin to be able to put a little weight on my foot but it could be a month or so before I can claim I am healed or go without some sort of bandaging on my leg. The bone is setting but isnae done yet and ye didnae want to cause it more injury by using it too soon."

"That poses a bit of a problem but I suppose we could spend the time looking for the boy. Ye cannae go anywhere without the lad and he could be in some danger."

"Nay. Ye dinnae need to. I ken where he is. Bethoc has him. The house is nay the best place for a lad but 'tis better than being stuck here with me and I having no way to protect him."

"What is wrong with the house?"

"Father has a heavy hand."

"Should I fetch him? We can protect him," said Simon.

"Nay, he is safe enough. No one kens where he is and that is the most important thing at the moment. There is naught to cause them to look at that house, either," Callum said.

Robbie returned and Callum watched him carefully put the brush back. "Hope ye did that right. She will notice and, if 'tis wrong, it will frighten her."

"Frighten her?" asked Simon.

"She fears the men who did this to me have found me. They were, are, looking for me. She has already confronted them once."

"They came here again?" asked Robbie.

Callum nodded. "Think the fools suddenly realized they had nay bothered to see if I was actually dead, that they had just assumed I was. Probably suspicioned they might have erred after they lost the boy. Suspicion they think I have taken him again. A logical assumption."

"How did they lose the boy?" asked Uven as he hefted a jug of cider, took a sip, and filled a tankard with some.

"Her father took him. She doesnae ken how, only that he showed up with the boy. But she did say the mon is acting unstable. Goes out every night. Mayhap he fears they watch him." He glared at his leg. "I can do naught about it, naught to hunt down the men who threaten Cathan. Naught to make certain she doesnae get caught in the midst of all this and hurt."

"Then someone needs to find out where these men are."

"Aye, now give me some of that cider."

As they drank, they planned how and where to hunt down the men who were such a threat. It was edging toward midafternoon when his friends finally left. Callum found himself relieved. This was about the time of day when Bethoc came round. The anticipation he felt made him both smile and shake his head.

It was not because she had saved him or tended his wounds. He did not believe it was even how she was treated at home. Although his life was dedicated to helping those who suffered such things, that mostly was a concern for children. Bethoc was no child and he had no knowledge of her brothers, nothing to tell him they were in bad need of a protector. Callum had to decide if what he felt was just a lusting or more before too much longer. She was not a lass one idled away a few enjoyable hours with. Bethoc was a lass you either left alone or married.

Bethoc took a careful look around before hurrying up the path. Half the way up she paused and stared at the ground. For a moment she could not understand what troubled her. Then she gasped. Someone had recently used the path, several someones in fact. Her heart suddenly pounding with fear, she raced up to the cave, tossed aside the brush, and rushed inside. To see Callum sitting there, calmly writing something before he looked up at her in surprise, nearly brought her to the floor.

"What is it, Bethoc?" he asked, and started to get up.

"Nay, no need to stand." She hurried back to the entrance, looked around carefully, and pulled the brush back against the opening before walking back to him. "Someone had used the path and I feared they had found you." She was struggling to rid herself of the feeling of panic that had overtaken her.

He reached out, grasped her hand, and pulled her down beside him. "It was my friends."

"They found you?"

"Aye. Seems Robbie noticed something and came up the path to have a closer look."

"I wonder what he saw. T'would be good to ken what was odd," Bethoc said as she began to unpack the food she had brought.

"I will be sure to ask him when he returns. Um, where is wee Margaret?"

Bethoc grimaced. "Colin has her again. He swore he

would ne'er leave her alone and made me leave her behind. It still feels odd to nay be carrying her weight. And I am trying to nay think about her. 'Tis best if there is some separation now that she is growing older."

"But ye probably willnae stay long, either. Like last time."

Bethoc leaned against him. "Foolish. I ken it. Colin is a good lad and she has obviously decided she likes him. Yet all I can see is those four wee babes and think on how, if I hadnae been there for her birth, there could have been five. I must teach myself nay to cling to her with the idea that I am just keeping her safe."

He turned her face up to his and brushed a kiss over her mouth. "Ne'er think on what-ifs, lass. What if I turned right instead of left, I might nay have been caught. And beaten. And had my leg broken. For everything that happens there are many what-ifs. They dinnae matter. Ye were there and she has lived to be a fine little lass who demands kisses on her forehead for being a smart lass."

She laughed and nodded. "True enough." She lightly patted his broken leg. "I think I have come up with a better way to wrap your leg and will bring the things I need on the morrow if I can."

"This serves. I can now put some weight on it. Just a wee bit, enough to make moving about a lot easier, but I ken it will get better."

"Aye, but what I have planned will serve better, I am certain of it. It will hold it more firmly. Although, as ye say, ye are healing nicely."

"Will it make it easy to ride with?"

"Ah, aye."

She did not like to think of him leaving, which was foolish. The man could not remain captive in a cave so that she could visit him now and then. He was a laird, after all, and must be eager to get back to his lands and his people. He had a rich life somewhere else he needed to get back to. Now that his friends had found him, he would gather up Cathan and go as soon as he could ride. Knowing that, she settled against him, enjoying the closeness that would soon be gone. She tried not to think on how much she would miss it.

"Ye could come with me," he said, shocking himself for a moment, then realizing it was what he wanted. "Ye and all the others."

"Ye cannae take eight others with ye. E'en with your friends, there isnae enough room. And what would ye do with eight strays plus Cathan?"

He idly wondered why he was not relieved that she obviously saw his suggestion as no more than a kindness. He should be. It was a large responsibility to take on and he had enough of those. Nor was he sure of just why he was so reluctant to say thank ye and walk away from her.

"I have a lot of strays at my keep. I collect them," he added, and smiled.

She leaned back a little and frowned at him. "Ye collect them?"

"Aye. When I was a child I swore I would always protect the wee ones. I was a child of the streets after my mother died. A feral boy, Payton called me, and I was certainly that. Got taken up by an evil mon and, at eleven, was close to being killed because I was getting too old and too rebellious, but the mon's wee wife saved me. She got me and several others out of there and got Payton to help us even while she was still wet from her husband trying to drown her. Fool forgot she could swim.

"Ye wonder on how I understand what is happening. Weel, I lived it, Bethoc. And so much worse. If not for

Payton and Kirstie I would be long dead." He gave her a quick kiss when he saw the sadness she could not hide. "But I survived and have done verra weel 'til now. I found my true family and my grandfather turned out to be a laird. My father was his only son. It saddens me that my father was killed but at least I ken he had hand-fasted with my mother first so I wasnae a bastard cast aside like too many are."

"So ye were legitimate? That must have eased your mind."

"Nay at first for I didnae ken the worth of it, but, aye, it did. Grandfather and I got along weel and I ended up living with him. He died a few years ago and I was his heir. So, I am now a laird. 'Tis an odd thing to get accustomed to. Cannae forget where I began so am often astounded by it."

She smiled. "I suspicion ye are a verra good laird and none care where ye began."

"T'would seem so. I do wonder at where your mother began. She was at court, after all, when she met Brett so she must have come from a good family, one with standing enough to be invited to court."

Bethoc frowned. "I have little knowledge of her beginnings. There were things said from time to time that implied she had married beneath herself, or wouldnae have if she hadnae been with child. I think my father may have been paid to take her as a wife."

"What was her maiden name?"

"I dinnae ken."

"She ne'er told ye?"

"Nay but that may be because she felt her family was lost to her. Also, my mother was nay weel. She could, weel, drift away a lot of the time. Ye could see her eyes go cloudy and then there was no talking to her. Or, if ye tried, her answers made no sense. I used to fear I would become like her but then, weel, I realized she was just broken and I didnae ken how to fix her."

"Sometimes it cannae be done. The dreams are so much better they cannae leave them to face what life really is. I have seen it happen. Sometimes what is broken stays broken."

"I ken it and she did, right up until she birthed Margaret and then, for one bright moment, she was clear-eyed and fierce."

"She had someone she needed to save."

"Aye, I suppose that was it." She did not say that she often wondered why her mother had never felt the need to save any of the rest of them, why it was only Margaret who had awakened her enough to fight for the life of her child. "I had best be on my way," she said as she stood up.

Callum stood up as well, and as quickly as he could, then took her by the arm. "Ye said Colin was a good lad," he said as he pulled her into his arms, liking the way her hair just lightly brushed the underside of his chin. "There is nay need to run home and ye ken it."

"Aye, I ken it, but 'tis hard. I have been toting her around, sleeping with her at night, and playing with her most of the day for o'er two years. Ne'er apart. It will be a while before I can do so with ease."

"I ken it." He brushed a thumb over her lips and watched her eyes turn a dark blue. "Just a moment more," he whispered, and kissed her.

Bethoc held him close as she gave herself over to his kiss. The feel of his mouth made her weak. She could feel the heat of him invade her body. The way he was moving his hands over her, stroking her back with his thumbs brushing against the sides of her breasts only added to that heat. When he slid his hands up and over her breasts, she shook from the intensity of the feeling that ripped through her. Then he shifted position and suddenly it was over.

"Ah, damn, I forgot for a wee while that I am, weel, impaired," he said as he lifted his head and smiled at her. "Sorry, but I turned in a way my leg disagreed with."

"Oh, is it hurt again?" Bethoc moved, thinking to look at it, when he tightened his hold on her.

"Nay. T'was but my leg warning me I am nay ready."

"Nay ready for what?"

"For ye, Bethoc."

She could not think of a thing to say as a blush heated her face, so she hurried out of the cave, taking the time to very carefully put the shrubs back. Then she found something to brush off the path as she went down it. By the time she started walking through the wood to home, she was able to try to understand what he meant.

It was more than kisses. That much she was sure of. Then she thought of the hard ridge she could feel beneath his kilt when he held her close and wondered on it. What she needed was someone to ask but there was no one. She could not ask the boys although she had the feeling they would not know all that much more than she did.

Ignorance was a hard thing, she decided. Then she thought on the horses she had seen once, years ago, and gasped. Callum could not be thinking of mounting her like a horse. The noise the female had been making did not bring her any warm feelings of anticipation. No woman would ever get married if that was how it was done.

Then she shook her head. It could well be the same but she doubted it was exactly the same. She needed to cease wondering about it and just leave it up to him. One thing she was certain of with Callum was, if she protested, he would stop. He would never knowingly hurt her.

Once home she collected Margaret and walked back to the fire to think about the evening meal. She suddenly thought on how often she did that, how many hundreds of times she had come in and fixed a meal. Sitting at the table, she watched Margaret play with the mats she had left there and actually considered not making anything, just putting bread, cheese, and meat out on the table.

It was a lovely thought, but she quickly shook it away. True, she brought that to Callum but he was captive, trapped until his leg healed. Kerr Matheson was not and would not be pleased. He would expect a hot meal, demanded one no matter what the weather.

She still had a little time, however, and decided to go out and see what the boys were doing. Once outside she looked around and sighed. The boys had done a lot of work over the years. Around the house was a very tidy garden and beyond that were fields, full of plantings that were close to being harvested. Anyone would be proud of such a place yet Kerr spent little to no time here.

Bean walked up to her, wiping his sweaty face on his shirt. "Looks good, aye?"

"Aye. I fear I ne'er just stood here and saw what ye had done. 'Tis quite wondrous."

"Keeps Da in drink and women. And lets him play the dice."

"And that is so wrong." She shook her head but he kept talking.

"Weel, we have beds and food. Suspicion he thinks that is enough."

"It isnae though. He could allow us to go into town

now and then or give ye a wee bit of coin to save or spend. Ye do all the work."

"Nay, it isnae enough and ne'er has been," he answered in a hard, angry voice and then he took a deep breath and let it out slowly. "'Tis the way of it though."

"I think we should make that our words on a shield." She smiled when he laughed. "One day this will change. It has to."

Bean nodded and then headed into the house. She did not think he believed her. She had not asked Callum anything, either. It was something she had to consider. This was now two of the boys who had expressed a wish for an end to this, the days of working all day but never gaining any benefit. Bethoc decided she would speak with Callum as soon as she could. She owed the boys that much. If she had to swallow a little of her pride to get them a better life, it was a small price to pay.

Chapter Seven

Laughing at the way Margaret was running through the garden with Cathan at her heels, Bethoc decided it was a beautiful day. The sun shone bright and warm, the sky was blue yet decorated becomingly with white fluffy clouds, and all the boys were in the garden for play, not work. It saddened her briefly that one of the reasons it was so wonderful was because Kerr Matheson was not there. That, she thought, was too sad for words.

So was the fact that she never referred to him as her father any longer, not even in her head. He was either Kerr or, at times, her foster father. She did not even speak with him unless he spoke to her, which he rarely did. If it was not for the boys, she would be like some stranger in her own home.

Kerr was bad, there was no question about that, but he had not been in the beginning, not even with her, a child he knew was not his. She suspected some money had changed hands for him to marry her mother and take her away, take her where no one her family knew well could see her shame. Yet he had not been like he was now. He hit, but rarely. Perhaps some of his anger came from living with a woman who forever dreamed

of another man. Her mother had given him no chance
to reach her.

Now you never knew when he would strike or why.
Now he was silent and cold and they all waited for
something to happen. He had not said a word about
the stone on the grave next to her mother or the re-
planted bushes that now thrived. That had surprised all
of them. Every night he slipped away and most nights
returned drunk. What was he doing? She could think
of no reason for him to be disappearing into the village
so often.

She looked at Colin who was now almost completely
healed with few obvious bruises. He had been such a
mess even when he began working again. She still
could not understand how nothing could be broken
but silently thanked God for that gift. His ribs had been
badly bruised though, causing him a lot of pain. He did
not even look at Kerr now, treating the man as if he
were not even there. Bethoc feared for him each time
Kerr was home. She thought the other boys did as well,
for they answered Kerr far too quickly when he asked
something.

"Ah, ye are thinking of your mon," said Colin as he
sat down beside her.

"I dinnae have a mon," she muttered and the tingle
of a blush rushed over her face as the other boys
laughed.

"Mayhap I should go to see this mon ye say ye dinnae
have."

"Nay. It wouldnae be a good idea to have too many
people going to the cave. Too great a chance of someone seeing us. He isnae healed enough to face the men
who attacked him and they are looking for him."

"It has been a long time."

"Eleven weeks." And she had missed him, only able

to make fleeting visits because of her worry about Colin and then her concern that her father may have dragged them into something very dangerous.

"That isnae good, is it?" Bean asked as he sat down on her other side. "Shouldnae he be better?"

"Oh, he is better, but he *did* break his leg. The bone needs to heal." She frowned. "And I promised him I had something better to put on his leg. I really need to do that." She stood up. "I think I actually have the time today."

"Leave wee Margaret here. She is having fun and I can watch o'er her," said Colin.

Bethoc was about to refuse the offer when Margaret smiled at Colin. If the child was happy to stay, perhaps it really was time to loosen the ties a little bit. There was no doubt in her mind that Colin would keep Margaret safe from their father. He had proven himself already.

She nodded and went to collect her things. Bethoc selected the carefully cut slats of wood and stuffed the long cloth strips into her bag. For a moment she paused to test the weight of the wood to be certain it was as light as she had imagined. Satisfied, she shoved them into the bag as well and then began to load up a basket with food. That was something she was sure he was running out of.

After making certain her father was not returning, she hurried away. This time there was no sign that his friends had been there and yet she suspected they had been. She was embarrassed to admit that over the last weeks she had not taken the time to ask about them.

Once at the cave, she slipped inside, covered the entrance, and turned to look at Callum. He grinned at her and she was immediately suspicious. There was an air of mischievousness about him. She walked over, put down her things, and then sat down next to him.

"No Margaret?" he asked.

"Colin is watching her again. He is finally weel enough to manage her e'en when she is playing so he doesnae e'en have to get any of the others to help him."

"Ah, so all healed."

"The last bruise I was concerned about has faded away." She touched her forehead just above her right eye. "I feared it could prove worse than his badly bruised ribs."

"Aye, 'tis a bad place to be wounded. So ye can stay longer this time?"

"I have come to redo your bandages. I was just wondering why ye look so pleased with yourself."

"I made my friends fetch me a lot of water and had myself as proper a bath as ye can have with only buckets to work with."

"Ye didnae get your bandages all wet, did ye?"

"Nay so I suspicion it is a wee bit rank under there." He grimaced. "It was a sore temptation to just rip them all off and scrub it but I resisted."

"Thank mercy for that." She pulled the boards and strips of cloth out of her bag. "Ye best sit verra still for these though it shouldnae hurt at all."

She took off the sticks and carefully unwrapped his leg. When she removed the last of the bandages, she studied his leg for a moment and then gently bathed it. As she patted it dry she took the chance to feel the bone.

"I dinnae feel any sign of the break," she said. "'Tis staying in place and that can only be a good sign. I think we may be close to it being completely healed."

"It is looking a wee bit withered and pale," he said, grimacing at the difference between it and his unbroken leg.

"Aye, and will probably be quite weak for a while e'en after it heals."

After wrapping his leg just once again, Bethoc carefully placed the wood around his leg, laying the strip of cloth underneath and having him help hold some in place. Once she had tied the top and bottom she began to wrap another long strip of cloth around the whole thing as tightly as she could and tied it off. She studied it, thinking it looked a bit messy, but it was holding.

"How is that? Does it hurt?"

"Nay. 'Tis fine." He frowned. "Why do ye think this is better?"

"Because it covers all the part of the leg that is broken. I thought t'would mean less chance of wobbling and, mayhap, damaging what has begun to heal. Colin is making something in a thick, hard leather that ye will be able to use soon." She looked at him. "I confess, I am nay sure about all of this, but it worked weel for when Colin broke his arm."

"If it worked for Colin's arm, t'will work fine for my leg." He patted the bed. "Come sit."

She did and settled in comfortably beside him when he put his arm around her shoulders. "So, have your friends accomplished much?"

"Nay as much as they would like but they are getting close to success."

"What are they looking for besides the men?"

"Some proof of their crimes. They would like to take them to the magistrate and know they will be punished. We could punish them ourselves but then ye have to explain what ye did and why. If ye come up against someone trying to make his mark or who is verra precise in how he interprets the law, explanations and justifications are nay easy."

Bethoc shook her head. "It all sounds much too confusing."

"Aye, it can require a lot of dancing about, cajoling, subtle threatening, and the like." He turned her face up to his. "I am a master of the subtle threat."

Laughing, she slipped her arms around his neck. "Are ye now? I am nay sure that is something ye should be so proud of. Would it nay be easier just to tell the truth?"

"Och, aye, but I have seen an innocent mon dragged to the gallows, proclaiming his innocence with every step. No one would heed him and he hanged. What troubled me most was no one cared about the man they killed when they found the truly guilty one. And that is a dark tale when I have a bonnie wee lass in my arms."

Despite all her efforts to control it, Bethoc knew she was blushing. Compliments were not something she dealt with well, having received so few in her life. A grunt of satisfaction for the meal she served was as close as she got. Before she could even think of what to say, he kissed her.

This was why she missed him so when she had to stay away, she decided. The companionship was wonderful, but his kisses were what she hungered for. She readily opened her mouth to welcome his tongue, that soft ache he always caused growing more demanding. Her body wanted something but she did not know what, knew only that she had to get closer.

When he pulled her onto his lap, she was startled but his kisses soothed her. She adjusted herself and straddled him as he kissed her throat. The way he bit her gently then softened the sting with strokes of his tongue had her trembling in his arms. When he kissed her again, she dared to parry the thrusts of his tongue with hers. His hold on her tightened and he made a noise deep in his throat, a soft growl of approval. Bethoc was so pleased with that it took her a moment to realize he had loosened her gown and tugged it down to expose her breasts. Then he put his hands on her, flesh against flesh, and she did not care.

Callum was aching for her. He did not think she was aware of it but she was rubbing herself against him. Her plump breasts begged for kisses and he gave them, savoring the breathy sounds of surprise and delight she made. He wanted her and her innocence did not sway him. Neither did the fact that he would have to take her like this, with her on top. He ran his hand up her slim leg, slipping beneath her skirts, but instead of the bare skin he expected to find there, he touched cloth. He wondered why she was wearing braies but, as he kept her distracted with kisses, he worked hard to undo them.

Bethoc could not think straight. The scent of cinnamon surrounded her. When he took the hard tip of her breast deep into his mouth to suck on it, she clutched at his head, holding him even closer. Through the haze of passion that was now clouding her mind she became aware of the fact that she was now naked beneath her skirts. She tried to form the words to say something but, suddenly, his fingers were there, stroking her, and the words were lost. Each teasing touch made that ache she could not name become greedier.

Then his hand slipped away and she whimpered a protest.

"I am going to take ye, Bethoc," he whispered as he kissed her ear.

"Take me where?" she asked, shocked by how husky and low her voice had become.

He laughed softly. "Paradise, I hope."

She gasped when she felt it, something trying to ease inside of her. Everything within her stilled as she realized what it was. It was certainly a lot larger than what the boys had. Bethoc also recognized that it was the hard ridge she had been rubbing herself against. She had only just realized she had been doing that and wondered why, then decided that it had felt good. She was not sure this would but, before she could consider protesting, she felt a sharp sting and she cried out. Callum went still beneath her.

"Sorry, lass, that is the way of it, I fear." He grasped her by the hips and held her in place as he kissed her and pushed inside her. "I wish it wasnae. Doesnae seem quite fair."

Bethoc felt full. Full of Callum, she thought, and would have smiled except that his kisses would not allow it. Slowly the ache returned and the pain faded. She wriggled and he groaned.

"Still hurt?" he asked, his voice hoarse and tense.

"Nay." She frowned as she thought about how she felt. "Just full. Full of Callum."

"*Jesu.* Now ye move," he whispered as he grasped her by the hips again and moved her.

For a moment she left it in his hands but her body soon demanded control. He finally let go of her to use his hands to caress her breasts as he kissed her on the mouth, her throat, her breasts. Bethoc could feel that aching tightness inside her growing stronger with every move she made. He grabbed her by the hips again to move her faster. She suddenly felt the tight ache break apart and her whole body shuddered from the force of the feeling that swept through her as she cried out. Callum slammed their bodies together a few times and then held her there as he groaned, and she felt something warm enter her before she collapsed into his arms.

Callum held her close as they both struggled to catch their breath. It had been more than he had anticipated. He prayed this changed nothing, did not make her shy away from him, because he fully intended to do it again. As he lightly stroked her back he wondered if he had found the woman meant for him. He liked her, a lot, and now they had made love, which he also liked a lot. Callum was just not sure if all of that equaled love, the one thing his foster parents insisted was essential for a good match.

Bethoc wriggled and, even though it stirred his interest, he let her go. He grinned at her blushes as she struggled to fix her dress then tried to discreetly dismount. When she turned to look for the braies he had tossed aside, he pulled his kilt down and sat up to reach for them where he had tossed them to the bottom of the pallet. After handing them to her he watched as she somehow managed to don them without exposing too much skin.

"Why do ye wear those?" he asked.

She grimaced. "Several years ago I had a bad tumble in the garden and my skirts flew up. The boys either laughed or kept asking me where my, er, dangly was."

"Your dangly?" he choked out as he struggled hard not to burst out laughing.

"They were just little boys. Aye, dangly." She shook her head when he laughed so hard he fell back on the pallet. "The older boys laughed too. But, after that embarrassing moment, I decided, weel, why cannae *I* wear what they do? Couldnae see why I shouldnae be able to."

"Nay, except few lassies do. A lot of the Murray women do though."

"Really? Why?"

"Same reason ye do, I suspicion."

"I am pleased to hear I am nay the only one to think of it. Weel, I really must be getting home now," she said, trying desperately not to appear as if she was fleeing the place.

There was no denying that was exactly what she wished to do. It had been wonderful while they had been doing it but now she could not think of a thing to say or how to act. Bethoc was desperately afraid she could all too easily make a fool out of herself.

He stood up and reached for his walking stick. She stood there looking as if she was wanting to bolt out the opening so he put his arm around her waist and gently kissed her until some of the tension began to leave her body. What he had done was make her feel unsure, awkward, and that was the very last he had wanted to do.

"Ye arenae planning on staying away, are ye?"

She rubbed her hands over her face, suspecting it gave away all her thoughts. "I cannae believe I just . . . I dinnae do that sort of thing. I didnae e'en ken what it was!"

"I noticed." He touched a kiss to the tip of her nose. "I am sincerely praying that ye will do it again with me though."

"Ye are?"

"Dinnae sound so surprised, love." He started to walk her to the doorway. "I quite enjoyed myself."

She blushed and looked away. "Weel, aye, it was nice." She frowned when he clasped his hand to his heart and staggered a little. "What?"

"Nice? Ye wound a mon with faint praise."

"Now ye are just being silly," she grumbled. "T'was wondrous. Happy now?"

"Aye." He kissed her on the cheek. "Ye could say it with a smile though."

"And now ye are teasing." She shook her head but a grin tugged at her mouth. "I have to go."

They talked a little more as she opened the way out and he prayed he had eased that embarrassment she had felt, eased it enough that she would not avoid him. Callum watched her leave. She looked around a lot before she stepped out and as she walked, which pleased him. He also surveyed the area carefully. Once she was out of view, he sighed, put the bushes back in place, and returned to his pallet. Callum prayed he had not frightened her away for he already wanted her back.

Her smell still lingered on his bedding and he sighed again. Bethoc had not only been a virgin, she had been completely ignorant. He was astounded that he could have been yet it was obvious Matheson had never let her leave the house. Her mother had been too lost in her dreams to teach her child anything and he could not see her father telling her anything either. Looking at how she had lived he supposed it should not surprise him that she could be so completely innocent at her age, an age where she should have been married or at least contemplating marriage.

Old memories stung him before he could stop them and he found himself feeling as if he had sullied her with his touch. He had not been innocent of much of anything since he was a small child. When he had reached an age to be intrigued by women, he had done all he could to get as much knowledge as he could. For a man like him to touch such a pure innocent seemed wrong.

Callum cursed, shaking away the moment of doubt.

He could not change anything in his past and he had done no harm. There was nothing to feel guilty about. He was just put off his stride by Bethoc's innocence. It was not something he encountered often in a woman for it had never been what he looked for. He had hunted experienced ladies who would allow a man in their bed for a while and then he could walk away. No bonds, just some pleasant memories.

He settled himself more comfortably against the wall. Before this went any further he had to decide what he was going to do about Bethoc. She was more than just an evening's entertainment. That was about the only thing he was sure of.

She had had a hard life with Kerr Matheson and that tugged at his sympathy, his need to shelter those who suffered from abuse. Yet he deeply admired her. She cared for all those children, only Margaret being truly related to her. Despite her hard life she was kind and he knew well that kindness was difficult to hold on to when living under a man's fists. And she still found things to take joy in. Yes, he deeply respected her and admired that quiet strength she revealed.

There was a lot to like about Bethoc but he knew that was not what had him thinking he could take her to his home, to settle her at Whytemont. The way that thought kept slipping into his head was driving him mad. Callum could not understand what it meant. Did he think he could keep her as his mistress and she would care for the various strays he tended to collect? A heartbeat later he knew the answer to that absurd question was no. But he still needed some explanation for his urge to take her home with him.

"Ye look thoughtful," said Simon as he strode into the cave, followed by Robbie and Uven.

"And ye are back sooner than I expected," said Callum, silently thanking God they had not returned earlier.

"We happened upon a verra helpful maid in the second tavern we entered. Ne'er forget to pay the wenches weel," Simon said. "She was verra angry at a certain scarred fellow because he gave her so little. Anyway, she said he and his friends were weel kenned to be the sort who did most anything for coin. Then the friends pulled him away from her charming company. They have gone off somewhere but she is sure they will be back."

"The question is, what have they been hired to do?"

"Nothing good. Him and the four men with him are brutes. Men who hire themselves out to do the dirty work, like killing, and ye get no blood on you."

"Then we wait. At least we ken where they will be soon. Better than having to search the land for miles around just to get a sighting." He sighed. "Anyone for a game of chess?"

"Bored, are ye?" said Uven as he moved to sit on the pallet and watched Callum set out the chessboard.

"I have been stuck in a cave for weeks." Callum felt no more needed to be said.

"Ah, true. I fear I would nay remain as sweet of temper as ye have."

"I dinnae understand how ye can say I am sweet-tempered."

"Ye arenae ranting."

Callum stared at his cousin as Uven studied the move he wanted to make. "I dinnae rant."

Uven just laughed as he made his move and waited for Callum to take a turn. "Aye, ye do, and what is happening here would have been sure to get ye enraged.

We will sort it out. I have learned enough about the men to ken they are nay the smartest group. They will err or we will get lucky and we will have them."

"I pray ye have the right of it, Cousin. I want this over and done."

Chapter Eight

Something began to trouble Bethoc as she drew near her house. She kept looking around but saw no one. Yet she began to creep toward her house, careful to stay in the shadows and use the trees for cover. She had just been to visit Callum, anticipating time spent in his arms after three days without him, only to be disappointed to find his friends there. Now she wondered if she might have a need of them soon.

She stopped at the edge of the tree line and alarm hit her so hard it sped up her heartbeat, leaving her feeling winded. There were five horses tied up in front of the house. She looked all around the house but saw no sign of the riders or, she realized, her brothers. Taking a deep breath to steady herself, she darted across the open area and crouched beneath the tiny window at the side of the house, the one closest to the woods.

Bethoc was just about to peer inside when a cry of pain caught her attention. She felt her heart leap into her throat and prayed it was not one of the boys. If those five horses meant the men who had hurt Callum were here, she feared for her whole family. Men who would do what they had done to Callum were not the sort to show mercy to anyone, even children.

"I told ye! I dinnae ken who ye are talking about!"

Her father's voice was high with fear. Bethoc looked at the five horses again and her heart sank. The men who had hurt Callum and taken Cathan had obviously found out who had stolen the boy from them. She might not consider Kerr Matheson her father any longer but her heart still clenched with fear for him. This could not end well. And where were the children?

Risking the very real possibility of being seen, she took a deep breath and inched up to peer in the window. Kerr was tied to a chair and all five men had their backs to her. She could see no sign of the children in the house. Then, suddenly, her eyes met Kerr's. He quickly averted his gaze but she had seen his fear. She had also seen a brief flare of hope, one that had died too swiftly. She wondered if it had been because Kerr could not believe she would help him or because he had the sense to know she could not.

"Fool, we ken ye took him," said the big man standing in front of Kerr. "Seems ye have a habit of taking lads and working them. Ye took the wrong lad this time. Tell us where he is."

"I dinnae ken."

"Where are your children? We ken ye have a large brood of them here."

"I dinnae ken. They should be here." Kerr looked around. "Ye must have frightened them away." His eyes widened with terror as he looked at the knife the man pulled out.

"Ye need persuading, do ye? We have gotten real good at persuading people. Been practicing." He laughed and it chilled Bethoc to the bone. "They gave up all they knew real quick. Now"—he grabbed Kerr's hand and put the knife against his ring finger—"where is the lad Cathan?"

Tears streaming from his eyes, Kerr said, "I keep telling ye, I dinnae ken."

She clamped both hands over her mouth and dropped to the ground when the man cut Kerr's finger off. Kerr's screams assaulted her ears. A part of her wanted to rush in and demand the men stop what they were doing. A smarter part of her kept her in place, letting her know she would accomplish nothing by doing so, would just get herself killed.

Caught by indecision, she heard them ask again. To her astonishment, Kerr again denied any knowledge of the boy and screamed as he lost another finger. She could not understand why he was not giving the boy up.

After the fourth scream, Bethoc decided she needed to move away. She could not just sit there and listen to him suffer. She scrambled across the yard and crouched down in the trees. It was not perfect for she could still hear his screams and pleas, just not as loudly. Bethoc knew that would have to be enough. She could not leave until she knew the children had left and for that she had to get around to the back of the house. That was going to have to wait as there was no place to hide there, even for a moment.

Snuggling down into a shallow between the thick roots of the tree, she waited. Waited in hiding as Kerr Matheson died a slow, torturous death. Waited as five men learned nothing from him and searched the house. By the sounds she could hear they were destroying much of it. They came out the back and searched the whole garden, taking no care for the plants as they did so.

Then they began to search the trees. She huddled

down even more, pulling leaves over herself. Fear was a growing knot in her stomach as they searched and then one cried out. She dared a quick look and saw they were near the route of escape Colin had shown her and prayed he had been more careful to hide his trail from then on. He was a smart boy, she reassured herself, and would know he had to try to hide his trail.

Cautiously inching out after the men ran to their horses and raced off down the trail, she tried to think of what to do next. She decided going into the house was dangerous and she certainly did not want to be caught there. Nor was she eager to see what they had left of poor Kerr. Following Colin's escape path put her too close to the enemy and could mean they ended up between her and the children, which would be useless if not dangerous. The only other thing she could think to do was get back to Callum and, she prayed, all his friends, for they could help her and the children if it was needed.

Staying within the cover of the trees, she picked up her skirts and ran. Every step of the way, Bethoc watched for the men after Cathan. They were on horses, which gave them some advantage but it also made them much easier to see and avoid.

She halted just inside the trees and looked around. Colin's route to the cave was long and winding, which it had been planned to be. He had told her how to follow but even as she had acted like she was paying attention to his words, she had been thinking how lost she would be if pressed to use it. As far as she could tell, she was there before the men. Taking several deep breaths, she bolted for the path up the hill. She moved just enough brush to get inside and hurriedly put it back. When she turned to speak, she found all of Callum's friends were still there and so were Colin and all the children. Choking back a sob, she rushed over to Colin and hugged him.

"Here now, Bethoc." Colin awkwardly patted her back. "I told ye we would come here. Ye didnae need to fret yourself sick."

"Aye, but those men were there and they saw some sign in the back, right near where ye showed me how ye would escape and they have followed it. I feared they would end up between ye and me."

"Robbie," Callum said, "think ye best get the horses up here. And the path up here should be brushed clear. How quickly do ye think they can follow the path ye took, Colin?" he asked as his friends moved to do as he asked.

"Nay quick at all," said Colin. "I made it twisted as I could, going round on itself in places, walking in the water in others, and walking on rock as much as we could. Nay matter how good they are at tracking, they will have to keep stepping off the path to search out where the trail they just lost starts up again."

"Good lad."

Bethoc let go of Colin, hugged the other boys, and then picked up Margaret and hugged her. She had been so terrified for all of them she realized that, blood or not, they were her family. Now she feared they would still have to place their fate in others' hands. After what they had just done to Kerr, she knew these men were not ones she could face alone.

"How did ye get away?" she asked Colin.

"Da came back to the house and told us to get out, to run, far and fast," Colin replied. "He looked scared. Real scared. I dinnae ken why I did it, but told him he should come too. He said nay, said he wasnae good to us but will be now. Said he had stains on his soul. Asked him if he meant the bairns. He said aye, that he had smothered them as soon as they were born. I just left him there. We grabbed what we could and we ran, just as he told us to. I carried Margaret and Bean carried Cathan so we could move faster. I just left him," he whispered in an unsteady voice, "and he is dead now. Aye?"

"He is dead but he ne'er gave ye up to them."

"Suspicion that was what he meant about being good to us now. It was bad?"

"Aye," she whispered, hearing his screams and pleas. "It was verra bad."

"Then mayhap he cleaned some of the black off his soul."

She stared at Colin for a moment, thought of all Kerr had suffered without telling them anything, and nodded. "Aye, mayhap."

Callum stepped close and put his arm around her. "Ye were there."

"Aye," she said, and knew she wept, could feel the sting in her eyes followed by the warm wetness of tears on her cheeks. "Only saw a bit but heard too much. And yet he ne'er told them," she said in wonder.

"Poor lass." He kissed the top of her head.

"I did naught to help him."

"And what would ye have done?" snapped Colin. "Rushed in to be killed at his side?"

"Nay, of course not." She glared at him. "I could have distracted them or something."

"How? By making them hesitate as they planned how to kill ye, too? Ye couldnae do anything. *We* couldnae do anything."

"The lad is right, Bethoc, e'en if he could be gentler in the saying of it," said Callum, and gave the poor boy a hard look of reprimand. "Ye had five large, hardened men and ye, a wee lass, or the lads, all small, all weaponless. Nay, sad as it is, there is no cause for guilt here."

Robbie returned with the horses. "Simon's clearing the path. No sign of the men yet."

"Good." He looked at Colin. "Seems the lad here gave them a treacherous path to follow."

After putting the horses in the back of the cave with Stormcloud, Robbie walked up to Colin. "Winding with lots of rocks, a bit of water?"

"Aye," said Colin.

Robbie patted him on the shoulders. "Good. If they are good trackers, ye delayed them, and if they arenae, they may ne'er get here." He looked at Callum. "I saw a spot at the top of the hill I can safely watch for them."

Callum nodded and Robbie collected a bow and a quiver of arrows before he walked out.

"He means to shoot them?" asked Colin.

"Only if he has to. The moment he shoots one, they ken we are here and we dinnae want that." He released Bethoc and crouched down in front of Cathan. "And how have ye been doing?"

"Fine," the boy said. "It wasnae so bad there."

"Glad to hear it. As ye can see, I was nay fit to be caring for ye. How did ye get away from the men?"

"They were drinking and I slipped outside but then got taken by their da." He glanced at Colin then looked back at Callum. "He kenned they would be looking for me but I think he thought he could hide me."

Callum nodded and looked at Bethoc. She still looked badly shaken. He hated to think of what she might have seen or heard but did not ask. The others did not have to hear it. He could tell she grieved for the man but was not sure he understood why. It was possible it was just years of thinking of him as her father that did

it and he could respect that even if he felt the man did
not deserve it.

Simon came in and put the bushes back then
glanced at Bethoc. "Is that the way they go?"

Blushing faintly, she went to the doorway and made
a few adjustments. "I was trying to make it look as if
they were growing here and nay just tossed in front of
the cave. They are dead now but dead things still hang
on to where they are growing from."

"Ye wanted it to look natural."

"Aye." She stood up and brushed off her hands. "I
dinnae suppose I ought to cook anything."

"Nay, though 'tis tempting. There is cold meat,
cheese, and bread in the basket ye brought. There is
enough for everyone to have a little." He rubbed his
thigh in his broken leg. "I need to sit down, I fear."

Bethoc hurried over to lend him a hand. He looked
a little pale and she suspected he had spent most of the
day standing up. Once he was settled with his back
against the wall, she took his walking stick. She was
thinking of putting it somewhere he would have to ask
for it before he could get up and walk around, when she
took a good look at it. It was now covered in carvings
the like of which she had seen on ancient headstones
in the graveyard.

"What have ye done?" She touched a carving of a
dragon that curled sinuously around the stick. "This is
beautiful." She traced her finger over the carving.

"I was a wee bit bored," he said, smiling faintly at the
way she kept tracing his carving and trying to ignore
the tightening of lust in his groin, something he was
too tired to do anything about.

She gave him a cross look and set the walking stick
next to his bed. Then she went about the business of
setting all the food out. Carefully dividing it up left

everyone with a nourishing but small meal. As she passed out the food she noticed that Colin was seated next to Simon while Margaret sat on his other side. Setting aside the food meant for Robbie, she took hers and Callum's over to him and joined him on the pallet.

Callum bit back a smile when Bethoc joined him on the bed as if she belonged there. He had no intention of pointing that out, however. It would make her too aware of what she had done and she would leave. It was good that she was so comfortable with him and he wanted to do nothing to spoil that.

"What should I do about your friend Robbie's food?" she asked.

"Leave it. He will return soon, once he is certain those men didnae track the boys here."

"How can he be certain of that?"

"He can ken how long it would take for them to get here according to all the boy Colin told him, even if the fools get badly lost. He has a skill for things like that."

She had absolutely no idea how, but said, "Weel, that is convenient."

Once done with his food, he took her hand in his, and asked, "Will ye introduce me to the boys?"

"Oh! I am sorry I didnae do that. Just thought they had introduced themselves."

"Nay, they just burst in and told us what was happening. Then ye arrived."

She sat up and signaled the boys to come over to the pallet where they lined up nicely. "Ye ken Colin, aye?" Callum nodded and shook the boy's hand. "He is the eldest at sixteen. Bean stands next to him and is fourteen. Then there is Liam, the boy with all the freckles, who is twelve. Gavin is next at ten. Georgie here"—she rubbed the boy's head—"is newly turned eight.

Magnus is six and has a knack for recalling whatever he has seen. Then there is your Cathan."

They were a varied lot. Colin looked most like Bethoc even if Callum knew they were not related, only his black hair was straight. Bean was fair-haired and blue-eyed. Liam had red hair and brown eyes to go with his many freckles. Gavin was surprisingly hand-some even at ten with his thick, rich brown hair and smoky gray eyes. Magnus was the sort of child who could get whatever he wanted with his curly blond hair and wide brown eyes set in the face of a little angel.

Bethoc had a fine horde of boys to care for, he thought. He also suspected they would stay with her until they were old enough to set out on their own and, even then, would not go far away. A man who took her on would have to take on the whole lot of them. It would be a daunting chore.

Yet Callum realized even that did not stop him from thinking of taking her with him when they finally cleared this mess away and he could return to his lands. What he really needed to think on was what he intended to do with her when he got there. There was something between them, something that pulled at him, but he was not sure what. Until he was, and knew in his heart what he could offer, it would be cruel to take her away from the only place she had called home.

One thing he was sure of was that he had never felt for another woman what he felt for her. He wanted to give her things, to take care of her, and keep her safe from the harshness of the world. He certainly had liked bedding her, gained more pleasure from it than he had ever had, even including his first time with that tal-ented dairy maid. But more than that, he had no urge to get up, dress, and leave when it was done. In fact, he had dreams of waking up in the morning curled around her, waking her up slowly with kisses so that they could make love again in the early morning light.

Margaret appeared at the side of the pallet, went around to the side that was not wounded, and crawled on the bed. She inserted herself between him and Bethoc and settled down, closing her eyes. Bethoc said nothing, just idly played with the child's curls and sipped her cider. Nothing could make the situation clearer to a man than that. If he took Bethoc with him, he took on the whole family. It was another reason to be absolutely sure what he wanted before he gave in to impulse.

"They are gone," said Robbie as he walked in and Bethoc held his food out to him. "Thank ye, lass."

"Where do ye think they went?" asked Callum.

"My guess would be back into the village to have an ale. Got weary of going in circles trying to find the lads."

"Ye dinnae think that is the last of them though, do ye?"

Robbie shook his head as he finished off his meal in a few bites and poured himself some cider. "Nay. They want something from the lass and they dinnae seem to be the sort to give up. I was thinking o'er it all but the only thing she has is that house and land."

"Why do ye think they wanted something from me?" Bethoc asked. "They asked after Cathan, nay me. Weel, they did ask where the children had gone but I suspicion that was because they thought Cathan was with them."

"Did ye hear everything they asked?"

"Weel, nay, I went into the trees and hid."

Robbie just shook his head. "I think they wanted Cathan but I think they wanted more. Lad was at your house for a long time yet they ne'er came after him. Now they show up? For a lad who can gain them only a payment or two? One they think Callum has already taken back to Whytemont? Nay, there is more to this. And ye were the one who could get them more. The only more there is is your house and land."

Bethoc frowned. "They cannae take that, can they?"

"I have nay idea but my gut says this is more."

"More what?" asked Callum.

Robbie frowned, dragged his hand through his hair, and said, "I dinnae ken. Just more. More than killing that mon," he added softly so the boys did not hear. "Doesnae have the taste of revenge. May just be Cathan but I begin to wonder if they have e'en given the boy much thought e'en though they asked after him. I cannae explain it. Just say I really feel this is more complicated than we believed."

"Then we had best find out what the 'more' is." Callum scowled down at his leg. "I hate leaving this all to ye and Simon. Makes me feel useless."

"Only lasts a while and then ye will be back on your feet ordering us all around again." Robbie grinned. "Me and Simon can look about. Leave Uven here in case the men come sniffing round."

"Thank ye," muttered Uven.

"My pleasure. Nay sure what we can find or what we are looking for but could turn up something."

"Just beware of those men. They may wonder what ye are about and attack."

"We will ask enough about ye to have them thinking that is all we look for but, aye, a close eye will be kept on them."

They tossed a few ideas around for a while but nothing very useful. It was going to be a search for something, some hint that could lead them to the truth of what was going on, and that was hard to make plans for.

Robbie wandered off to make his pallet and lie down. Callum turned to speak to Bethoc and grinned.

At some point during all the talk, she had settled down next to Margaret and gone to sleep. The sight of her and the tiny girl curled up together caused a pang in his heart and he wondered why. As he awkwardly moved so that he, too, could lie down, he realized he was really going to have to sort out what was happening to him. He had, after all, seen many a woman and child curled up asleep and never felt such a pang, a longing. Finding her hand, he held it close and smiled. This was not as much fun as his dreams played out for him, but it would do.

Chapter Nine

The sight of the house broke Bethoc's heart but she steadied herself. She looked around before stepping out of the trees but saw nothing, neither the men who had killed Kerr nor an angry Callum. She had thought to bring Colin with her but had suspected he would protest such a move as much as Callum would. Knowing neither of them would like what she was doing did not make her stop, however.

She had slipped out of his bed before dawn had fully broken. It embarrassed her to think she had fallen asleep so thoroughly and done so in his bed. Only Margaret's presence had made it innocent. The fact that she had heartily wished it had not been all so innocent also embarrassed her. When had she become a wanton woman?

Assured no one lurked about the place, she hurried up to the house. The smell of death, of blood and pain, hit her hard. She stood in the doorway taking deep breaths for as long as she dared before stepping inside. Kerr was still strapped to the chair and he was a mess. They had taken not only his fingers and toes, but his ears and one eye before he died. He had not been a good man but no one deserved to die this way. She felt her stomach roil and fought to be strong.

She grabbed a blanket from the bed and was about to spread it out on the floor to place her father's body on it when she heard horses. Going to the door, she peeked out, relaxing when she saw that it was not the men who had butchered Kerr. It startled her when two men hastily dismounted and grabbed her. Bethoc stared at the officious-looking man who slowly dismounted and wondered what trouble she had stepped into now. He kept staring at her as he signaled a third man to go into the house.

"What are ye doing?" she demanded as they dragged her into the house.

"Looking at what ye have done," the man leading them inside said. He looked at Kerr's body and then gave Bethoc a look of disgust even as one of his men ran outside gagging. "Ye couldnae just cut his throat?"

Bethoc was speechless with shock for a moment and then choked out, "I didnae do this."

"Do ye see anyone else here?"

"I but came here to bury him! I couldnae abide the thought of him tied to the chair."

"Burying is a good way of hiding what ye have done."

"I didnae do this!"

"Yet ye were going to bury him."

"Of course I was. He is dead. He shouldnae be left to just rot in a chair. He was my father."

"Was he?"

"What do ye mean by that?"

"Seems he was fond of telling the world and its mother that your mother was already carrying ye when he wed her. 'Tis why they allowed a mon like him to have such a fine lass. Why they gave him this land. Said she finally gave him one bairn, a lass, and it wasnae ye he was talking about. So where are the others?"

"The others?" Bethoc felt a cold wave of fear, wondering why these men would care about where the boys were.

"All the laddies that run about here, working the land for this fool. The laddies he stole."

"Ye kenned that? Ye kenned it and did naught?"

"And what should I have done? They were cast-off children. He did weel by them. And now this is how ye repay him."

"Are ye nay heeding me? I didnae do this! Look at the mon. Do ye think I could wrestle him into that seat, tie him to that chair, and then do that to him? Do ye think I could even lift him?"

"Tell me where the others are," he demanded, and grabbed her by the chin, his eyes fixed on hers as his men wrapped Kerr's body in the blanket she had put down.

"They ran away when the men arrived," she said, beginning to think speaking to this man was akin to banging her head against a wall.

"What men?" he demanded and made a sharp gesture to signal his men to carry Kerr's body out of the house.

"The five who came here and killed Kerr."

The man frowned. "The ones who heard the poor mon's screams and told us to come here?"

"A tall mon with a scarred face? Rode here with four others who looked nearly as rough as he did?"

"Aye. Those men and they sent us here. To catch a killer. Came to warn the sheriff like honest men should. Come along now," he said even as he began to have her dragged out of the house by his men who had just returned.

"They lied! They were the ones who did this to him."
She tried to pull free of the men's hold.

"Cease, woman! Ye have been caught. Now we will
take ye up for punishment."

"Dinnae ye mean justice?" She knew the men had
decided on her guilt but hoped to shame them into
what they were supposed to do. "Ye are the sheriff and
ken weel I deserve a trial, a chance to prove my innocence."

"Ye will get the chance to tell us exactly what ye did,"
said the sheriff. "No less."

"Ye mean tell ye that I did it," she snapped.

"Aye," he said flatly. "Ye and nay other."

Bethoc began to fight the hold they had on her like
a wild thing. To her dismay, all the men joined in
trying to hold her still. All the while she loudly denied
killing Kerr, protesting her innocence over and over
again. When they tied her hand and foot and tossed
her over the back of a horse, she was still protesting.
They gagged her with a barely clean cloth, the sweaty
smell of it making her want to vomit. Only her fear of
choking held her back, even as the men mounted their
horses and rode back to the village, adding more abuse
to her uneasy stomach.

She thought briefly of Kerr. They had taken his body
although she had no idea why. She dreaded the possibility that the boys would return and see the blood left
behind. And a part of her, the one that had lived in the
man's house for so many years, felt sad that no one was
burying him. Or that they might never know where he
was buried.

Once at the jail, she was dragged inside and the
sheriff sat at a table. The officious man calling himself
the sheriff demanded that she confess to what she had
done as he tore the gag off her mouth. Bethoc yet

again swore that she had not touched Kerr. He nodded and mumbled something about changing her mind. That did not sound good, she thought, and sat tensed and ready for trouble. She heartily wished she had told Callum where she was going.

"Where is Bethoc?" Callum demanded, walking cautiously as he tested the leather boot without a foot that Colin had strapped to his leg.

"I think she went to bury Da," said Colin. "I saw her slip away."

"And ye didnae stop her?" Callum could not hide his shock.

"They had already killed the mon. What more could they do? I kenned they must be gone by now."

"I dinnae ken what else they might try to do, but they also asked after all of ye. They could decide to look about the house themselves, to see if they missed something, since they had lost your trail." He felt bad when the boy turned pale but he had no time to coddle him now. "Robbie, I need to go after Bethoc." Callum held on tightly to his fear, keeping it under control, and patted Colin on the back. "I will get her back," he promised.

Robbie brought Stormcloud and his mount to the cave. "I will ride with ye."

Callum opened his mouth to argue, took one look at his friend's face, and shut it. Robbie had that determined look on his face. It meant there would be no moving him in his decision. It could be annoying but Callum suspected it was what had saved him when he was a small, much abused child. He quietly followed the man as Robbie carefully moved the horses through the opening to the cave.

The ride to where they assumed Bethoc's home was took longer than Callum liked. Since he did not know where she lived, and Colin's directions were not easy to follow, he could not really complain, no matter how much he wanted to. When the small cottage appeared, he tensed. The door was wide open and it gave him a bad feeling. Callum told himself it was just because she had rushed inside but he could not shake his unease.

He stopped in front of the house and dismounted cautiously. Robbie was already striding into the house as Callum grabbed his walking stick to follow him. The chair and the blood surrounding it was the first thing that caught their eyes.

"This is where they tortured and then murdered the mon," Callum said.

"Then they took him off with them."

"Them?" he asked Robbie.

"Aye. More than one horse was here. Lots of tracks and footprints. Think one set of them might be your lady's."

Callum immediately went outside to study the ground. The closer he looked the more alarmed he became. There had been at least three men and some sort of struggle had taken place. Then the prints he had judged to be Bethoc's disappeared.

"I think they have taken her, too, Callum," said Robbie.

"But *who* has taken her?"

"Weel, I am fair certain it isnae the men looking for ye. I suspicion she has been taken up by the magistrate's or sheriff's men, or whate'er passes for the law round here." He clapped Callum on the back. "We can follow the trail. They made no attempt to hide it."

"Aye. If we hurry we can see who has her." Callum went to his horse and sighed as he had to have Robbie help him into his saddle. "E'en if it is the law, we cannae leave her in their hands for long."

The ride into the village was another too-long trip that left Callum annoyed. There was no sign of the men who had taken Bethoc. He feared they were wrong, that it was the men who had attacked him. The only thing that stopped him from immediately believing that was that they had not found Bethoc's body and he was certain those men would have tortured and killed her in their attempt to find him. He resolutely ignored the little voice that whispered they could have taken her elsewhere.

To his consternation, but also relief, the trail led straight to the sheriff's. As Robbie helped him dismount, Callum considered the approach he needed to take. Despite how much he wished to simply demand Bethoc's return, he knew he would accomplish more by being cautious in word and deed. Taking a deep breath, he prayed for strength and followed Robbie into the sheriff's.

Bethoc had been sore by the time the horse stopped and the rough way she had been brought to the cell had not helped. The way they had dragged her into the stone building, down some narrow steps, and along a hall to the cells had given her no chance to ease her aches and pains. A bundle of rags huddled in the corner of one of those cells caught her eye but, before she could look closer, she had been dragged around a corner and thrown into a cell. A quick look around as she pulled herself to her feet revealed that she was all alone. A shiver went down her spine.

"Now, perhaps ye will tell us why ye killed your father," said the sheriff.

"Do ye nay ken? I have said, and I will keep on saying, I didnae do it." She fought to keep her voice quiet and calm when she had the strong urge to scream at him in fury.

"Weel, we will have to see what ye have to say about it all, later." He looked at the man behind him. "William?"

"Aye, sir."

The man who stepped forward made Bethoc bite back a gasp. He was huge with a wild mop of brown hair, and muscles so big she was surprised he could move. The way he stepped into her cell showed that he could move just fine and the barrel he brought in proved his muscles were not just for show, either. Bethoc heard a splashing noise and knew it did not bode well for her.

"See that she tells us the truth," the sheriff said.

"I am telling ye the truth. I—didnae—kill—him." The sheriff started to walk away and she ran up to the bars of her cell. "All ye have to do is think for a moment on what it would take to subdue Kerr Matheson and ye would ken full weel that is wasnae me!"

The sheriff and his men did not even hesitate in their walk away from her. She cursed and turned around only to find William standing there. It took all of her willpower to stifle a scream when he grabbed hold of her. She struggled with all of her strength but it was of no more worth than a fly struggling in a spider's web.

He approached the wide-topped barrel and she realized it was full of water. Before she could protest, he flipped her around so that she was upside down, and did it so quickly and neatly, she knew he had had a lot of experience. With her hands tied Bethoc could do little to fight him but she tried anyway.

"Huh," he grunted. "Braies. Takes all the fun out of me work."

She opened her mouth to call him a depraved fool only to shut it fast and take a deep breath as he plunged her into the water. Bethoc went still, concentrating fiercely on just holding her breath for as long as she could. Despite all of her efforts not to, she began to thrash as her lungs ached with the need to take in some fresh air. He pulled her up just as she lost the fight and then held her upside down as she coughed out the water she had swallowed.

"Ye ready to confess?" he asked.

"Aye," she gasped out. "I didnae kill Kerr Matheson."

"Ah, lass, I dinnae think that is what the sheriff will be wanting to hear."

He dunked her in the water again and again she gave the same answer to the question. His calm manner never changed and that infuriated her. It was a useless rage for it changed nothing.

By the fifth time she was put into the water she was sure she would drown. She could not hold her breath any longer. She was exhausted and her body ached from rough handling. When the water flooded in as she gasped for air, Bethoc thought of Callum, of how she would never see him again, and then wished she could kill William. He pulled her out and she hung limply from his grasp. When he set her on her feet and she collapsed, retching painfully as her body fought to rid itself of water, she wondered how long she could endure this. Rolling away from the mess she made, she began to slip into unconsciousness, and welcomed it.

"Answer the question, lass," came William's voice from above her.

"I didnae kill Kerr Matheson," she replied in a weak,

unsteady voice, "and if your fool sheriff would just think for a moment, he would see that truth." She thought she heard him sigh as she slipped into the blackness.

Callum strode into the sheriff's office with as much grace as he could manage. Three men were there. He assumed the man seated at the table he faced was the sheriff and looked him over as he fought to contain his anger, an anger he knew was born of his fear for Bethoc. Just because it was the law who had her did not mean she was safe. The man seated before him looked overfed and smug.

"I seek a person I believe ye have just gathered up, Bethoc Matheson," he said.

"Do ye now." The sheriff folded his hands over his rounding belly. "Weel, the lass is here because she killed Kerr Matheson, her own father."

"That mon wasnae her father."

"All the more reason for her to be killing him then."

Robbie kept close to Callum's side as he strode up to the table. "That lass didnae kill anyone."

"Men told us there was something going on at that house so we went out there. Found her standing o'er the body. No one else about. She had a cloth all laid out for his body and was planning on burying him. Verra suspicious that."

"She went there to bury the mon. How is it suspicious?"

"Hiding the proof of her crimes. Did ye ken she cut the mon to pieces?"

"Ye did have a good look at the lass, aye?" When the sheriff cautiously nodded, Callum continued. "And ye actually believe she could do all that to a grown mon?

Could subdue him, get him in a chair, tie him up, and then slowly kill him?"

Callum could see the man had doubts but he needed someone to take the blame for the killing. He wondered if someone wanted Matheson's land. With Bethoc convicted of his murder it could all be taken away so easily. It could prove difficult to pull her out of this mess even if the sheriff could see the one accused was an ill fit.

"Weel, we think she had the lads help her," the sheriff finally said. "We are looking for them too."

"Are ye now? So ye believe they all turned on the mon?"

"They were naught but cast-off bairns when he took them in. Ye ne'er can tell how such as them might act, now can ye?"

Callum felt a sharp rise in his anger and fought it back down. "Who were these men who sent ye out to the house?"

"Five rogues who have long been round the village. Leader is a big fellow with a scar on his face."

"I would like to see Miss Bethoc Matheson now."

"Nay, no one speaks to her until she is ready to tell me the truth."

Before Callum could speak, Robbie took him by the arm and forced him to start walking away. "What are ye doing? We have to get Bethoc out of here and away from that fool idiot of a sheriff."

"I ken it and we will." Once outside by the horses, Robbie stopped and looked at Callum. "It is time for the laird of Whytemont to demand things. That is a mon who would bow before such things."

"That was what I was about to do."

"Ye dinnae look much like a laird right now."

"This is nay a time to be worrying o'er what I am

wearing," Callum snapped even though a quick glance revealed he was wearing some very ragged clothes.

"Aye, it is. The sheriff is a fool, nay doubt about that, but he is one who recognizes, e'en fears authority. Men like that often do. But they need the show of it. And we are going to go back to get ye rigged out weel enough to put on a fine show. And while ye do that, I am going to go and try to get Sir Simon Innes." Robbie helped Callum mount up.

"Ye ken Sir Simon Innes?" Callum asked in surprise. He had heard of the man from Payton but did not know Robbie had actually met him. "The laird of Lochancorrie?"

"Aye, played chess with him a few times. He was at Tormand's and I stopped there for a wee visit once when returning from Payton's. Good fellow." Robbie mounted his horse and they started back to the cave.

"Do ye think he would, or could, help us?"

"'Tis a puzzle and he likes puzzles. It cannae hurt to try, aye?"

Callum nodded. He then prayed that Robbie was right as the more he thought on the matter of Bethoc in jail, the more he felt that is was greater than the sheriff's need to blame someone for a murder on his watch. Any fool could see with a look at Bethoc that she could not have killed a man, could never have done what was done to Kerr Matheson. She had neither the strength nor the stomach. Someone knew only Bethoc had a claim to the land and this charge of murder would put an end to it.

When they reached the cave and Robbie rode off to try to get Sir Simon Innes to help, Callum washed and donned the clothes that fully revealed his place as laird of Whytemont. He looked at the boys who now stared at him as if he was a stranger and felt he had done well.

Then he sat down on the pallet, thinking of how to tell them what was happening with their sister, a sister he knew was almost a mother to every one of them. When Margaret hurried over to sit with him, he sighed as she snuggled up next to him and decided to do the children the honor of telling them the full truth, no matter how hard it was.

"Your sister went back to bury your father. Someone had told the sheriff there had been a murder at the house and he arrived as she was working to bury him. They took her up for his murder. They have put her in a cell and I mean to get her out."

"Bethoc?" Colin said. "They think Bethoc killed our father? That is . . . that is," he stuttered, "bollocks. 'Tis nonsense."

"Weel, aye, 'tis," Callum agreed. "I begin to think there is something else going on here."

"What? What could they possibly want with her? What does she have?"

Callum grimaced. "I have to wonder if someone wants the land. Seems they all ken none of ye are his own children, that he brought ye in from the streets."

"Or was given us by our mothers," Colin said. "Me and Bean were naught but bairns. Either we were abandoned or orphaned. Only he kenned and he ne'er told us."

Giving Margaret a kiss, he set her down, and then stood up. "The men who broke my leg were the ones who told the sheriff to go to your house. Sheriff spoke of five men and the leader with a scar on his face. Sounds too much like the ones who attacked me to be a coincidence."

Bean frowned. "The matters are nay connected."

"I ken it but I am thinking the rogues took on a new job. They were nay sure they had killed me and they had lost the boy. So they needed to stay near until they were certain and got the boy back. Suspicion they got a chance to do some other work while they did that. They would have been fools to say nay."

Colin nodded. "Aye, true enough. What is your plan?"

"Weel, as ye can see, I have donned my best so I am obviously the laird I claim to be."

"Ye are a laird?"

"Aye." He waved a hand as if to brush aside further questions. "It might help to bestir the sheriff to reconsider. If not, I am taking the smaller boys with me so that he has further visual proof of the ridiculousness of his charges against Bethoc. Robbie has ridden to fetch a mon who can help if need be, a mon who was called the King's Hound once because he was so skilled at solving such crimes. I have others I can call on if it proves necessary. I but ask that ye all be patient."

When all the boys nodded, Callum turned to Simon. "I would like ye to stay with the lads left behind." He stared hard at the man, who nodded, letting Callum know he understood he was to make certain the older boys remained hidden. "And Uven, if ye could drive the wee cart that the lads told us is at the house, it would help. I ken it is a sorry vehicle for ye, but it will hold the lads. We can collect it from the house as we go."

Uven nodded. "We will get started now. Come along, lads." He scooped up Margaret. "And ye, my bonnie wee lass."

Callum started to say they should not take Margaret and then shook his head, smiling faintly. "Aye, her too."

They hurried out of the cave and Callum followed only to have Colin grab his hand and ask, "Have they hurt her?"

"I dinnae ken."

"But ye think they have."

"I fear they may have, or will, but I truly dinnae ken, am trying verra hard to nay think on it. But, aye, 'tis a possibility. They want her to confess."

"She willnae. She did naught."

He ruffled the boy's hair. "That I am sure of and it does make me fear for her. I do swear, if they have done her any true, hard injury, I will see that they pay for it."

Chapter Ten

Bethoc groaned, opened her eyes, and then scrambled to the far corner of the cell where she was wretchedly ill. Still shaking, she moved away from the mess she left and slumped against the wall, fighting to breathe deeply and slowly until the waves of sickness passed. She had been tossed in with the gray lump of rags she had noticed while being dragged off by the sheriff.

The fear that had not left her since the sheriff had arrived at her house took a sharp leap upward. Had they thrown her in with a man? Bethoc could not believe the sheriff would put men and women together. Then she narrowed her eyes as she stared at the lump and began to relax. Something about the size and shape of the heap of rags told her it was a woman or a child. There was also a scrap of graying lace among the scraps of clothing. She prayed she was not imagining the faint movement that indicated breathing.

As she worked up the strength, and courage, to poke at the rags and satisfy her curiosity, she thought of Callum. A small voice in her head insisted he would find her and save her. Another voice, that of her common sense she suspected, said there was nothing he could do except work up a good defense, do his best to prove she was innocent. He was going to find that difficult to do when the sheriff was so certain she was guilty.

For a few moments she thought on how there might be a way to defend herself that she had not used yet. Saying she had not done it and pointing out how she simply could not have done it was not working for her. Then she sighed. Bethoc doubted the sheriff would care whatever proof or logic she presented him with. He wanted a killer and had decided she would do. The question was why he was so unable to be reasoned with.

The pile of rags shifted and Bethoc froze. Slowly it rose up and leaned against the wall. One small, delicate hand lifted to brush away the dirt and fabric covering the face. Bethoc found herself staring at a young woman who, despite her bruises, was stunning in her beauty, from her wide blue eyes to her full-lipped mouth. A bath, some decent clothes, and her wounds healed and the woman could make kings bow before her.

"Ah, William has tried drowning ye, has he? First time?"

"Aye." Bethoc frowned. "He will try again?"

"Four times they dragged me down to that cursed barrel. Then they got brutal."

In an attempt not to think about what "got brutal" might mean, Bethoc asked, "Who are ye? I am Bethoc Matheson."

"Laurel MacKray. The sheriff thinks I killed my husband. Thought of it often enough but I couldnae do it. He was a nasty bastard but I am nay a killer. Who wants that sin on one's soul? Didnae do it when he did get killed. But the sheriff willnae listen."

"Nay. He willnae heed me, either. He thinks I killed Kerr Matheson, a mon many ken as my father."

"Hates women he does, ye ken. The fairer the lass the more he hates her. If she speaks up, the hate for her grows. The only ones he hates more than women is the magistrate but he cannae beat or rape that mon, can he."

Bethoc gasped. "The sheriff raped ye?"

"Him, William, and those two fools who trot after him everywhere." Seeing the horror on Bethoc's face, Laurel shrugged. "They dinnae ken who they are dealing with. My husband could do me more hurt even when he was sober." She looked curiously at Bethoc who was still pale with shock. "That these things shock ye so badly tells me ye have lived a sheltered life. Aye?"

"Weel, aye, I rarely was allowed to leave the house, though that has changed a bit of late."

"Ah, ye met a mon." She gave a laugh that made Bethoc shiver. "Watch him. The bastards are verra good at hiding the monster within. My husband was wondrous handsome, all right, and his monster appeared a fortnight after our marriage. Fool in love, I was. Told myself he had just lost his temper, he would control it better in the future. He didnae. And, since someone killed him, I assume he showed some other lass his monster."

"Nay, Callum isnae like that."

"They all are."

"Nay, he takes in the bairns, and occasionally their mothers who have been mistreated. Margaret adores him and she avoids men usually as our father was one to beat us, badly, from time to time. He didnae hit her but she saw him hitting the rest of us too often."

"Margaret?" Laurel asked.

"My sister. She is but two years and some. Nearing

three. My mother died bearing her and made me swear to never leave her." Bethoc frowned. "This will be the first time I have been away. The lads will be there but I have ne'er left her and she may nay be able to understand. She must be scared."

Laurel reached out and patted Bethoc's hand. Bethoc was astounded that after all she had endured, the woman could still be kind, still sympathize with someone in any way. It was at that moment she decided that Callum would be asked to do what needed doing to set Laurel free and see it done.

"There is something verra wrong with all of this."

"What do ye mean?" asked Laurel.

"The mon doesnae care about anything ye say. He has decided ye are guilty before he e'en hears what ye have to say. It makes no sense."

"Ah, nay, it doesnae, but I dinnae think the why makes a lot of difference to us. Whatever moves the sheriff he decided we were guilty and that is all that matters."

Her thoughts quickly turned to Margaret and the boys. Not only must it be difficult for Callum and his friends to deal with so many children, but the children had to be concerned for her. She prayed someone would take the time to comfort any of the children who needed it. Margaret would be badly in need of it to still her fears.

Callum walked into the sheriff's room with Margaret by his side and five little boys marching behind him, Uven guarding their backs. He noted the sheriff's eyes widened a little but then his face took on that almost petulant look of self-righteousness the man favored. Callum's free hand clenched on his walking stick. It took a lot of control to deal successfully with such fools, and Callum's temper was on a very frayed rope.

"What game do ye play, sir? What are these brats doing in my house?" the sheriff demanded.

"Try to speak more civilly, sir, ye are scaring the children." Callum patted Margaret's back as he picked her up. "Ye asked me to bring in the brothers and I have."

"Those bairns are nay them! What about the big lads? I ken weel that Kerr had some."

"The boys were with me all day," he lied without hesitation or shame. "As ye can see"—he patted his broken leg—"I have a lot of need of assistance. And ye obviously havenae seen the lads for they are nay so verra big."

"Then where were those bratlings if nay helping to kill Kerr Matheson?"

"These lads were working in the fields as they do every day when nay aiding me. If they had happened to see or hear anything, which I doubt, the men killing Kerr would have gutted and killed them as weel." Callum nearly smiled when he noticed the sheriff getting a look of panic in his eyes, obviously seeing too many holes in whatever plan he had devised. "I cannae stress enough that none who were in the area could have killed Kerr Matheson. Bethoc and these lads certainly wouldnae have tortured him. There are five men riding about with a growing list of crimes attributed to them, yet ye dinnae e'en ask for their description."

"Who the hell are ye?"

"Sir Callum Murray MacMillan, laird of Whytemont."

"I can give ye a verra good description of the five men, sir," said Magnus as he stepped up to the desk. "The leader was as tall as Sir Callum, had long brown hair and a brutish scar down his face that killed one eye but left the other a sort of muddy brown. The second man was taller, bone thin, had a hooked nose. He was missing two fingers on his right hand, last two of them. The third was shorter and square, so thick with muscles he might have had trouble moving about. He was fair with blond hair to his shoulders and little blue, blue eyes. Fourth fellow wasnae much of anything, ye ken?"

"Nay, I dinnae. What does that mean?" asked the sheriff, shocked by the boy's precise description yet fascinated.

"Ordinary people and all," replied Magnus. "He was nay too tall or too short, nay too thin or too fat, either. Hair was nay too short or too long save to say he had brown hair. Plain brown hair. And ordinary gray eyes. The last mon had a beard, it was black and streaked with silver but his head was bald. He also had a boil on his neck though it could break at any time and disappear so may nay matter. There, now ye can go look for them and let our Bethoc out."

Callum could tell the man had recognized the ones Magnus described. The way the man's eyes had briefly widened with certain descriptions gave him away. And that was why Bethoc was in jail, charged with murder, and, if this man could do it, would be convicted. The sheriff knew who Magnus spoke of and knew they had killed Kerr Matheson but planned to blame Bethoc for it. He either needed to impress his master or enrich him. It was hard to believe that flashing the fact that he was a MacMillan, a clan this area knew well, and laird of Whytemont could break that need. It should have worked and the very fact that it had not made him suspicious.

"If I catch such men and if they prove to be the

killers, then we will let her go," said the sheriff, still looking a bit dazed by Magnus but sounding firm.

With a shake of his head, Callum said, "Ye are making a verra big mistake, Master . . . ?" He looked at the man and waited for him to give up his name.

"MacDavid. Patrick MacDavid."

"Thank ye. I will remember it." He finally saw the man pale a little. "Now I would like to see Miss Matheson." When the man started to protest, Callum asked very quietly, "Is there some reason ye dinnae wish me to see her? To assure her that I am working to set her free?"

"Of course there isnae," snapped the man as he stood up and snatched some keys from a hook on the wall. "Ye will see that she is just fine. We dinnae mistreat our prisoners."

Callum fell into step behind the man, wincing as he heard the children walking behind him but he did not have the heart to tell them to wait for him. Uven moved up beside him to keep a close eye on the two men who flanked the sheriff. The two men said nothing but continually looked back at them as they went down the stairs. Margaret slipped her small hand into his and held on tight as they went down the well-worn steps. He tried hard not to think of how many had made their last walk on these steps but now he wondered how many had done so and been completely innocent.

"Bethoc?" she asked, staring up at him.

"Aye, we are going to see Bethoc now."

The moment the sheriff stopped before a cell Margaret ran up to the door and grabbed the bars. She struggled to open the door but Bethoc hurried over to her. "Nay, Margaret. 'Tis locked," she said.

Margaret spun around to glare at the sheriff. She

stamped her foot and pointed at the door. "Open! Now!" she bellowed.

It was difficult not to laugh, especially at the sheriff's shocked face, but Callum managed and grabbed hold of Margaret. "Now, lass, we told ye Bethoc was in jail, aye?" She nodded and her bottom lip began to wobble. "That means the door stays locked. Ye can still see her and talk to her though." His heart broke a little as two fat tears trickled down her cheeks but he set her down and she walked over to the bars to stick her arms through them and grab hold of Bethoc. He watched as Bethoc quietly talked to the child.

Bethoc tried to explain things to Margaret and thought the little girl understood most of it but the fat tears that kept trickling down her cheeks broke her heart. "I need to speak with Callum now, sweetling."

When Margaret kissed her and stepped back, Callum went up to the door. He glanced back at the little girl to see her standing next to Magnus, a fierce look on her face as she glared at the sheriff. It was hard not to laugh as the man began to look increasingly uncomfortable.

Then he turned all of his attention to Bethoc as he clasped her hands in his. She looked wet and tired. The tired he could understand. The wet, though, confused him. He lightly touched her gown and frowned when he found it wet.

"Why are ye so wet?" he asked.

"We always wash the prisoners down," said the sheriff quickly. "Vermin, ye ken. Dinnae want them in here."

A lie, Callum thought, and looked at Bethoc, but she just smiled at him and said, "Ye are looking verra fine."

"Thank ye. I decided it was time to be a laird again.

Doesnae appear to be working as I had hoped," he added in a whisper, "and I mean to find out why. There is something amiss here, something bigger than we can see right now."

"Weel, while ye are doing that, mayhap ye find out what ye can about Laurel MacKray accused of killing her husband. And, nay, I dinnae think she did it, but he is dead and her land is forfeit to the magistrate. They have been verra hard on her in here."

"Is she that pile of rags o'er there in the corner?"

"Aye. She went that way the moment she heard ye approaching. She does it whene'er she hears anyone approach."

"That is enough whispering," snapped the sheriff. "Ye can talk so all can hear. I will have nay conspiring with the prisoner."

"I mean to get ye out of here, Bethoc." Callum ceased whispering but talked softly nonetheless. "Robbie has gone to get a friend of the Murrays who can help."

"How long do ye think that will take?" Bethoc had no wish to see what would happen to her after the fourth dunking in the water barrel.

"He told me the mon was close at hand so nay too long. And now that Magnus has told us what the men who did it look like, I can watch for them as weel. Though I did give a fairly good description of them myself."

A ray of hope shone in her heart and refused to be snuffed out. "The sheriff willnae like that. Any fool could see it would be nigh on impossible for me to do it but I dinnae think he cares who did the killing at all."

"Nay, I dinnae either. If Robbie brings who he is after, I am thinking more than the sheriff will find themselves in a pile of trouble." Out of the corner of his eye he caught the man nudging closer in the hopes of catching every word. "So, hold on, Bethoc," he said clearly. "Ye will be out of here soon." He turned toward the sheriff. "I would suggest it might be verra wise to be certain she is treated weel." Before the sheriff could answer, Callum walked out.

The boys ran up to the cell and grinned at her. "I told him," said Magnus, pointing at the sheriff, "what they all looked like so he will go after them now. Then ye can be free."

Bethoc could tell by the sheriff's face that he had no intention of following that plan but she did not tell the boys. She took care to reassure them as well as she could. Then gave them each a kiss and sent them on their way, watching as they ran up the stairs, Uven right behind them. She had to smile for she doubted Callum's cousin had ever expected to be made a child tender. Then she looked at the sheriff and froze. The look the man gave her did not bode well for him obeying Callum's order to treat her kindly. Bethoc hoped Callum could work fast with all the new information he had.

"Your laird doesnae rule o'er this village, woman. Nay matter how weel ye pleasure the fool, he never will." The sheriff smiled in a way that was definitely not friendly and marched off, his guards staying close.

"Was that your mon?"

Bethoc jumped a little in surprise as she turned around to look at Laurel. "I dinnae have a mon."

Laurel laughed. "Och, ye certainly do. That was Margaret, aye?"

"Aye, that was my wee Margaret."

"A beautiful wee lass, and she kens what she wants."

Bethoc laughed as she moved closer to Laurel and sat down. "I need to keep a watch on that and get her to, er, soften her demands." Laurel laughed. "She can be verra forceful."

"Och, nay," Laurel said, laughter still in her voice. "She just hasnae learned the correct ways to get what she wants when she wants it. Or how to properly show her anger and disgust with an oaf like our sheriff. She is a lass with wit and strength. It already shines in her. It just needs honing. The lads look to be fine little lads, as weel."

"They are. These troubles have shown me that. They need more than working those lands for naught though and now it appears I may have lost them a chance to finally have that. They will lose the only home they have e'er kenned."

"Ah, because it will be taken."

"Aye, as yours was and, I suspicion, as those women who sadly hanged lost theirs."

"Ye think this is something to do with the lands?"

"'Tis a thought and it would explain so much. Callum feels sure something else is going on here. He also thinks it might have to do with what is being forfeited by the women arrested."

"It would have to be someone beside the sheriff though. And I cannae believe it of the magistrate. Dinnae ken the mon weel but he is said to be kind and just. This is neither."

"Callum and his friends will sniff it out."

The sound of heavy, slow steps quieted both of them. Bethoc watched Laurel disappear into a pile of rags again and wished she could do the same as William appeared at the door and smiled. She decided she loathed that smile and would like nothing more than to have the strength to wipe it off his face. When he opened the door and pulled her out, she prayed she faced no more than she had before. Terrifying though it was, it would not be death by the command of a foolish man she now suspected was trying to satisfy a greedy man.

"They have been doing something to her," said Callum later that night as Uven came to settle down on the pallet. "I dinnae ken what but her gown was wet."

"Ye dinnae think it was what he said."

"Nay, I think he was lying and she cleverly changed the subject."

Uven frowned. "No bruises or other signs of injury?"

"Nay, not that I could see. Yet what would leave her in a wet gown?"

"Plunging her in the water. Was her hair wet too? I didnae look."

"Aye, it was, though nearly dry. So what are ye thinking they are doing to her?"

"Dunking. The dunking could be used to get her to confess. Dinnae think there is anyone who isnae afraid of drowning, aye?"

"Aye," Callum agreed, his anger simmering inside him as he recalled the fear he had felt when he had thought he would drown. "They put her in water until she feared she was going to drown, didnae they? And for that she was supposed to say, 'Oh, aye, I killed Kerr.'"

"I believe that is how 'tis done, aye, though I have only ever shoved a mon's head into the water until he thought he would drown. He did tell me what I wanted to ken though."

For a moment Callum forgot his anger and stared at Uven. "Just when were ye holding a mon's head under the water to get information and why?"

"King's business."

"*Jesu*, Uven, that is a good way to meet God early."

Uven winced. "I kenned it nay long after that and got away. It was exciting but, aye, a good way to get yourself killed." He crossed his arms under his head. "Aye, had a lot that I liked what with that excitement, the danger, and, oh, the lassies who smile favorably on such men. Then a friend was killed. After I was done grieving for him, I looked at all he had lost, all he would ne'er have, and weighed it against what he had accomplished, none of it for him, only for the king, and it didnae weigh in weel. For king and country, aye, in a battle, a war, a true fight with good, clear reasons. The other things, the spying, watching fools who think they are so much better and should be king? Nay. That sort of thing also turns on ye when ye least expect it and ye can get killed by the ones ye used to call friend. I walked away. Too many secrets. Too many lies."

"Verra wise, especially when ye find out the one the king names an enemy isnae always a true threat to the throne."

Uven laughed. "Och, aye, true enough."

Callum smiled but then sighed, unable to hold fast to any humor. Those men at the sheriff's had been using torture to get Bethoc to confess to a crime she had not committed. He was not sure what they were doing since they would have to submerge her completely to get her gown as soaked as it was. She had to have been so afraid, he thought, and that stirred his anger. He had not protected her.

"If she gets but one wound, one bruise, I will beat the whole lot of them into the dust," he finally said.

He glanced over at Uven and sighed again. His cousin was asleep. He would obviously be sharing his bed tonight, just not with the company he would prefer. Settling down as comfortably as he could, he closed his eyes. Callum knew rest was needed if he was to be able to free Bethoc. If naught else, he would need his wits sharp.

Sleep was almost upon him when he felt a small weight jostle the pallet then curl up at his side. Callum opened one eye and saw Margaret huddled up against him, half on his chest. He put his arm around her in the hope that he could keep her from rolling off the pallet. Although there was no whining, no crying, he knew the child missed Bethoc. He missed Bethoc. Silently he swore to Margaret that he would get Bethoc out of that cell even if he had to raid the place, grab her, and then flee.

Chapter Eleven

Waking up and retching was getting tedious, Bethoc decided as she crawled away from the mess she had made. She always held the fear that William would make a mistake and she would actually drown. Nothing she did could ease that fear. Her belly hurt as did her lungs. The rest of her body ached all over. She feared sitting around in damp clothes would bring on a fever as well and, if she got a fever in this wretched place, it could kill her.

Perhaps she should have told Callum what they were doing but she had eluded his every question about her damp clothing and her weariness. One look at the sheriff was enough to make her believe that, if she spoke up, it would be far, far worse for her and that was terrifying. She had nursed Laurel after the men had taken her away and she lived in fear of the same thing happening to her.

"Better now?" asked Laurel as she sat up and looked at Bethoc.

"A bit. Getting the water out helps."

"That was the fourth dunking," Laurel whispered.

"I ken it. All I can do is pray Callum returns with what is needed to set us free."

"Us." Laurel laughed and it was not a pretty sound. "Ye really think he can free me?"

"Aye. If there is any proof ye didnae kill your husband he *will* find it."

"I pray ye are right because I fear I will soon say whate'er they want to hear just to make it stop." She began to softly weep, quickly covering her face with her hands.

Bethoc staggered over to sit beside her and hold her. She had wondered when the woman would break and marveled at her strength. The fact that no one came for her or spoke up for her certainly did not help. Laurel had no hope to cling to and was losing the need to hold fast to the truth. If she gave that up, she would hang for a murder she had not committed. Bethoc suddenly wondered how many other women had done so, wondered if they had broken and confessed to a crime they had not committed just to get the men to leave them be. It was horrible to consider.

After a moment Laurel sat up again and wiped the tears from her face. "I am sorry."

"Ye have naught to be sorry for. They should be beaten within an inch of their miserable lives."

"That would be a pleasure to see. Nay, I apologized because I failed in my promise to myself. I promised I wouldnae break down like this and add to any fear ye may have."

"And ye did verra weel but I was still terrified. It is like something alive inside of me so dinnae hold strong for my sake. And I can do naught but marvel at the strength ye have shown. The sheriff really isnae interested in the truth, is he. He doesnae care if we did it or nay."

"Nay, he wants us to confess. Then we hang and his

laird takes our lands." Laurel huffed out a cynical laugh. "He can have mine. I dinnae want them. Too many dark memories. Do ye ken, he ne'er offered us money for it? No one came by to e'en ask me or my husband if they could buy the property. I dinnae understand that."

"Nay, it makes no sense."

"'Tis almost as if he wants to be verra sure there is no one to lay claim to the land, to mayhap argue his rights to them."

"Weel, my boys have a right to that land. And, it was my mother's kin who gave it to Kerr. So, e'en if they can say I am nay his daughter, Kerr still had the right to pass his land o'er to whomever he wished. And, then there is Margaret. She *is* his child. Nay doubt about that."

The moment she said it, Bethoc was hit by a wave of panic. Margaret could be considered the true heir if Kerr had written no will, had never bothered to state who would have the farm after he was gone. Yet Margaret was still just a child, she thought as she fought down the panic gripping her. A child too young to be a threat. She would not be a child forever, though, which meant, if she was not gotten rid of soon, she would become a threat to whoever was after the land.

"Bethoc!" snapped Laurel. "Margaret is safe with your mon. He willnae let anyone get to her."

It took several slow, deep breaths before Bethoc could crawl past her fear. "Of course, Callum will care for her. I suspicion he has already seen the danger. I wish he would come. Then I could be certain of it. Or warn him." She frowned. "Yet why would the laird, if it is the laird, do this? Doesnae he own all the land anyway?"

"Most of it. People pay a rent fee. But nay every inch. Some ancestor could have gifted the land to someone for some brave deed done or e'en sold it off when the coin was needed. The people would then have papers saying so."

"Papers?"

"Aye, something signed by whatever laird gave it or sold it, mayhap ones e'en carrying the king's seal." Laurel frowned. "I dinnae ken where Robert put his. He had some and was verra proud of them. He kept them close. Some ancestor saved a laird's son and was given the land."

"How was Robert killed?"

"He was gutted out behind some tavern. It was an appalling wound and he suffered a lot before he died. Unfortunately, the only word he said clearly was my name. So they took me up. I was at home but no one stepped forward to say they saw me there, which was an odd thing. I was working in the garden until late, then shortly after that, I was sitting out there because it was a fine evening and cooler out there than inside. Someone should have seen me as all my neighbors have a clear view of the back of my house. Now I wonder if they e'en asked or if my neighbors e'en ken where I am." She shook her head. "How did they gather ye in?"

"Some men told the sheriff they heard screaming and were sure murder was being done at my house. So the sheriff says. So they came out to look and found me." Bethoc sighed. "I didnae much like Kerr and kenned he wasnae my father but I played the game for years. Mayhap that is why I couldnae abide him left tied to a chair with pieces of him scattered about his feet. I went back to bury him."

"Ye lived with him all your life. Sometimes that is enough."

"I suppose so but it proved to be a foolish mistake." She shook her head. "I didnae ken what the men were after so I cannae say why they tortured him so badly. There is this boy Cathan who they took from Callum. They did ask after him. I fear I saw that much. They obviously thought Kerr kenned where he was or learned that he was the one who took the boy away from them. I only kenned who the boy was because Callum spoke of him."

"A verra tangled mess. Whoever is doing this no doubt sees it as an easy way to get the land." She frowned. "There is a verra greedy mon at work here and this town is corrupt, I think."

"Weel, Callum will uncover it all. We can only pray he can do so in time to help us."

"This must be the most corrupt village I have e'er entered," said Sir Simon Innes as he entered the cave. "Did ye find any papers?" he asked Callum as Robbie handed him a tankard of ale.

"Aye and it appears Kerr saved everything anyone ever wrote down for him." Callum scowled at the box he was slowly working his way through.

At Sir Simon's instructions, they had ransacked the house searching for proof of ownership, for any official papers at all. All of them had searched, the boys proving to be invaluable. It was surprising how many small places there were in the house and they required a small, agile boy to search them. In one of them was stuffed this box. Callum assumed Kerr Matheson either had a crook to reach it and pull it out or had used one of the boys when he was too young to recall it later.

"Ah, I think I finally have something useful," Callum muttered as he thumbed through a set of papers that had been tied together with a heavy ribbon.

Sir Simon sat down on the pallet beside him and held

out his hand. Callum gave him the papers and waited tensely. The man had immediately responded to Robbie's request for help. He was clearly a man with a strong sense of justice and a sharp curiosity about puzzles. Although he had not said so, Callum believed Sir Simon had dealt with a similar trouble for he recognized the problem and knew exactly what they needed.

"Aye, this is what ye need," Sir Simon said. "The land was bought and paid for by Kerr Matheson's late wife's parents. I suppose one must give them some credit for nay just tossing the lass out into the street even if they did choose badly when they bribed Matheson into marrying her."

"I suspicion he presented a fine image for them back then," said Callum. "And, to be fair, he may have thought she would come to love him but she disappeared into dreams about Brett Murray, the one who gave her Bethoc."

"Now we can free her but this does naught for that other poor woman. Ye are sure she is innocent?"

"Bethoc is and what we learned about her husband's murder makes me believe Bethoc's instincts are right. She has been treated poorly. I need to get Bethoc out of there before they treat her the same."

"We need to find at least one of those five men."

"Ye think he would confess or turn on his companions?"

"They tied a mon to a chair and cut bits off him until he died. They attacked ye, a lone rider, as a group. They were after a little boy, one they probably intended to kill or kenned they would be asked to do so. All for what, I suspicion, would seem a pittance to us. Aye. It may take a wee bit of persuasion, but any one of them will confess and point fingers at anyone involved in a vain attempt to save their own miserable lives or e'en just to be sure they dinnae hang alone."

Callum nodded and began to understand how this man had risen to become the king's man and gain such a fearsome reputation. "Then we best hope our Simon and Uven find the bastards for I cannae wait long when I can use these papers to free Bethoc."

"Ye fear they will abuse her."

"Aye," Callum said between gritted teeth. "I doubt my threats will deter them."

"Nay, nay for long. So we best make an effort to get those men."

"Will two of them do?"

Sir Simon and Callum were startled by Uven's voice, not having heard him enter. Right behind him came Robbie dragging two tightly bound men. Sir Simon strode over and stared down at the two men Robbie dropped to the ground and Callum quickly followed.

"Ye caught the leader," Callum said, nudging the scarred man with the toe of his boot.

"Have we?" Uven shrugged. "Mayhap he will ken something useful."

"What happened to the other three?"

"One escaped although I am nay sure he will live long with the wound he has. The other two are dead. They proved reluctant to come along willingly." Uven grinned.

"Weel, at least ye left two to speak."

"Ah, knocked them out first then tried to persuade the others."

Sir Simon grinned. "Good work. Now we wake them and get information."

Robbie walked off and brought back a bucket of water, which he dumped on the men's heads and Sir Simon laughed softly. "Thank ye."

Consciousness was regained slowly and then Sir Simon crouched down next to the scarred man. Callum saw the expression that had undoubtedly struck terror into the hearts of many. The scarred man could not successfully hide all his fear as he looked at Sir Simon.

"Why did ye take the boy Cathan?" Sir Simon asked.

The man's voice was calm even if his face was cold and threatening. It revealed a great control over himself. That was terrifying and it was evident the scarred man thought so as well. Callum knew he would never want to be questioned by the man if he was hiding something.

"His family wanted the boy back," said the scarred man.

"Why?"

"'Cause he is family."

"And holds both coin and land."

"Aye."

"Yet his mother, when she ran to Whytemont, gave the rights of guardian to Sir Callum MacMillan."

"She was sick and not in her right mind," the scarred man spoke as if reciting a hard-learned lesson.

"And was that the reason ye beat the laird of Whytemont and tossed him into the water to drown?"

"What? I . . . He wouldnae give us the lad!"

Callum fought the urge to say something because he suddenly saw what Sir Simon was doing. Lulled by easy questions he had ready answers for, ones that could be answered without incriminating himself, the scarred man was thrown off when given a hard one and blurted out the truth. He was eager to see how the technique would work in getting the information to set Bethoc and Laurel free.

Sir Simon settled down on the ground, sipped his drink, and then began to question the other man, tricking him into also confessing the attack on Callum. Callum sat down on the ground to watch. It was as good as a play. Sir Simon showed no reaction with each hard truth he pulled out. He quietly listened and then pressed for more.

"I must say, it has been a long time since I have uncovered such a putrid mess. Corruption, bribes, murder, anticipated murder, and the use of helpless women to steal land." Sir Simon stood up, handed Robbie his empty tankard, and brushed his hands off. "Ye will, of course, hang but ye will have a lot of company on the gallows."

"No one will heed ye," the scarred man said but the taint of panic was in his voice.

"Oh, aye, they will. Ye see, I am nay just a knight or a laird. I was served as the king's mon. They called me the King's Hound. Unflattering but useful."

When Sir Simon walked away, Callum followed. "Ye, sir, are a marvel."

Sir Simon laughed. "Thank ye, but there is naught marvelous about it. Ye make them calm with easy questions they have readied, practiced answers for, answers that will nay hurt them, and then abruptly slip in a hard one. They almost always falter then. Only the truly evil can evade the trap and these men are naught but hired brutes."

"So we take them to the sheriff now?"

"Och, aye, and I will enjoy presenting them to the sheriff." Sir Simon smiled. "From what ye have told me of the mon, that fool will break fast and give us a flood of information. I feel there will be a lot of men in positions of power who will fall soon. The fact that it involves the taking of land implies it. Then mayhap the people in the village will breathe easily again."

"Thank ye for this, for coming so quickly."

Sir Simon waved away the thanks. "Too many similarities to what happened to my wife Ilsabeth to resist. Women are too often seen as nay more than easy prey. Few risk standing up for them, either. And if what ye say is true, she could be a cousin. But this has felt good. I do like to keep my hand in, keep my skills sharp. Now, let us load these fools on a horse and go get the women free."

"I pray we are in time."

"Aye." Sir Simon's face darkened. "We will be or someone will pay."

As they tossed the men on the back of their own horses, Callum felt his tension grow. He could not forget that huddled bundle of rags that was Laurel, a poor abused woman unfairly accused. Each day that passed, he could see Bethoc becoming that. It had only been four days since he had seen her, but he thought that three too many. Her place in that jail ate at him until he found himself making plans on how to break her out of the jail. He was glad he did not have to carry out any of those plans and he prayed the delay did not cost Bethoc too dearly.

Bethoc slumped against the wall and breathed a sigh of relief. The footsteps had not been coming for her. They had been dragging in another poor woman. She felt sorry for her as it was possible they were blaming her for some crime she had not committed as well. If so, why was no one taking any notice? Did they think there was some outbreak of murderous rage among the women in town? Did all these women have no one ready to stand for them? Why was there no one in town simply asking about what was happening?

"Laurel? Was there no one to stand for ye? No one to ask why?"

"Nay. My family was pleased about my marriage but then they, weel, drifted away. They still had six children and Robert wasnae verra welcoming. What hurt was that my own mother believed I did it. She visited me here once and berated me for nay quietly enduring whate'er Robert did."

"Sorry." Bethoc sighed. "Do ye think the woman they just dragged in has anyone?"

"Nay. That was Lorraine Halliday. Orphaned. She had a husband much like mine so I suspicion there were nay too many friends. I dinnae ken what she has that they want, though. Mayhap the building the shop is in." She shrugged. "I wonder if we can find out what she was taken up for. I dinnae ken her weel enough to e'en guess."

"They have quite a nice business going here, dinnae they," Bethoc muttered.

"Oh, aye. I wonder who leads it all. I just cannae believe it is the laird."

"Mayhap one of his sons. Does he have sons?"

"Four. Aye, it could be one of the younger ones. It doesnae matter. 'Tis still too late for Yolanda."

"Yolanda?"

"A woman who was here when I was brought in. She wasnae much older than me. They hanged her a few days ago for the murder of her husband."

"Oh, *Jesu*," Bethoc whispered. "'Tis what we face, aye?"

"Aye. I just dinnae ken when. She had a wee boy, too, and constantly wept for him."

Bethoc tensed. "A boy. Do ye ken if she said what he looks like? Ye ken Kerr liked to get boys to work his fields and I may ken who the lad is."

"Aye, she always spoke of his big brown eyes. She

had them too. Big eyes, deep brown, and so full of expression until these bastards killed all the life in them. And I guess he was a clever wee fellow. She was so proud of him but ne'er saw him again before she was hanged."

"Do ye ken how old he was?"

"Five? Six? He wasnae a bairn. Why?"

"Aye, I think Kerr had him, took him, whate'er. Ye ken the boy who stepped forward to describe the five men I blame for Kerr's murder?" Laurel nodded. "That was Magnus. He is six and he has those eyes. Big, brown, full of expression. He has been with us for seven months now though so it doesnae fit, does it?"

"It may. I only caught a glimpse of him but if he has anything of his mother in him, I would recognize it once I got a good look at him. I still see the look in her eyes as they led her off to her hanging, see them in my sleep. The resignation, the depth of the sadness, was heartbreaking. She kenned she was going to die, her good name now blackened by a crime she didnae commit. And, at times, when she talked of her lad, I got the feeling she spoke of a dead child or one lost to her for a while."

"If fate allows it, I will get ye that look at him."

Both women tensed as footsteps echoed in the hall. Laurel whimpered faintly and disappeared into her disguise as a pile of rags. Bethoc felt her heart start to pound so fast and hard she feared it could break free of her chest. They had not given her as much time to recover from a near drowning as they had before. She was terrified Laurel was right about what followed the fourth dunking.

The sheriff and his two silent guards stopped before her cell. There was a look on the man's face that told what she feared was going to happen. So did the absence of William. She stepped back and kept trying to step back as they unlocked the door and walked inside. The two guards leapt forward and grabbed her by the arms. To her shock, Laurel suddenly came alive and leapt at the men, her hands curved into claws.

"Bitch!" screamed the sheriff as Laurel's nails scraped his face before one of his men pulled her off.

The battle was short but vicious. All the men were bleeding slightly before Laurel was knocked back against the wall so hard she lost consciousness. Bethoc kept struggling in an attempt to get free and go to her aid but the sheriff's men just tightened their grip on her. As they dragged her out of her cell she saw Laurel move and breathed a sigh of relief.

"Sir Callum said ye had best nay leave a mark on me," she said.

"Then we will hold ye verra gently," said the sheriff and the way the guards laughed chilled her blood.

So terrified she could think of nothing else to say, she concentrated on doing what she could to stop her progress down the hall. They passed a cell and she saw a woman sprawled on the floor, coughing and choking as she emptied her lungs and belly of water. The men did not even glance at the woman. At that moment her hatred of the men hardened. It would not do any good, would not save her, but it was there in her heart, cold and hard and begging for vengeance.

"Are ye nay e'en going to ask for my confession?" she demanded as they shoved her into a room.

"Ye will give it to us before long," said the sheriff.

"But I am ready to give it now and save ye all the trouble of pulling it out of me."

"It willnae be any trouble."

The two men yanked her back and tossed her down onto a bed. Bethoc fought hard but they managed to get her hands and feet tied to the posts. Then she looked at the sheriff, who smiled coldly, and began to pray for Callum to arrive. She just wished there was some small chance her prayers would be answered.

Chapter Twelve

Callum helped carry the men into the sheriff's and frowned when he found a strange man in the sheriff's seat. "Where is the sheriff?"

"He is busy now. I am William and ye can tell me your business." The man leaned back in his seat and crossed his impressive arms over his chest. "What do ye want?"

"I have the men who killed Kerr Matheson and murdered Robert MacKray."

"Aye?" The man stood up and looked over the desk, peering down at the two bound men. "Why do ye think they are guilty?"

"Because they told us," said Sir Simon. "They confessed it to me."

"And who are ye?"

"Lord Simon Innes, laird of Lochancorrie, and I used to be kenned as the King's Hound."

The way William reacted told Callum he had heard of Sir Simon. He paled and carefully moved back to sink down in his chair. His big hands clenched the arms of the chair. For a moment he stared at Sir Simon in silence, his wide eyes showing fear, and then he cleared his throat.

"What do ye want?"

"I want Bethoc Matheson and Laurel MacKray released. Here are the guilty men so ye can set the women free. They are clearly nay guilty. Now, where are they?" demanded Callum.

"Down the stairs. Miss Matheson is being interrogated," he said as if relating a lesson well learned.

Callum felt alarm tighten in his belly and took off. He heard Sir Simon order William to watch the men and, a moment later, he heard his three companions following him. He reached the cell she had been locked in and Laurel rushed up to the bars. There was a bruise on the side of her face and her lip was bleeding. The sight caused Callum to taste the sour wash of fear.

"They took her off!" Laurel cried. "Ye have to go get them, stop them."

"Where?" he demanded as Sir Simon stepped up and unlocked the door, causing Callum to wonder why he had not thought of snatching the keys before running off.

"Follow me," Laurel said, and took off running down the passageway.

Hurrying after the woman he had only ever seen as a pile of rags with an occasional sight of a blue eye peeking at him, Callum realized Laurel MacKray was beautiful. He caught sight of another woman in a cell, weeping as she stood at the front of her cell watching them. He glanced back to see Sir Simon stop to talk to the woman but Uven and Robbie stayed hard on his heels.

Then they reached a closed door and Laurel began to frantically try to open it, pounding on the door when it would not budge. Callum gently nudged her aside and signaled to Uven and Robbie. Those two men kicked it open quickly and as Callum rushed inside the sight that met his eyes caused rage to sweep over him. The sheriff was settled between Bethoc's legs, his manhood in his hand, and he was reaching for the braies she wore. He yanked the sheriff off of Bethoc and tossed him into a wall. Uven and Robbie quickly took down the two guards as Callum bent to untie Bethoc's hands and feet from the narrow bed they had put her on.

Bethoc just stared at Callum as he freed her, unable to believe he had come, and just in time. He gently took her into his arms and, despite all her efforts not to, she burst into tears. She knew they were caused by both the fear she had fought to hide and pure, joyous relief. Rape had come too close. The men's blatant lust had left her feeling dirty.

"Ye are safe now, Bethoc," Callum said, holding her close and rubbing her back.

"I ken it." She pulled away and wiped at the tears on her cheeks. "I need to cease being weak. How did ye get here in time?"

"We found the true killers and had just brought them in."

"So, ye think that will free me? And Laurel?" She glanced at her friend to see Laurel being kept out of the way of the guards by Uven.

"And Lorraine Halliday," said a tall, dark man as he stepped into the room, Lorraine staying close behind him.

Laurel and Bethoc both broke free of the men they were with at the same time and ran to each other. For a moment they just hugged. Bethoc felt a sharp sympathy for Laurel. She had been saved that final degradation, but had a better understanding of the terror the woman had suffered. To be so helpless was not something she wished to ever feel again.

"Did they . . . ?" began Laurel.

"Nay." She pulled back from Laurel and looked at the room. "They have been doing this for some time."

"Aye, I fear so. What better way to torture a woman, to make her swear to whatever ye want her to. I would have broken soon," she added softly in a tremulous voice.

"I think it is to be ended now," she said quietly as she watched the tall, dark-haired man who had brought Lorraine in walk over to the sheriff. "That is a verra serious mon, one who willnae abide lies or evil games like this one."

He smelled like an old pine, she thought, one of those big, sturdy old trees that stood no matter what storm battered them. She tensed and glanced around then told herself not to be an idiot. People could not tell what she was thinking. Her odd little skill was still a deep, dark secret.

Turning, but keeping an arm around Bethoc's waist, Laurel watched the man crouch by the sheriff. "Nay, he doesnae, but we shall see," Laurel said softly.

"Awake?" the man asked the sheriff when he groaned and opened his eyes.

"Aye, aye. Who are . . ." The sheriff began to sit up and caught sight of Callum. "Ye threw me! Weel, ye will pay dearly for that, sir. I dinnae care if ye are a laird. Ye dinnae lay violent hand on a sheriff."

"Sit," said the man crouched near him as the sheriff started to get to his feet.

The sheriff gaped at the man. Then, slowly, his

expression changed from shock to wary confusion. He carefully sat down.

"Who are ye?" he asked.

"Sir Simon Innes, laird of Lochancorrie. Ye may ken me from a position I once had as the King's Hound." He nodded slightly when the sheriff paled. "I have a few questions I would like ye to answer."

"What questions? And what are these women doing out of their cells?"

"I believe ye have the answer for that."

"What do ye mean? I am just doing my job."

"And what part of your job says 'interrogation' includes the base use of a woman put in your care?"

His words were soft yet so cold, Bethoc was not surprised when she shivered. It pleased her to feel Laurel do so as well, although she feared ugly memories of this room might have some part in it. She slipped her arm around Laurel's shoulders and gave her a little squeeze.

"I wasnae doing that! I was just holding her down as I questioned her."

"Ah, I see, and that works weel, does it? I am still rather curious as to what part your penis played for ye had it in your hand with your kilt hiked up high. Going to beat the truth out of her and forgot your stick, did ye?"

"Nay, I didnae. Ye . . . I . . ."

Sir Simon surged to his feet and then yanked the sheriff up. "I have some men ye need to meet."

Uven and Robbie grabbed the guards. Callum went to collect up the woman but it was Laurel who went to Lorraine and led her away. He took Bethoc by the hand, pleased to find no resistance. It was clear what she had been through would not cause her to fully reject him.

"I was in time, aye?" he asked as they followed the others.

"Aye." She managed a brief smile. "My braies confounded them."

"Another reason many a Murray lass wears them. I think it was Elspeth who said they can buy ye a few moments to get free."

"Or have some men kick down the door so they can all rush in and start tossing men around."

"Aye, that too." He gave her a quick kiss on her cheek.

Bethoc was feeling safe again and she savored the feeling. "Ye have some powerful friends," she murmured with a nod toward Sir Simon.

"Ah, weel, Robbie fetched him. Seems all this reminded Sir Simon of when his wife was wrongly arrested. He is wed to a Murray lass. Elspeth's daughter in truth. Two strong reasons. I also think it has been a while since he has had a good puzzle to solve."

"Was he really the King's Hound?"

"Aye. He had a reputation for being honest and unrelenting in his search for the truth. Beginning to see why," Callum said as they reached the sheriff's office.

The sheriff looked at the two men tied up on the floor and all the color drained from his face. He staggered to his chair and sat down. Uven and Robbie shoved the two guards against the wall and stood watch over them. It was then that Callum realized William had fled.

"William has taken to his heels," said Callum.

"I doubt a mon who looks like him will be hard to find if we need him," said Sir Simon and then he looked at the sheriff. "I believe ye ken these two men."

"Aye," the sheriff muttered, looking as if he was about to weep.

"Weel, they have confessed to attacking Sir Callum here, of torturing and murdering Kerr Matheson, and of gutting Robert MacKray. They also claim ye were aware of all of it." He glanced at the scarred man. "Who are ye?"

"Ian MacDuff." He tilted his head toward the other man caught with him. "This is Dougal Marr."

"Are ye weel acquainted with the sheriff?"

"Aye, but he isnae the one we work for."

"And who would that be?"

"Nay sure but he is close to the laird, mayhap e'en one of the mon's sons. What did I care? His money was good."

Sir Simon took a deep breath and let it out slowly then quietly asked, "And Master Halliday?"

"What of him? He is dead. Got his throat cut, didnae he?"

"Strange that ye ken how he died."

"Why? 'Tis a village. People talk."

"Mistress Halliday, might I ask just when your husband died?" Sir Simon politely asked.

"Sometime in the night. They found him in the fields outside of the village," she replied. "The sheriff and his men found him round dawn and then came to take me up."

He looked at the sheriff. "Ye have quite the profitable business working here, dinnae ye. Kill the mon, take up the wife for murder, and confiscate all the property."

"Ye cannae prove that."

Sir Simon smiled. "Oh, I could but I dinnae really have to. What I do have is enough to set the women free. I also have papers to prove Matheson's property was fully his, sold by the laird himself. I suspicion I will find papers at the other houses. Your hirelings didnae search weel enough." The glare the sheriff sent Mac-Duff was enough to confirm Sir Simon's suspicions that they worked together.

"There were three others," said Laurel. "They have been hanged!"

"Weel, we will see their names cleared as weel. 'Tisnae nearly enough but at least they will be recalled as murdered nay murderers. How about the magistrate? Is he part of all this?"

"Part of what?" asked the sheriff, and he jumped when Sir Simon slammed his hands down on the table and leaned toward him.

"Dinnae play with me, sir. I can pull in a near army of men to dig out all your secrets. Who is the magistrate here and is he a part of this?"

"The magistrate is Sir Walter MacKray and he doesnae ken anything. He but passes judgment on the prisoners we bring him." Every word sounded as if it had been pulled out of the sheriff, an unwilling confession.

"I see." Sir Simon straightened up and looked at Callum. "Can ye watch this lot? I believe I should go inform the magistrate that he sent three innocent women to their deaths."

"I will go with ye," said Robbie as he stepped forward.

"Ye cannae leave three men guarding five. Best if ye stay here," said Sir Simon.

Robbie nodded toward the sheriff. "He could be lying. Magistrate could be part of it all."

"I dinnae believe he is lying."

"Two of the men are tied up."

"Robbie, I . . ."

Robbie walked over to the sheriff's two guards, grabbed their heads, and slammed them together. He walked back to Sir Simon even as the two men slumped to the ground unconscious. Bethoc stared at the men, then glanced at Laurel and Lorraine and all three women looked back at the guards while fighting not to laugh.

"Numbers are better now. We can go," Robbie said.

"Of course." Sir Simon made it out the door before he started to laugh.

Callum shook his head and looked at Uven who said, "Robbie's idea of a solution to the problem."

"Simple and direct. Do ye think the magistrate is part of it all?" Callum asked.

"If Sir Simon says nay, then nay. He has a good ear for a lie." Uven looked at the sheriff. "He kens this fat fool is lying."

"I havenae killed anyone," protested the sheriff.

"Nay? Ye took up three women, accused them of murders ye kenned they didnae commit, abused them, and when ye tired of that, saw them sentenced and hanged." Uven looked at him in disgust. "That was murder."

The sheriff stuttered as he struggled to protest that charge.

"Hush," snapped Uven. "Nay more lies. We willnae heed them. Ye are worse than that scum," he said as he pointed at MacDuff. "They got the blood on their hands but that doesnae make yours clean. Enriched yourself nicely, I wager. Either from what the woman had or by helping yourself to some of the pay meant for these fools."

MacDuff sat up straighter and saw the truth in the sheriff's face. "You bastard!"

Uven ignored that and asked the sheriff, "Did ye get to keep one of the properties?"

"Nay! I kept none of the lands. They all went to . . ." He abruptly closed his mouth.

"Ah, nay, there is at least one more player in this game. Best to give up the name. We will find it out anyway," said Callum.

The sheriff kept his eyes lowered and shook his head.

"I am certain we will find out soon. Sir Simon has a true skill for ferreting out the truth. Aye, ye may nay have wielded the knife but ye are a part of these killings, a verra big part. Ye are also all foul rapists."

"They were willing," the sheriff protested.

Laurel marched over to the table in front of him and mimicked Sir Simon, slapping her hands down on the table, causing the sheriff to jump. She leaned forward and spat, "Willing? Ye tell yourself we were willing?"

"Ye didnae fight, did ye?" The look in her eyes made him lean back as far as he could without moving his chair.

"'Tis hard to fight three men, even harder to fight when ye are tied hand and foot. Women who have had much of their strength sapped from their bodies by being nearly drowned repeatedly in William's barrel, from getting only one plate of slop a day, from the fear of kenning ye are innocent but no one is listening so ye will hang. Dinnae ye dare use the word *willing* when ye speak of what ye did, ye fat bastard. Dinnae ye ever dare."

Bethoc hurried over to take Laurel by the arm. She could feel the woman shaking and knew she would soon start weeping. That would later humiliate her so Bethoc put her arm around the woman's waist and led her out of the room. She could hear the soft sound of Lorraine as the woman hurried after them. Callum gave her a stern look that conveyed the clear message that she was to go no farther than just outside the door and then the door behind them.

"*Jesu*," muttered Laurel and she covered her face with her hands. "The hatred I feel for that mon kens no depth. I could feel it rising up to choke me with its venom." She took a deep breath and then wiped the tears away before looking at Bethoc. "Thank ye for getting me out of there. I wouldnae have wanted him to see my tears."

"Because he would have thought them a sign of weakness, nay the fury they truly reveal," said Lorraine as she stepped up to lightly rub Laurel's back.

"Exactly." Laurel kept taking deep breaths and letting them out slowly. "I am better now."

"Are ye certain?" asked Bethoc. "Better enough to go back in there?"

"Mayhap it would be good to give me a few more minutes."

"Then we will take a few. He cannae get anyone to believe his lies, ye ken. All those men saw me tied to the bed, skirts up, with the sheriff on top of me and ready. They ken what he was about. Two of them are lairds. One used to be the King's Hound, and all are knights. He is done, finished. I just wish we could learn who has been the one ordering this, the one picking the lands to take."

"I really think it is one of the laird's sons," said Lorraine.

"That would explain why no one is telling." Laurel frowned. "'Tis the youngest, I would wager. He has always been a little bastard, wanting what is nay his, bullying people to get his way, and nay paying his tab at the tavern. A shame, for the laird is a good mon and so are his other three sons. His lassies are pure angels.

I have seen the youngest son being mean to them, too. Aye, I will bet it is him. I think this will all soon end," she said as she cocked her head, listening. "That Sir Simon returns with more than Sir Robbie the head cracker."

Bethoc laughed and then Sir Simon came into view. With him he had a well-dressed man who looked as if he was about thirty. The man's eyes widened at them and then he stared hard at Lorraine.

"Lorraine?" he asked, and stepped closer, causing Sir Simon to halt.

"Aye, Sir MacKray," she replied, and blushed when he took her hands gently in his.

"Weel, if I didnae already ken the mon, I would wonder if he had killed her husband," murmured Sir Simon as he moved next to Bethoc and watched the two step away to have a fierce whispered conversation.

"'Tis a bit of a surprise." Bethoc looked at the man. "Ye found him quickly."

"Ah, I would like to say it was my great skill but I fear it was just good luck. He was about to come in as Robbie and I stepped out. Probably caught wind of her arrest, now that I think on it. So, Robbie and I took him o'er to the tavern and had a chat." He sighed. "He is horrified about those other three women and I believe I actually saw his friendship with the sheriff die. I feel badly for him as he is a good, honest mon who believes in the law and justice."

"I have a feeling he will be getting all the sympathy he could want," said Bethoc as they watched Lorraine stroke his hair when he bent his head in shame.

Sir Simon chuckled and then took a few steps closer to the couple. "We had best go, Walter."

"Of course. I will speak with ye later, Lorraine." He kissed her cheek and followed Sir Simon.

"My, my," drawled Laurel when the door shut behind the men, and she grinned when Lorraine blushed brightly. "Ye willnae be a widow for long."

"Nay, ye misread the situation," Lorraine protested. "I have kenned Walter since we were bairns together. That is all it is."

"Lorraine, that mon is nay looking at ye as if ye were his childhood friend."

"Truly?" Lorraine looked wary yet hopeful as she looked at Bethoc for some response.

"Truly," Bethoc said. "Now let us get back in there. I dinnae want to miss this."

"Walter is terribly upset," whispered Lorraine.

"He is probably an honest mon and his name has now been smeared by what these fools made him a part of."

Bethoc opened the door to see a pale-faced sheriff staring at Walter. It looked as if the man was finally seeing the full cost of the games he played. It reached far wider than the death of three women, something she doubted bothered the man at all. What he was beginning to see was how deeply it appalled others.

"Walter . . ." the sheriff began.

"Nay, dinnae call me that. 'Tis only my friends who have the right and ye are nay longer counted amongst that number. My God, ye have put blood on my hands! Innocent blood! Ye used me to help ye play this vicious game and I curse ye for that. Now, tell me who set ye on this ruinous path," the magistrate said in a voice that held all of his authority.

"Angus Keddie," said the sheriff in a sad whisper.

"Lock them up. I need to step outside. I need, I crave, fresh air."

Walter MacKray walked out. Lorraine looked after him with sad eyes. Laurel and Bethoc moved to flank her as Sir Simon, Callum, Uven, and Robbie started to drag the prisoners out. They each elbowed Lorraine lightly.

"What?" Lorraine asked but she could not keep her eyes on them, instead she constantly looked in the direction the young magistrate had gone.

"He would welcome a friend right now," Bethoc said. "A shoulder to cry on."

"Someone to say 'there, there,'" added Laurel.

"Someone to say it will be fine, or get better."

"Aye, someone who can raise his spirits. Pat his back. Mayhap kiss his cheek."

Lorraine laughed. "Ye do recall that I am but a day widowed?" When she got no response from either woman, she laughed and headed out after the magistrate.

"There. That wasnae so hard," Bethoc said, and exchanged a grin with Laurel. "Are ye going to be all right?"

"In time. Aye, I will recover. I am thinking I might sell my lands and leave this place though." Laurel sighed. "But there is time to think that over. Now, I fear, we must go and break the laird's heart."

Chapter Thirteen

The laird of Dunburn bowed his head and slowly shook it. They had laid out the whole nasty plan and who was involved. His eldest son and heir stood behind him, his hand gripping the man's shoulder. He too looked stunned but even as Callum watched, the look turned to one of belief, then resignation, and finally anger. It was a blow to the heart they had delivered and nothing could be said to soften it but they were not being openly argued with and the son's face told him it all came as little surprise.

Laurel finally moved to pour the man an ale and hand it to him. "Here, m'laird, drink."

"Ye were one of them, aye?" he asked as he studied her.

"I was, aye. My husband was killed and I was accused of his murder."

"I am so sorry, lass. So verra sorry."

"Nay, if ye mean for the loss of my husband, dinnae trouble yourself. He was a brute and nay a great loss. He didnae deserve what he got, mayhap, but I willnae miss him. And none of this was your doing. 'Tis I who am sorry for what ye must do now."

"Laurel," Bethoc hissed softly, "ye shouldnae speak of your husband that way."

"Why? 'Tis naught but the truth. I dinnae miss him."

"'Tis disrespectful."

"Weel, if he comes back and does something worthy of respect, I will give him some. For now? Huh." When Bethoc looked up, Laurel asked, "What are ye looking for?"

"God to strike ye down for speaking ill of the dead."

"Hah! It isnae God who is welcoming that mon." She turned back to the laird who was watching them and smiling faintly. "Oh, 'tis good to see your spirits are better. The ale helped?"

"Aye, the ale helped."

Callum leaned closer to Sir Simon. "They did that on purpose, aye?"

"Aye." Sir Simon grinned. "And they have a fine rhythm to it. The laird was buried under his grief but he is out of it enough now that we can tell our tale."

Sir Simon began to speak to the laird. Bethoc listened for a while then turned to Laurel. The rags she wore were no longer needed to hide in and she suspected Laurel would like to put something else on. She could do with a change as well, as four dunkings into the water, the dress left to dry on her body, had left it shapeless and itchy. They would both feel better after a change. Perhaps Lorraine would as well, she thought.

"We need to wash up and change," Bethoc said.

Laurel looked down at herself and grimaced. "Och, aye. It was useful, I think, even when it went to rags but now I want it gone. Didnae save me though. Nay, it needs to go. It and the smell of the prison. And those men," she whispered, and smiled faintly when both Bethoc and Lorraine grasped her hands. "How do we get away?"

"Ask," Bethoc said, and stood up. "We are going to Laurel's to clean up, if ye would be so kind as to excuse us," she said to the laird.

Robbie glanced at Callum who nodded. "I will go with ye."

The three women got up, spoke politely to the laird, and followed Robbie out. The man seemed to have elected himself the guard of everyone, Bethoc thought with a little smile. And he could be very insistent about it.

"Do ye have to stomp around after everyone?" she teased him.

He gave her a sideways glance, looking down at her. "Seems a reasonable thing to do."

She laughed and shook her head as Laurel led them to her home. It was a small, neat house made of stone with a fine garden in the back. Inside it was tidy but not richly furnished. Leaving Robbie to watch the door, all three women went to the room in the back of the house that Laurel said she had set aside for bathing. They heated water and talked as they prepared the first bath for Laurel. As they scrubbed her hair, rinsed it, and scrubbed it again, Laurel was revealed to be a redhead. Bethoc decided the woman was a lot more stunning than she had first realized.

Lorraine went next and Laurel disappeared to collect gowns for them to wear. By the time it was Bethoc's turn, she nearly tore her own gown in her rush to undress. Laurel returned with gowns for each of them. When Bethoc put on the one chosen for her, she was pleasantly surprised to find that it fit and looked at the taller Laurel in curiosity.

"My younger sister visited us for a wee while last summer," Laurel said, and then smiled. "It was nice. For a short while I enjoyed being the lady of this house and my husband was on his best behavior."

Bethoc patted her on the arm then frowned as she tied back her damp hair. "I wonder how the men are doing convincing the laird of what his son has done."

"He was certain of it the moment they told him," said Laurel. "The decision they seek now is what to do next."

The laird was heartbroken but holding up well, Callum decided. The man never argued anything they said and Callum kept waiting for the man to explode in fury and refuse to believe a word. He did not. He knew he had a bad one but had obviously held out a hope that whatever he had seen in his child would never manifest or would just be petty things, easily ignored. It all had to be unbearably hard news to bear, however.

Just as Sir Simon asked where the young man was, he walked confidently into the hall. It surprised Callum a little that the young man was so plain, so ordinary, and not just because, at sixty, the laird was still such a strong, imposing figure of a man. Two other young men stepped in and halted as they studied Callum, Sir Simon, Uven, and the magistrate all seated there near their father. They showed a curious caution that was missing in young Angus Keddie. Despite how much sympathy he felt for the laird, he was going to enjoy crushing the cockiness the young man wore so proudly.

"Who are these men?" asked Angus, flicking a dismissive hand toward them.

"These men are more important than ye think," said the laird in a hard, cold voice that quickly put a dent in the young man's confidence. "That one"—he pointed at Sir Simon—"is Sir Simon Innes, laird of Lochancorrie, and do ye ken what he used to be called? The King's

Hound." Angus paled a little but his father did not hesitate in continuing the introductions. "Sir Callum MacMillan, laird of Whytemont, Sir Uven MacMillan, and I believe ye ken our magistrate. Seems your wee game has been uncovered, lad." He patted his eldest son's hand and that man quickly left the room.

"What game are ye speaking of?"

Callum had to give the young man praise for how well he acted shocked. He noticed the other two young men had edged their way into the room, hands on their swords as they eyed Angus warily. If the fool was in some war with his father he had failed miserably in gaining any support from his brothers, for Callum had finally seen the familial resemblance that marked them as the laird's sons. He would not be surprised to learn the young man had long been a thorn in his brothers' sides.

"It appears there has been a rash of husband killing in our village. The wives have been taken up for the killings. So far three have been hanged. 'Tis odd that I heard naught of this, aye? But, I didnae. Ne'er heard a whisper of their crimes, their troubles, or their fate. Wonder why that is. Magistrate?" He glanced at Walter.

"I was informed by your son Angus that ye had been told, even that ye felt certain the women were guilty," Walter answered quietly, the paleness of his face telling Callum that it would be a long time before he forgave himself for the hanging of those three women.

"Weel, why should ye hear of all these troubles, Father? Ye have sons to deal with such petty problems."

"I doubt those women thought them petty problems," said Walter.

The look Angus gave Walter was so full of spiteful menace, Callum was glad they would soon take Angus down. Even if Walter was too sunk in guilt to see it,

Callum did, and a quick look at Sir Simon told him that man had seen it too. The way the laird had narrowed his eyes told Callum the man was also aware of the threat. The youth had grown overconfident but he suspected killing six men and having three women already pay for some of the murders had made him cocky. That and he put too much faith in being the laird's son giving him some shield against actually paying for his crimes.

"They killed and they paid for it. All of them confessed."

"Nay," said Walter, anger beginning to harden his voice, "the three ye had brought in recently are crying nay and naught changes that."

"They will. The sheriff can be verra persuasive."

"Aye," said Callum, "tying a lass to a bed and having three or four men use her as they will can make a lass confess to anything."

A glint came into Angus's eyes that told Callum the man would have enjoyed being part of it and he ached to strike him down. The image of Bethóc tied to that bed, the sheriff between her legs ready to take her, was not one he could easily forget. Any man who revealed an interest in such a thing deserved to be pounded into the dust.

"Cease picking at Walter, Angus, 'tis beneath ye, though I begin to believe little else is. Ah, and I believe this is what I need," the laird said as his eldest returned looking enraged, with several papers in his hands.

Silence reigned as the laird read the papers, though he kept one hand on his eldest's arm. Callum judged that wise as the man looked eager to strike at Angus. The other two brothers edged closer, reading the papers over their father's shoulder. The way their eyes widened and they glared at Angus made Callum think they might know, or knew, someone mentioned.

"Ye killed David," said the laird, and he stared at his son as if he did not know him.

"What? Nay! I ne'er killed anyone. What are ye talking about? David was my friend."

"Then ye had your hirelings do it, but he is dead all because ye wanted Boswin Cottage. Tell me, have ye already moved in or have ye set up a mistress there?"

"Nay, I didnae kill David."

"Then why do ye have the deed to Boswin Cottage? Is that why ye also have the deeds to Colin Knox's and Ian Fearn's farms? Ye killed David"—he paused as Angus stuttered a denial—"or had him killed. Colin and Ian as weel. Then ye had the sheriff take their poor wives and accuse them of murder and then ye saw to it that they hanged. What happened to David's bairns?"

"I dinnae ken what ye mean. Why should I ken what happened to them?"

Angus cried out and fell to the floor when his father suddenly rushed at him and backhanded him, demanding, "What happened to his bairns?"

"I dinnae ken."

The laird looked at his other two sons who had come in with Angus. "Find them and find out if Knox and Fearn had any bairns. It cannae give them back their parents but we will make certain they are raised weel, cared for until they are of an age to take possession of what this worm I bred tried to steal."

"Nay, Da, I didnae . . ." Angus began as his two brothers rushed off.

"Shut it. And ye nay longer have the right to call me Da. Nay longer have the name. Ye are nay my son. Ye are nay a Keddie and ye nay longer reside at Dunburn. As soon as I replace the sheriff ye are his problem."

"I could hang!"

"Aye, ye could. Right now I wouldnae lift a finger to stop it." He walked back to his seat as his eldest son dragged Angus off. The laird stared at the papers for a moment before looking at Sir Simon. "The other women are freed, aye?"

"Aye," replied Sir Simon. "The sheriff and his guards as weel as two of the five men who did the killing are locked up tight. A big fellow named William is running free but I doubt he will be hard to find. I am sorry this trouble has come to ye but it had to be stopped. As for the two women now freed whose husbands were killed, weel, ye will have no trouble o'er that."

"Ah, they dinnae grieve the loss."

"They werenae verra good husbands, nay. And I am now done with this so I willnae be pressing ye to do what may be impossible for ye."

"That is verra good of ye. Dinnae fear though. Whate'er happens he will ne'er be unwatched again."

"I think that is best." Sir Simon stood up and the others followed as they all shook hands with the laird.

When the laird went to Walter, he clasped him by the shoulders after shaking his hand. "I am truly sorry, Walter. I picked ye as a magistrate because I kenned ye were a deeply honest mon, one who could be fair, honest, e'en kind."

"I sent three innocent women to their deaths."

"Nay. Nay ye didnae. My son sent them there. Ye did naught but what ye should when given a preponderance of proof by men ye trusted, the sheriff, his men, e'en Angus. Remember that. They lied, they twisted justice. Ye have naught to feel guilty about. Put the blame where it belongs."

"Aye, my laird."

They were almost out the door when Walter suddenly

stopped and turned back. "My laird? Ye will be in need of a new sheriff. If I might venture a suggestion, I think Artair MacReavie would be a good one."

"Aye, I will consider it. Thank ye, Walter. God's speed."

"*Jesu*, that was hard business," said Uven once they were outside.

"Nay as hard as it could have been," said Sir Simon as he mounted his horse. "The mon listened and believed. We were fortunate that the laird had already seen what evil lived in his son. His brothers kenned. Each one of them. Even before we spoke they had guessed who we had come for."

"Aye, a good mon, the laird. He didnae deserve this blow."

No one argued and they made their way to Laurel's house only to find that Lorraine and Bethoc had left. Hearing that Bethoc had talked of stopping at her house, Callum rode there. He suspected Walter would be visiting Lorraine when Sir Simon and Uven headed back to the cave. The thought that all he had to do was send Robbie off and he might have some time alone with Bethoc caused Callum to nudge his horse into a faster pace.

"I could have done that," Robbie said from his seat at the table.

"Kerr was my father in the only way he kenned how, and this needed cleaning up. I dinnae think the lads should see it." Bethoc scrubbed the last of the blood off the floor, tossed the scrubbing brush into the bucket, and set back on her heels. "Why would any person do such things to another person?"

"They wanted him to tell them something. Pain and

fear loosen the tongue," Robbie replied, and drank some ale.

"So poke at him a wee bit, threaten to cut his belly and pluck his innards out one by one, or mayhap cut off another bit he was so proud of." She glared at Robbie when she saw he was grinning.

"Bloodthirsty wee wench," he said. "What they did meant less blood, but plenty of pain and fear. I suspicion they wanted him to tell them where Cathan was and when they didnae get what they wanted they turned ye o'er to the sheriff who was more than willing to add ye to their game."

Bethoc shook her head as she stood up and stretched. "Six men dead, mostly innocent men, and three innocent women hanged. Laurel and Lorraine's husbands were nay good men, but they are dead and didnae really deserve that. The same with Kerr, although he did redeem himself in the end. All dead and they would have hanged us, too. For what? These places are nay worth that much."

"All together, with mayhap a few more added to the lot, aye, they are."

"Mayhap, but I still dinnae understand how anyone could do such a thing."

Robbie had no answer, and she took the bucket of bloody water into the back garden and tossed it under the bushes. To make certain no stain remained, she got a fresh bucket of water from the well, washed her hands clean in it, and then tossed that under the bushes. Pleased that the boys would not have to confront Kerr's blood when they came home, she walked back inside only to discover Callum sitting where

Robbie had been. A quick glance around revealed no sight of Robbie.

She looked at Callum and he was grinning, a definite glint in his eyes. Bethoc managed to subdue a blush but her heart picked up its pace. He smelled of cinnamon and she knew what that meant. A part of her was not sure it was wise to give him what he so clearly wanted yet a bigger part of her was very eager to do so.

Callum stood up and slowly walked over to her. "We are actually alone. No boys, no little girls, no sheriff and his men, no ladies. Wonder what we should do with this precious time?" He reached out and pulled her into his arms.

"I believe I ken what ye think we should do," she said, making no effort to break free.

He kissed her. It was a slow, seductive kiss and Bethoc swiftly gave in to the power of it. She curled her arms around his neck, bringing her body up hard against his. He lifted his head enough to kiss her neck then nip at the lobe of her ear and she shivered with pleasure.

"Where is your bed?" he asked, his voice soft, deep, and husky, caressing her.

Bethoc pointed toward her small bed. He kissed her as he walked her backward toward it. His kiss was still seductive yet there was an increasing ferocity to it. Something inside of Bethoc rose up to meet that ferocity and she reveled in it.

When the back of her legs hit the edge of her bed, she gave a little squeak of surprise. Callum chuckled softly, lifted her up into his arms, and set her down on the bed. Even if she had felt inclined to say anything there was no time to do so before he joined her on the bed.

"Your leg," she said as he took off his shirt.

"Is fine." He began to undo her gown. "Has been fine for a while now. Thinking it is healed."

"I could check the bone for ye."

"Later." He looked at her breasts, the tips hard and beckoning to him. "Much later."

Bethoc cried out softly when he began to kiss and lick her breasts. She threaded her fingers into his hair and held him close. The feel of his warm lips against her skin clouded her thoughts and heated her blood. She smoothed her hands over his broad back, delighting in the warmth of his skin, the taut muscles beneath her hands. Even the weight of him sprawled in her arms was welcome.

He slowly kissed his way up to her mouth. Bethoc ran her hands over his back, down as far as she could reach, as she luxuriated in the power of his kisses. No one had spoken of love, even hinted at marriage, so she knew she was doing something everyone would consider wrong. Bethoc realized she just did not care. Some things were worth becoming a social outcast for.

Callum stripped her of her clothes so skillfully she was barely aware of it until she realized they were skin to skin. For just a moment she was intensely aware of the fact that she was utterly naked in front of a man, she who had not been naked in front of anyone since she was a tiny infant. Before that realization could dampen the passion she felt, Callum's hand slid over her belly and between her legs.

She tensed, shying away from such intimacy, but then he kissed her. His kisses soothed her even as they roused her dimming desire, pushing it back to full life. Cautiously, yet with a strong hint of greed, she opened herself to his stroking fingers and shuddered with the pleasure he gave her.

When he moved his mouth to her breasts, she wove her fingers into his thick hair to hold him there. Her body was on fire. Even though they had only made love to each other once, she knew she was going to have to have him inside her soon. She moved her hands down his back and stroked his backside. He groaned and she ran her fingernails over his hips. Then he was there, where she needed him. The hard ridge of his manhood rubbed against her and she felt the aching need in her grow greedy.

"Callum," she whispered and he brushed his lips over hers.

A moment later he thrust home and she cried out softly in welcome. He kissed her as he moved slowly. Bethoc reveled in the slow tightening in her belly as she wrapped her legs around his waist. She had the wild thought that she could do this for hours but then the demands of her body began to grow fierce. Callum moved faster as he kissed her throat. Her legs tightened around him and then the tension broke, pleasure sweeping over her. She held on tight as he slammed into her several times before joining her, calling her name as he spilled himself inside of her.

As Bethoc's breathing slowed, she idly ran her hand up and down his back. A soft protest escaped her when he separated them. He nuzzled her breast and then rolled onto his back, pulling her into his arms. Bethoc settled her cheek on his chest and closed her eyes, enjoying the lazy aftermath.

"One of these days I will be able to take my time," he murmured, then chuckled at the curious look she gave him. "There is a lot we can share, loving." He kissed her.

She was not sure what his words meant. It sounded as if he planned to keep her with him for a while. He did not know about her special skill, one the horrified Kerr had called witchery. He had to be forgetting about all of her responsibilities. She wished she could be so selfish, to just say farewell to it all, and reach out for whatever he wanted to share with her for however long he wanted to share it. That was not something she would ever be able to do, however, but she said nothing. The hard truth could wait to be told only when it was absolutely necessary.

Chapter Fourteen

"Ye are coming with us."

Bethoc stared at Callum. They had enjoyed the last week, slipping away to be together, making love when they could, and just being free of the crowd that surrounded them most of the time. But reality was back; she was not free and never had been. There were seven children who needed her.

"Ye need to meet your real father, lass."

Those words drove her heart into her throat. She had never really given much thought to her father since she had learned it was not Kerr. The man had never been a part of her life and, after one and twenty years, she doubted he would abruptly change his mind. She was not sure she wanted to start some kind of relationship with him, either.

"Nay. He wouldnae want a grown daughter rapping at the door."

"Aye, he would." Callum took hold of her hands, ending her nervous wringing of them.

"There are the children to worry about. I must needs . . ."

"Nay, ye dinnae. Robbie will stay with the older lads

so no one will try to take the house and the others will come with us. Colin and Bean intend to stay here. And ye ken weel that Laurel would dearly like to take young Magnus into her home."

"I ken it. I have been trying to be unselfish, to, weel, let go of the lad." She frowned when he grinned. "'Tis nay funny."

He kissed her. "I wasnae laughing. I was just thinking that ye sound like me when one of my strays has a chance to go to a new home and have a proper family." He sat beneath the tree and tugged her down beside him. "Magnus seems to truly like Laurel."

"He does and I think he wouldnae mind being her boy. She is certain he is Yolanda's boy. I am wondering if they have talked of the woman at all but keep forgetting to ask. And he hasnae been part of this family all that long, nay like the others."

"Robbie likes Laurel too. I am thinking that is why he is staying for a while."

"I am nay sure Laurel is wanting a mon."

"Neither is Robbie looking for a lass but he is wondering and he means to give it a try."

When he put his arm around her, she leaned against him and sighed. "Ye insist I meet with this mon Brett Murray, dinnae ye?"

"The mon is your father."

"One I have ne'er met. Dinnae ken e'en in passing. I cannae see that he will want that changed."

"I do but nay just for him. The clan is a large one, Bethoc, and a good one to have a friend in. Ye dinnae have to stay with him. As ye say, ye are a grown woman, but he didnae desert your mother, e'en gave her a way to contact him, so he showed that he wasnae deserting ye, either. That shows he would ne'er have left her with child and unprotected. His own family would have been most upset with him if he e'en tried. Mayhap he would like to ken what happened."

"I ken it. I was thinking on it last eve, thinking on how different my life would have been. Then I thought on the boys and I am nay too sorry I ended up here. I would have been raised as a Murray and nay here to meet them. That would have been a tragedy, I think. They needed me."

He nodded. "Aye, they did. I am thinking though that ye need to meet your father. Ye need to do that for ye, to see what ye sprung from and all that."

"I am nay a small boy like ye were, Callum. I am old enough to find it simply comforting to ken I have one and he didnae treat my mother poorly, would have been there for us if my mother had contacted him." She turned and gave him a quick kiss. "But, aye, ye are right. After my mother, mayhap it would be good for me to ken the other half of my parentage."

Callum took her into his arms and kissed her hard. "Mayhap we should go back to our place by the burn."

"Too late, ye randy goat. I need to make a meal. And, we should be more careful. Someone could discover us there."

"Bethoc, they ken where we go." He laughed at the look of horror on her face.

"How could they?"

"Weel, I suspicion it has something to do with me telling Uven to make sure none of the lads wandered off and went near the burn the first time I took ye there."

Bethoc was stunned. She had thought it was all their little secret. Now it appeared everyone had known what they were doing. The times she had worried about being discovered had been an unnecessary loss of peace of mind. Everyone had known that she and

Callum were down by the burn doing something they should not be doing and had politely stayed away. She was not sure how she felt about that.

They all knew, she thought, and blushed. Did they think she was being a fool or, worse, was just a whore? She realized next that they had known all along and not one had treated her differently.

She frowned before she could get too lost in that embarrassment and worry. No one had acted differently around her or Callum. They all acted as if everything was just as it should be. That could only mean one thing. Not one of them cared what she and Callum were doing near the burn. Bethoc found that hard to believe yet she could not ignore the facts. She turned to speak to Callum only to find him sprawled on his back, hands behind his head, and his eyes closed.

"Callum?"

He opened his eyes and grinned at her. "Have ye stopped fretting? Mayhap sorted it all out?"

"I wasnae fretting; I was merely thinking on it."

"Ye were fretting."

She decided to ignore that. "They dinnae care."

Sitting up, he put an arm around her shoulders and kissed her on the cheek. "Nay, love, they dinnae."

The last of her confused emotions melted away. "Weel, I guess I had best go and ready something for everyone to eat then." She took a deep breath to steady herself and tried to speak calmly. "And to ready some food to take with us when we leave."

"I am thinking we will go alone to see Brett. Leave the boys here with Robbie, Uven, and Simon and just the two of us go there. Then ye can meet without anyone's expectations muddling things. Talk freely and all that."

"How long will it take?"

"Weel, if we dinnae stay long, it could be done in two or three days. Then back here, collect the lads and Margaret, and head off to Whytemont. What do ye think?"

She thought about it for a few minutes. It would mean she could meet the man with none of her family to worry about. Also, she would have a few nights alone with Callum. They got little of that. There was always someone around, some child who drew her attention. Selfish it might be but she nodded. She was going to grab for it.

Bethoc stared at Banuilt as they approached and felt her stomach slowly tie itself up in knots. This was madness, she decided. She was too old to go looking for a father. And how would the poor man explain her to his wife? The very last thing she wished to do was cause trouble for him with his wife. She was just about to turn her horse around when Callum reached over and grabbed her reins.

"Nay, ye willnae turn coward now," he said. "He is expecting you."

"Weel, he wouldnae be if ye hadnae sent word so fast. I am sure his wife isnae pleased."

"About what? That o'er twenty years ago the boy her husband used to be had a brief affair with a young lass? Or had a bairn? She has one of those by him so nay room for jealousy about that. Ye fret too much, love, although ye do astound me at times o'er what ye come up with to fret about."

"I am so pleased I amuse you."

"Didnae say amused, said astounded, but that bodes weel for our future."

She was about to ask him what future he spoke of

when he was distracted by the men on the walls of Banuilt. After what was a lot of bellowed nonsense the gates slowly opened. There on the steps into the impressive keep stood a tall, black-haired man. He had his arm draped around a much smaller woman with long hair that appeared brown except where the sunlight struck it and red shown through.

Callum helped her dismount and walked her over to the man she had come to meet. Her first thought was that if her mother had to lose herself in a dream, Sir Brett Murray was a good choice. He had to be inching toward forty but he looked a lot younger, his body lean and fit, his eyes a sharp bright green. She idly wished she had been gifted with those. His black hair, however, was as thick and dark as her own and, she was pleased to note, was as yet untouched by gray.

She was introduced to Lady Triona and found only an honest welcome. If the woman had been upset to discover her husband had a grown child, they had already argued about and settled the matter. Bethoc did feel a pang for her mother, however. If not for one lost piece of paper, she could have had this man instead of suffering under Kerr's fist for years.

Brett introduced his children Ella and Geordan. Bethoc wondered why the pretty little girl had a cat riding on her shoulder but Callum patted the animal as if that was normal. She did wish she had brought the boys though as they would have loved such a sight.

It was not until they were at the table in the great hall, children gone, the food enjoyed, and no one else in the hall that Brett finally asked, "How . . . nay . . . why did she ne'er contact me? I left the information she needed."

"I fear she lost it." Bethoc smiled sadly when his eyes widened in shock. "My mother was sweet, loving, her manners perfect, but I fear she wasnae"—Bethoc thought hard on what to say then shrugged—"too sharp of wit. She wasnae a dullard or the like, 'tis just that she . . ." Bethoc struggled to explain clearly.

"Dreamed a lot," Brett said. "She was one to get lost in dreams."

"Aye, exactly. E'en then?" When he nodded, Bethoc shook her head. "I wondered about that. It got worse as the years passed and I fear the mon her family made her marry didnae help."

"She had an unhappy life?" asked Triona.

Bethoc hesitated to tell the whole truth but Callum patted her hand. She looked at him and he nodded. If he felt Brett could deal with it, then she could tell. She softened it as much as she could but decided it was not enough when Triona's eyes filled with tears over the tale of the babies in the garden. Nevertheless, she continued until ending at Kerr's death.

"Poor lass." Brett shook his head. "If she had only kept that letter I gave her." He took Triona's hand in his and kissed it. "She didnae deserve that misery. E'en if I couldnae have wed her for some reason, the Murrays would have taken her in. Nay fixing the past though. I am sorry ye were trapped because of that one mistake."

"It wasnae good but it had its good parts," Bethoc said, "if that makes sense."

"Oh, aye," said Triona. "I have the same feeling about my first marriage. Ella's the good part."

Bethoc smiled. "The lads and Margaret are my good part. I didnae ken how or why Kerr took the lads from whate'er life they had but they did make life easier to bear. When ye have someone ye have to watch over, 'tis hard to get too lost in your own misery, aye."

"Aye, verra hard," Triona agreed, and smiled.

"So, Callum, I hear ye have had an adventure, one that required even Innes's skills," said Brett.

As Callum told the story, Bethoc fought to stay alert but weariness began to weigh on her. Triona quietly excused them, leaving the men to talk, and Bethoc was grateful. She was astonished by the room she was shown to, from the heavy drapes on the window to the feather-filled pillows.

"Aye, we are doing so much better at Banuilt now," said Triona after Bethoc exclaimed her delight over a tapestry on the wall. "A lot of work left to do but now we ken it can be done. Wait until ye and your lads see Callum's lands and home. Brett tells me 'tis verra nice."

"Weel, I am nay certain I will see it." Callum had spoken of it but she was still uncertain for he had never said what she was to be or do when she got there.

"Oh, aye, ye will. Your boys will too? Will ye take them all?"

Bethoc frowned. "It has been said that Colin and Bean wouldnae be going and Robbie would stay with them. I think Robbie hopes he can catch Laurel's interest as weel."

"Laurel?" Triona asked, and listened carefully as Bethoc told her Laurel's story and then she sighed. "I suspicion Robbie kens all this." Bethoc nodded. "Ah, good, then he kens he cannae woo her as he might another lass. And which boy does she want?"

"Magnus. She is certain he is Yolanda's child and she was hanged for a murder she didnae commit before we were able to stop that vicious game the sheriff played. Now all they can do is take the stain from her name. Since his father is dead too, that means he is an orphan. Magnus seems to like her weel."

Triona nudged Bethoc with her shoulder. "'Tis hard to set them free. Yet, mayhap ye should do it for

Laurel's sake. Give her that person she needs to care for so her mind doesnae rest too long on what was done to her. Give her someone to love so that she doesnae forget what that is."

"Oh. I should have thought of that." Bethoc sat on the bed, realized it had a feather mattress, and forced herself not to be distracted by that. "I ken she willnae keep him from the other boys or me. And she has a lovely cottage. And she wants to honor Yolanda." Bethoc sighed. "I need to let go."

Sitting next to her, Triona patted her clenched hands. "She sounds perfect for the boy."

"I dinnae want the other boys to think I am intending to hand them all off to someone."

"They have nay reason to think that. Just be who ye have always been with them and, nay matter what changes come, they will be fine."

"Thank ye, Triona. Ye have a true skill for seeing another's worries. And Callum says I have a lot of them." She frowned. "He says I astound him with the things I can think of to fret about."

Triona laughed. "I do the same. How does it feel to meet your father?"

"Odd. I dinnae blame him for anything, if that is your worry. My mother made the mistake, lost the only way to reach him and couldnae e'en recall what he wrote. It hurts a wee bit to say it but she truly wasnae verra sharp of wit. 'Tis why she ne'er once thought to leave, ne'er thought to help any of the lads Kerr brought home." Bethoc grimaced. "She truly did live in her dreams. Brett was her prince." She was startled when Triona collapsed in a fit of giggles.

"I am sorry." Triona finally got herself under control, wiped her eyes, and sat up. "Your mother's story is so sad yet Brett as a prince, weel, she was young. She was ill, I think. Ill in her mind. Mayhap only a little at first then more and more so as time went on."

"Aye, she was. She was so bonnie and so brittle. A sad woman who met a sad death." Bethoc saw Triona frown. "'Tis better than some of the other things I have thought o'er the years."

Triona patted her on the back. "Families. None are perfect. Ye are now part of ours so ye will discover that soon enough."

Her laughter followed her out of the room. Bethoc had to smile and shook her head as she dug her night shift out of her pack. As she dressed, she thought on the man she had the right to call Father. He certainly was good-looking, strong, and a laird. His wife was both wise and charming. What left her a little stunned was how he welcomed her, never questioning her claim. She rather wished she had been able to greet him with more warmth, then shook her head. Bethoc would just let things happen, no planning, and no fretting, which would please Callum.

Tugging on her night shift after having a quick wash in the still-warm water left by the maids, Bethoc got into bed. She groaned with pleasure as the soft mattress cradled her body and her hand was settled nicely against the soft feather pillows. This was luxury, she thought, and she would not allow it to spoil her.

"She isnae sure," said Brett after the women were gone. "Nay about me or about having a father."

"Weel, she is a grown woman. I dinnae think she e'er expected to meet the mon who fathered her."

"She has her mother's eyes."

"Ye can recall the lass?"

"She was my first. I was hers. Aye, I recall her. I

recall, too, that she was delicate, in body and, I think, in mind. Bethoc is similar to her in body but nay in mind. 'Tis hard to think of the life my child has led because her mother lost my letter."

"It was hard, nay question about that, but it didnae break her. It honed her." Callum smiled faintly.

"And ye mean to have her."

Callum was stunned by Brett's words and unsure of how he should reply.

Brett shook his head. "Ye look as if I just punched ye in the head. The lass is a grown woman. I have had naught to do with her raising. All I ken is that she has spent her life raised by a hard mon and cares for a lot of bairns that are nay hers. Her mother was nay help to her, lost in misery and dreams as she was. What I am trying to spit out here is that I dinnae have the right to demand anything of ye. I will ask though that ye dinnae hurt her. She has had enough hurt in her life."

"I would ne'er hurt her."

"Ye ken what I mean. Ye are keeping her close and ye ken what a lass can see in that."

"Aye," Callum admitted. "Do ye want the truth?"

"Always better."

"I dinnae ken what the hell I want." He frowned when Brett laughed. "'Tis true. I cannae say I love her. What do I ken about such things? Yet I cannae see nay having her about. When I saw that sheriff on top of her, I threw him into a wall and if she hadnae needed me to untie her, I would have broken him into pieces. I dinnae e'en care if she drags all the little ones with her if she comes with me to Whytemont. And I already ken I willnae heed a nay when I say she should come with me. *Jesu,* 'tis a confusion."

Brett laughed. "All I ask is that ye dinnae hurt her. I may have seeded her but I am nay a father to her. She is a grown woman. Who kens? If we see each other from time to time that bond will grow. But I am nay going to tell ye what to do. All I can think of saying, again, is just dinnae hurt her. She has had enough hurt in her life."

"Fair enough. Ye do believe ye sired her though, aye?"

"Oh, aye, nay question of it. Proud to call such a bonnie lass my daughter. But nay a bond. That must come with time and kenning each other. I look forward to it."

"Then we shall be sure there is regular visiting done."

"Ye ken where your bedchamber is?"

Callum nodded and left the room as fast as he could without looking as if he was running. His bedchamber was right next to Bethoc's and he had no intention of sleeping in that bed. That was not something he was comfortable revealing to her father, even one who said there was no bond yet. Once inside his room, he stripped off his clothes and washed up. He then threw on his plaid. Realizing he was intensely anticipating spending a full night in a bed with Bethoc, he grinned and slipped off to the bedchamber.

Bethoc woke to a hand on her breast. An instant of panic came and went quickly as she recognized the scent of Callum and even recognized his hand. She tried to push back against him but found the covers and turned to see him on top of them.

"What are ye doing out there?" she asked.

"Waking ye up." He stood up, shed his plaid, and climbed into bed.

Bethoc caught her breath when he shed his kilt. It

was only a brief glimpse of his naked form but it was more than enough to set her heart pounding. The man was perfection as far as she could see. He was all smooth skin and taut muscle. The hair at his groin and on his legs was more than enough to be manly and darker than the hair on his head, but it was the glimpse of what rose up from those reddish-brown curls at his groin that truly took her breath away. As he took her into his arms, she idly wondered what would happen if she touched it. He touched her between her legs, she mused, so it ought to be fine for her to return the caress.

Then Callum pulled her into his arms and sighed. Bethoc could not help herself: She laughed. It was such a happy sound.

"What is so funny?" he asked, kissing her shoulder.

"Ye sounded so content. I have heard the boys and Margaret make that same sound at times when they found something they think they lost."

"Ah, weel, my skin against yours makes me verra happy."

Bethoc relaxed in his arms, running her hand over his chest. Resting her cheek against his chest she inched her hand down to caress his taut belly. A moment later she gave in to her curiosity and went farther. When she clasped him in her hand, his whole body tensed. Afraid she had erred, she released him, only to have him take her by the hand and put it back.

"I thought I had hurt you," she whispered.

"Nay, just surprised me."

As she lightly stroked him he kissed her. He was hot silk in her hands, hard yet soft. It was obvious he liked her touching him. Even as she stroked him, she lost herself in the pleasure of his kiss and the fire he spread inside her with his own stroking hands.

Callum moved so that Bethoc was sprawled beneath him. Her hand fell away from him as she reached out to grab hold of him. He kissed her as he eased their bodies together. Resting his forehead against hers, he went still, savoring the feel of her heat surrounding him, the silk of her skin against his. He ran his hands over her legs when she crossed them over his back. Gently he kissed her forehead, her cheeks, and her nose.

"Ye are nay moving," Bethoc whispered.

"I ken it. I was making certain I kenned the right plan of attack."

"Attack?"

"Weel, there is a part of me that truly wants to go verra slow, to make it last as long as it can. Mayhap even hours."

"Hours?" She swallowed hard.

"Or"—he brushed a kiss over her mouth—"mayhap fast would be better."

"Or somewhere in between?" she asked even as he began to slowly move inside her.

Bethoc closed her eyes and savored the feel of him moving lazily, their skin brushing against each other's with every thrust of his body. It was not long before he began to move faster, his kiss growing fiercer. She felt her desire soar until it shattered and washed her in intense pleasure. Callum quickly joined her, her name a soft groan on his lips. Bethoc held him close until he left her, holding her curled up in his arms when he flopped onto his back.

Callum kissed the top of her head. "Still not ready for the slow."

She laughed. "Is it important to ye?"

"Aye and nay. I just want to give ye the most pleasure I can, to show ye all the things we can share. But, as long as my body is so greedy for ye, that is a difficult goal." He kissed her forehead. "And I ken ye dinnae understand what I am talking about but someday soon I will show ye."

Bethoc thought on that as she relaxed beneath his hand, which was idly rubbing her back. It certainly sounded interesting. She smiled a little and she started to give in to sleep, wondering what it would take to help Callum not be so greedy. Then she decided she did not want to dim that greed at all.

Chapter Fifteen

Standing on the walls next to Sir Brett, Bethoc stared out at the lands surrounding it. He had told her of all the trouble they had had in trying to keep it, but it was certainly land worth fighting for. The fact that it was not very accessible to the outside world appealed to her.

"'Tis beautiful, sir," she said and he smiled proudly.

"Aye, 'tis. It will grow more so." He turned round and leaned against the wall. "Ye can call me Father."

"Oh." She struggled to think of something to say when he laughed.

"I ken 'tis hard but Triona says we should do it. Until that gets set in our minds. Ye ken, when I was told about ye, I was both happy and sad. Happy to find a child I didnae ken about and sad about your mother. Then ye came here and ye were nay a child. I kenned how long ago ye were born but"—he shrugged—"occasionally the mind goes its own way. Dinnae ken what to do about that."

Bethoc smiled. "Aye, I understand that, *Father.* Mayhap Triona has a good idea."

"She often does. So, has Callum told ye about himself?"

She frowned. "Weel, I ken he had a hard childhood, a bad mon held him for a while, and that he took a vow to protect children. Then he met his family, became a MacMillan, and is now a laird. It isnae really verra much, is it," she murmured as she thought about it.

"Nay, but more than I had expected. He was horribly abused," he said. "And I tell ye this because I think ye need to ken. He can get, weel, enraged about certain things which might make ye wonder."

"I rather assumed that was what he meant. I ken 'tis something that can linger and leave scars. My mother had many so I understand how such things can mark a person. I have seen little of that in Callum although I do believe if my father had lived there would have come a moment that could have been a concern."

"'Tis good, then. Payton did what he could for the lad, gave him pride, skills, found his clan so that he had a name and kinsmen, but I do wonder sometimes if anyone can ever truly get past such things. Get past that anger."

"I have nay met Payton but he did a wondrous job. I ken what a constant simmering anger looks like in a mon. I have lived with it all my life. I ken that rage that bursts to life and strikes out for no rational reason. There is none of that in Callum."

"Weel, *Daughter,* that eases my mind. Naught like the word of an expert to soothe a worry." He caught her by the hand, tugged her close, and gave her a kiss on the cheek.

"Howbeit," she said, "I wouldnae hit my wife or child if he is close at hand."

"That goes without saying," he said as he started to

lead her down from the walls, "although I am thinking I would be more afeared of what my wife might do."

Bethoc laughed.

It was shortly after noon when Callum and Bethoc prepared to leave. She hugged Triona and kissed the children before turning to her father. Before she could decide what was the best thing to do, Brett hugged her. Something stirred inside of her and she realized it was a sense of belonging. There was also some sadness for all she had missed.

Callum left Brett with a promise of letters and visits, and Bethoc wondered how he could promise such things for her. She made no complaint though for she had already promised Triona letters. Then the ride took up all her attention.

They rode until the threatening night stopped them. Aside from a few rests for the horses, it had been hours, and Bethoc was feeling every single one of them as she dismounted. Home was not far away but neither of them wanted to ride in the dark and her backside desperately needed a rest. She rode very little and it was costing her now. Once the horses were settled she cautiously sat down before the fire Callum built and helped herself to some of the food he had set out.

"Ye are sore, arenae ye?" Callum asked.

Since the part of her that was sore was not one she wished to discuss, Bethoc blushed. "Aye, a bit. I can ride but I dinnae do it often."

"Weel, be sure to have a walk ere ye lie down for the night or ye will be worse in the morning."

Bethoc was not quite sure how she could be worse but she nodded in agreement. As they ate he spoke of Whytemont and she knew she would have to go there.

How long she might stay was all that was in doubt. It was not that he was commanding her to go, but the way he spoke of her seeing his home that swayed her. He so obviously wanted her to see the place, wanted to show her things he had, and pretty places there, that she simply could not say no.

Callum spread out a place for them to sleep as she cleared away the remains of the food. Then he caught her by the hand, pulled her to her feet, and began to take her on a walk. Bethoc could already feel her muscles stiffening up and prayed this would help.

"Poor lass, I fear ye will be a bit sore in the morning," Callum said as he put his arm around her shoulder.

"Aye, but I will be able to finish the ride."

"Just need a rest between this one and the next, aye?"

"That would be nice."

"So, tell me what ye have decided about Brett."

"I havenae decided much at all. Oh, we did agree to call each other Father and Daughter. Triona felt that would be good, would help us in building something. She thought it would work to make us recognize what we are and the rest will follow."

"That makes sense, actually. If ye both just keep saying 'sir' or 'miss' the realization that ye are more isnae settling in." He nodded. "Very clever woman is Triona."

"Aye, I think she is." Bethoc sighed as they returned to the bed Callum had spread out.

"Take off your gown and lie down on your stomach. I have some cream I can rub on ye that will help."

Bethoc did as he asked but was startled when he lifted her chemise and tugged off her braies. "Callum, I . . ."

"Dinnae worry, love, that is nay what I am thinking of. Where did ye think I would put the cream?"

A moment later he was rubbing cream into her backside and the top of her legs. The twinge of embarrassment she had suffered faded fast as the ache eased. She closed her eyes and listened to Callum wash his hands before joining her on the pallet he had set up. Then she realized there was still the feel of air wafting over her backside.

"Callum?" She started to reach back but he caught her hand.

"Nay, leave it for a while. Ye go covering everything up now and it will take off the cream. I will just lie here and admire your pretty backside until the cream has dried."

She groaned. "Ye are a rogue, Callum."

"Go to sleep, Bethoc. Ye need your rest. Dinnae fret"—he bent down and kissed her cheek and she could feel him smiling against her skin—"I will be sure to cover ye up properly before I go to sleep."

Since she was half asleep already, she made no argument, although she fully intended to make him pay for this later.

The ride to her house was nowhere as near as long as the one the day before and Bethoc was highly grateful for that. The cream had helped but it was not perfect and she badly wished to get out of the saddle. Then she noticed Callum had stopped and was looking not at her house but up the trail to the cave.

"Is something wrong?"

"Nay," he answered. "'Tis just that there is only one horse at your house, which means the others are at the cave."

"And ye wish to have a word with them."

"Well, aye, just a wee talk to plan the ride home."

"Go," she said. "I will go to the house and see how the boys and Margaret are."

"They might be at the cave too."

"Then Robbie's horse wouldnae be there. He would only stay if one of the children did."

"Ah, true. All right then, I will go up to the cave and have a talk with the others. Ye can send Robbie up there if he wishes it or I will see ye in a while."

To her surprise, he gave her a kiss farewell before he rode off. Touching her mouth, she then shook her head and rode toward the house. It concerned her a little when no one came out to greet her as she rode up.

Bethoc dismounted and cautiously walked into the house. Then she saw Robbie. She was relieved until she saw that he was tied to a chair. Frantically, she looked around but could not see any of the children.

"Run," Robbie said.

"I should free you."

"Run."

The urgency in the soft word finally reached her and she spun around. She was running for the door when a shadowy figure stepped into the doorway. Stopping quickly, she wondered which way to run next and wondered who she was running from. The rancid smell assaulting her nose told her she was about to face someone very dangerous.

"Weel, weel, look who has come home."

Shock almost stole her ability to move as the man stepped into the light, but sheer determination to survive kept her backing up until the next step back would land her in poor Robbie's lap. Angus Keddie looked wretched. His clothes were filthy, his hair was a snarled, dirty mess, and he smelled as if he had not bathed since they last saw him. It did not hide the smell of rot in him,

however. There was a look in his eyes that terrified her.
She knew it was madness.

"I thought ye would be hanged or in jail now," she
said, desperately trying to decide where to run and if
there was any way she could help Robbie.

"That is where I have been," he replied. "In jail. But
I grew weary of it. Ye shouldnae have put me there."

"Ye put yourself there. Ye killed men and women
who had done naught wrong."

"Do ye ken what it is to be the youngest of four sons?
Ye get naught. Ye are always the last to be thought of.
Weel, I decided I deserved something as much as my
brothers did and I went after it."

Oh, good, she thought frantically, he wanted to talk
and she wondered how long she could keep him
talking. "So ye decided to steal it all from innocent
people."

"Why should they have pieces of my father's lands
while I get nothing?"

"Because they paid for it?"

"They had no right. No right at all."

"So how did ye decide on who to kill and who to
leave alone?"

"Curious little thing, arenae ye. Weel, it willnae
matter what ye learn for ye and that big idiot in the
chair will soon be dead."

"So tell me."

"First I found out who had been gifted land. 'Tis astonishing how much my grandfather gave away. So
generous, people said he was. He was a fool! Ye dinnae
hand land out to peasants as if it was a treat for being
a good servant. So what if someone saved his son. So
he should! That is their job!" He shook his head.

"There were several other *gifts* I meant to retrieve but I couldnae kill the fools."

"They didnae trust ye or your minions?"

"They were ne'er alone."

"Ye didnae have to kill the wives."

"Oh, my dear, but of course I did. They would have been widows. I found out a long time back that they dinnae sell out just because they are alone now. And I needed someone to be the killer."

He sounded so calm, so eminently reasonable as he talked of his mad plan. It was as if he considered the people who had been gifted with Keddie land or bought it nothing but thieves. He could talk all he wanted and Bethoc knew she would never fully understand. Innocent people had been killed because he was disappointed in what he would receive from his father when the older man died.

Somehow she had to get away from the man but she had no idea how. Nor did she know how to get Robbie free yet she could not leave him behind. She was looking around the room as cautiously as she could when she caught sight of a movement beneath her bed. Her heart pounding with the fear that it might be one of the children, she tried to keep a watch on it without appearing to.

"Ye never said how ye got out of jail," she said.

"What does *that* matter? Weel, if ye must ken, it was my brother Keith's fault." He smiled and held his knife out as if pointing at her. "Came to visit me. Keith was always a fool. Big of heart, short on wit. Couldnae believe I could do what was said, wanted me to deny it or tell him why. Told him I didnae ken." He laughed and it made Bethoc feel cold. "Then acted all broken and sorry. Acted like I was trying to cut my wrist open on the bedpost, which was iron then picked up a piece of wood and was trying to stab myself. The fool thought I was really trying to kill myself." He laughed again and Bethoc prayed nothing would amuse him again for it was a horrible sound. "Fool bent o'er me and I caught him in my legs then strangled him. So here I am. Here to finish a wee bit of business before I run."

"Ye killed your own brother?" She chanced a glance under the bed but saw nothing and breathed a sigh of relief.

"Aye, and now I mean to kill ye and that big fool in the chair."

"Wait! What did ye do with the children of the people ye killed?"

"Dumped them on the streets of the next village. Probably too young to survive but"—he shrugged—"stupid people breed like bloody rabbits."

"They were just bairns!"

"Get his back to me."

Bethoc blinked and tried not to look at Robbie when she heard those whispered words. "Nay a kill to be proud of," she said, struggling to think of a way to get him in the position she assumed Robbie wanted. "Just toss them aside and let nature do the work for ye." If the narrow-eyed look he was giving her was any indication, she had succeeded in getting his mind off how many ways he could boast of his cleverness.

He lunged for her and she darted out of the way. The knife he held was long and looked sharp but she tried not to be distracted by it. As she waited for him to make his next lunge she tried to think of how many more times she needed him to move then decided it was useless. She could not plan what move he would take. He lunged again as she barely got out of the way in time, the knife slicing her skirts. For a moment he actually chased her but finally stopped. As she faced him again she realized she finally had him with his back to Robbie but was he close enough? To her surprise she discovered the fool was winded from the short chase.

"Out of breath?" she asked in surprise. "O'er a wee bit of dashing about?"

"Ye bitch! Ye willnae get away."

"Ye cannae e'en catch me without panting like a hard-run horse. I think 'tis time ye went back to jail."

She tried very hard not to watch Robbie for fear it would warn the man. Robbie pulled his hands from behind him and she wondered how he got them untied. Slowly, silently, he stood up. One silent step brought him up hard behind Angus. So quick she gasped, he grabbed Angus by the head, wrenched his head around, and she heard the awful sound of his neck snapping. She stared at Robbie.

"I think ye have killed him," she whispered.

"Aye, he did."

Bethoc's eyes widened even more when she looked toward the door. The laird stood there, flanked by two of his sons, one looking pale and bruised. He stared down at Angus who sprawled on the floor like a broken doll. Robbie stood tall and rubbed at his newly freed wrists.

"I am so sorry, m'laird," said Bethoc.

"Better this way. And he gave ye no choice. He wanted to kill ye, that big fellow, and would probably have even killed the wee lass peering round him."

She spun around to stare horrified at Margaret. The little girl smiled, stepped out from behind Robbie, and held up a rope. Suddenly Bethoc knew what she had seen under the bed.

"Margaret!" Even Bethoc could hear both a scold and relief in her voice.

"Fix," Margaret said, and looked at Robbie. "See? Fix."

"Aye," Robbie said. "Ye did weel, lass."

"Ye had her help ye?"

"Och, nay, ne'er thought of it. But I was struggling to get loose when I felt a wee hand slap mine out of the way and then she got to work. Couldnae say anything so just had to let her do it." He frowned. "An odd skill in such a wee child."

"Aye. Allow me to show ye her favorite toy."

Robbie watched Bethoc go to a big chest, open it, and then pull out a length of rope. The rope had a line of knots on it. He looked down at Margaret who was doing an odd little hopping dance and clapping her hands as Bethoc walked back and waved the rope at Robbie.

"How long has she been doing it?" Robbie asked, fascinated.

"Since she discovered fingers were good for more than sucking on. She saw that rope knotted on your arms and couldnae have resisted nay matter what crazed fool was dancing through the house. She had to untie that knot. Isnae that right, Margaret?"

The little girl grabbed the rope and yanked on it. "Mine."

"Say please." Bethoc sighed as the child just kept pulling on the rope and glared at Robbie when he looked like he was about to laugh.

Margaret got the rope, climbed up on Bethoc's bed, smiled, and said, "Thank ye."

Bethoc just shook her head and smacked Robbie on

the arm for laughing, but then noticed his shoulder was bleeding. "He stabbed ye?"

"Early on. Right after he tied me up. Thinking he meant to do some more poking at me but he heard something. Dinnae ken what but he suddenly dashed outside. Obviously, he hid and watched until ye walked in."

"Weel, we need to see to that."

"The laird is leaving."

She gasped as she recalled what she had to tell the man and ran out the door. "Laird! I ken where the bairns are."

The man turned from the horse they had draped Angus's body on and slowly walked back to her, so she said, "Again, I am so deeply sorry for what ye have had to suffer in all this."

He waved his hand to dismiss her condolences. "Ye saved me the hard task of signing the hanging order. What of the children?"

"He said he took them to the next village and left them in the streets. I dinnae ken how old they are but he implied some might be too young to survive long." He turned back to the horses and a moment later Keith, who still looked a little weak, rode off with Angus's body while the other Keddies rode hard for the next village. "God's speed," she whispered.

She turned back to the house only to stop at the doorway to look at the ones now walking up to the house. "Laurel," she called, pleased to see the woman walking hand in hand with Magnus. "Weel met. How are ye?"

"Verra weel." Laurel stopped and Bethoc quickly hugged Magnus. "He was visiting with me for the day."

They walked into the house and Laurel stopped abruptly to stare at Robbie, who was sitting down and looking pained. Bethoc was about to say something when Laurel ran over to Robbie. As she scolded the man and studied the wound in his shoulder, Robbie sent Bethoc a little grin.

It shocked Bethoc but as she watched Laurel tend his wound, she began to think his campaign to get her to notice him enough so he could woo her was working. It would be a slow, frustrating wooing, she suspected, but she also began to think Robbie knew exactly what he was stepping into. She then looked at Magnus who had gone to sit with Margaret.

The boy looked happy. He also looked remarkably clean. The clothes he wore were far better than any he got from Kerr. Laurel was clearly treating him very well. Bethoc knew she had to let him go to the woman, let him have a good, loving family.

"Bethoc!" cried Callum from outside, appearing a moment later in the doorway. "What has happened here?"

"Sit and I will get some ale." She looked at Robbie but he was keeping an eye on Laurel, using her diverted attention to send a big grin at Callum as the others walked in.

By the time the men were all seated and Bethoc had served them ale, Laurel and Robbie were able to join them. Bethoc sat next to Callum and let Robbie tell the tale. She added very little to it. The whole thing made her sad. The laird was a good man, as was his whole family except for the one and that one had tainted so much that was good about the laird's rule.

"The mon was quite insane," remarked Simon, shaking his head.

"Aye, especially if he thought he could tie up our Robbie and all would be fine," said Uven.

Robbie smiled and there was a sly twist to it that told her he was about to tell them about Margaret. Bethoc had a moment of unease and then inwardly shrugged. None of these men had revealed any problem with the child so she would assume, until shown otherwise, that even this oddity would be accepted.

She listened as he told his tale, and watched their faces. Laurel just laughed but the men looked stunned. When they all looked at her, she just shrugged.

"Margaret likes undoing knots," she said simply.

"But she is only two," said Uven.

"Actually, nearer to three now. I dinnae ken how or why she does it. I truly dinnae. All I ken is Robbie is free right now because Margaret cannae bear to leave a knot tied. I only just got her to stop untying gowns and boots. I will let her have her knotted rope."

"'Tis just that one always assumed it required a bit of skill yet she does it. Dinnae think that is supposed to be possible." Callum smiled at Margaret. "Ye are a clever girl."

Margaret hurried over to Callum, climbed onto his lap, and presented him with her forehead. He laughed and kissed her. After a brief subtle look at Robbie and Laurel he glanced at Bethoc and winked.

Bethoc had to admit it looked as if Robbie was not insane to think he had a chance and she suspected he was one who had a lot of patience, was more than willing to wait for what he wanted. She idly wondered if she should warn Laurel then inwardly shook her head. Robbie was a good man. Laurel deserved one of those. And, Bethoc thought, she deserved a little boy who clearly adored her.

It was not until Laurel took her leave that Bethoc let her know her decision. She followed her friend outside and took her hands in hers. The wary look Laurel gave her told her she was expecting a no and Bethoc smiled.

"Ye can collect up Magnus and his things tomorrow."

Surprise was Laurel's first reaction and then she burst into tears. Bethoc took her into her arms and patted her on the back, not sure what to do. It was several minutes, and a silent dismissal of a glaring Robbie, before Laurel calmed down.

Laurel wiped the tears from her face. "I dinnae ken why I did that. Mayhap because I have been so tense about this business. And, did Robbie come out here? I thought I heard him."

"Dinnae ken how. The mon walks as if all that is beneath his feet is clouds," Bethoc grumbled.

Laughing, Laurel nodded. "True. Are ye certain 'tis acceptable to ye?"

"Aye. Magnus hasnae been one of my boys for years as the others have. I think he also needs more than being amongst a crowd vying for attention. I think ye need him too. And from all ye have told me of Yolanda, she would have wanted ye to have him."

"I will come by on the morrow then."

Bethoc stood and watched Laurel until she was out of sight. It pinched to let go of Magnus but she knew she was making the right decision. Now it was time to see to her own life. There might be some more changes to come and she needed to be ready for them. She also needed to stop hiding from the urge to take a chance, she decided, and walked back in to join the others.

Callum smiled at her as she sat down next to him. Listened to her quietly tell Magnus he would live with Laurel and was pleased to hear no deep sadness or uncertainty behind her words. What he puzzled over was why she was so insistent that he know he could, and should, come back to visit Colin and Bean anytime he liked. Then he caught the look on Robbie's face and smiled.

She would be going with him to Whytemont, he was sure of it. Robbie would stay with the older boys and he wished his friend much luck. He was going to need a lot himself if he planned to keep Bethoc at Whytemont.

Chapter Sixteen

Whytemont was more than she had ever expected. It was not a towered castle like at Banuilt but it was not some simple fortified manor house, either. It was a bit of both, she decided, and was quite stunningly beautiful in its indecision. The walls enclosing it were thick and high but the gates were wide open.

Callum could not mean for them to live in such an elegant place, she thought. She glanced down at her gown and winced. Laurel had insisted on giving her one for her entry into Whytemont and it was lovely, a soft gray with white lace at the sleeves, but it was still a very simple gown. The boys looked worse even in their cleanest clothes. She noticed they had gone very quiet as well. They were as suddenly intimidated as she was, she suspected.

The only one undisturbed by such grandeur was Margaret. Bethoc had let the child ride in front of her for the last part of their journey. She stared at Whytemont and smiled at Callum. Bethoc could tell the child could not wait to get down off the horse and thoroughly explore the place.

Once inside the bailey, Callum helped her and

Margaret down from her horse, the white mare a gift from Callum he had had to work hard to get her to accept. The boys gathered around her as they waited for their baggage to be unpacked and the horses and cart taken away. Bethoc tried to ignore how everyone stared at her. The stares were not unkind, just curious, but she badly wanted to get away from them for she felt as if everyone was asking what a girl like her was doing with a man like Callum. Then a man and a woman came over, the man speaking kindly to the boys as the woman took her by the arm.

Callum hurried over and put his arm around Bethoc's shoulders. "Nay, Agnes, these people are with me. We will be needing a few guest rooms made up if ye would be so kind."

"Oh, m'laird, so sorry. I will see to it right away." She frowned at the four boys. "Do ye want one for each lad?"

"Nay. Just a bed for each and if ye have to split them up, mayhap it could be in rooms that are near to each other."

"And the wee lass?" Agnes reached for Margaret.

Margaret wrapped herself in Bethoc's skirts and growled.

"Margaret, ye must cease growling at people. 'Tis rude." Bethoc looked up to apologize to the woman, saw the laughter in her eyes and the tight press of her lips, and decided to just mutter, "Sorry."

It took clearing his throat before Callum could speak without laughing. "I will sort out something." The moment Agnes and her husband, George, took the boys away, Callum crouched down in front of Margaret. "Ye must nay growl at people, Margaret. Ye are nay a dog. If ye dinnae like or want something just say nay."

Margaret nodded and moved to stand beside Bethoc

and take her hand. Callum stood up and a heartbeat later a little girl with wild red curls raced up to him. She hugged his leg.

"Da?"

Bethoc felt a pain tear through her chest. The child had to be Margaret's age. She wondered where the mother was and why Callum had never mentioned he had a daughter. Bethoc did not know what hurt most, that he had a child or that he had not told her. Or, even worse, he had brought her to a place where that child's mother still lived.

"Sorry, Callum," said Uven as he rushed over and picked up the little girl. "She got away from me."

"Not to worry." Callum kissed the girl's cheek. "Shona? Would ye like to meet another girl? She is your age."

Callum carefully set the girl in front of Margaret. "Margaret, meet my niece Shona."

The two little girls just stared at each other until the little redhead pointed to herself. "Shona."

Not to be outdone, Margaret pointed to herself. "Mar-gar-et. Clever lass."

Turning around so the children could not see him, Callum quietly laughed. He sensed Bethoc come up beside him and smiled at her. She crossed her arms over her chest and shook her head.

"That child is going to be trouble," she said. "She just informed Shona that she is also a smart lass and a good lass."

"Is Shona impressed?"

"Struck speechless, I think."

He laughed and took her by the hand. "We had best get inside."

With Uven's help Bethoc got the girls inside. Callum showed them to a very nice room where they could wash up. She shooed Uven away as she washed the little girls then herself. As she brushed out Margaret's hair she had to marvel at the quarters they had been shown to. It was a big bedchamber with a huge bed facing a huge fireplace. Rugs warmed the floor and heavy drapes cut the draft from the windows. There were two doors aside from the one she came in, one on each side of the room. A quick look told her one led to another bedchamber and one led to another room obviously used to do business in. That was when it hit her. Callum had had them taken to his quarters, to the laird's own chambers.

Bethoc was frozen with panic. She took deep, slow breaths in order to calm herself down. She could not understand what the man was thinking. He was a laird, a fairly new and young one. His people had to be wondering what was happening. Their laird had placed a strange woman who arrived with five children into the laird's own chambers. Bethoc knew what they all thought; that she was his mistress.

Horrified by what he had inadvertently proclaimed to the people of Whytemont, it took Bethoc a long time to calm down enough to go face everyone in the great hall. As she led the little girls to the hall, she struggled to think of what she should say to him. She had no trouble being his lover, but she did not really wish their relationship to be so blatant, so well known by one and all. How could she face the people every day? How could she make a place for herself? And she did not think Callum would understand much of that worry.

"I think your lady has realized ye have put her in your rooms," said Uven when Bethoc entered the hall.

"Ah, I cannae tell how she feels about it though."

Callum studied her face as she approached. "I will have to ask her after we eat and retire for the night."

"Oh, dinnae think ye will have to ask. Think she will be telling ye clearly as soon as may be."

That sounded ominous and Callum frowned at his cousin but then Bethoc and the girls arrived. He assisted her in settling the girls at a table with other children then escorted her to a seat next to his at the laird's table. It was a quiet meal, almost too quiet, and it began to make Callum uneasy.

Most of the people had left and the remains of the meal had been cleared away when a tall, thin man stepped up to the laird's table. Relieved for something that might take his mind off why Bethoc was so quiet and what that meant for him, Callum smiled at the man. He had the feeling one of his strays was about to be leaving him.

"Weel met, Thomas," he said, and stood to shake the man's hand. "What can I do for ye?" he asked as he retook his seat.

"Me wife and I have taken a real liking to young Michael," he said, the faintest of tremors in his voice the only thing revealing his unease.

"Ye do ken what that means, aye?"

"Aye, we do. We only have the one lass, ye ken, and there is nay much reason to think that we will be blessed with another child. Met young Michael and thought there be the answer. Like him, too. He is a good lad."

"Ye arenae taking him just to help ye with your work, are ye?"

"Nay! I am nay so old I e'en need him for that. 'Tis true he will be a help, but he could even find something else he would rather work at. We dinnae care. Just really like the lad, especially me wife."

"T'will be about two weeks ere ye get an answer."
Callum doubted it would take so long but felt the need
to warn the man.

"We ken it. 'Tis why we are asking now. Give us time
to get the lad, weel, settled in before the winter comes."

"Good. If ye and your wife are absolutely certain
there is naught I can find to make me say nay, it will
give ye time to ready yourselves for the lad too."

"Aye, sir. Thank ye, sir." Thomas vigorously shook
Callum's hand and hurried out of the hall, clearly
eager to tell his wife.

"So another of your lambs goes home," said Uven.
"Good choice, I think."

"Oh, I think so too."

"Why two weeks?" asked Bethoc, frowning over the
conversation she had just heard.

"Ye ken I said I take in strays, aye?" She nodded. "I
do like it when they can be settled in a good home but
I always check to be certain it is good. Tom and Anne
have lived here all their lives so that information will be
easy to gain. If he or she had e'er worked elsewhere, I
will find out about that as weel. In truth, I dinnae
believe I will find one single reason why they cannae
have Michael as their own."

"Then why do it?"

"To make certain the children sheltered here go to
a good, loving home. And if I do it with one, 'tis only
fair to do it with all who ask. Oh, I ken no one can
be completely sure, but I do what I can. That and my
instincts."

"Ah, ye didnae smell a taint in him. Nay, I didnae
either." She took a drink of cider only to realize both
men were staring at her oddly. "What?"

"What do ye mean about smelling a taint?"

Realizing these men did not understand what she meant, Bethoc blushed. "Oh, nothing."

"Bethoc, ye are a Murray," Callum said. "I doubt it is nothing. Ye *smell* a taint?"

"I didnae with Thomas, but, aye, I can smell it, feel it. 'Tis why I ran to your rescue which, if ye think on it, was nay the wisest decision a lass with a child and walking alone would make." She shrugged. "I dinnae ken what happens. I just meet a person and 'tis almost like a smell, an unclean smell most often, or a need to shudder and move away. Angus reeked and made my stomach turn."

Callum sat back and studied her for a moment. "Methinks we best find a chance for ye to talk to a Murray or two. Many of them have such, er, gifts. Did Kerr have a taint?"

"Aye, but nay such a strong one. I wondered why because of the bairns, but he did feel guilt o'er that. I think t'was because he was just a very angry, unhappy mon. Nay actually evil though he had done evil things, just terribly disappointed in his lot in life. He smelled like soured milk." She found it wonderful to be able to speak so freely about what Kerr had always said was witchery, and she could see the men were just curious, fascinated.

"Does everyone have a scent to you?" Callum asked.

"Aye. Uven smells like the ocean." She smiled when he blushed. "Robbie smells like clean earth."

"What does that mean?"

"I am nay sure though I have figured out some of them. I have always thought that earth smell, clean, rich earth, just meant this is a good, honest person, one who will stand firm."

"Oh, aye, that is our Robbie," said Uven. "Stands

as firm as an ancient oak when he sets his mind to something."

"Aye." She smiled. "'Tis why, despite his size, I ne'er feared him. I ne'er questioned him watching o'er the boys. Ne'er once. I ken Laurel cannae smell him like I do, but I suspicion she does a wee bit. She was easy with him far too quickly for a woman who has suffered as she has."

"So, Robbie could gain what he wants because he smells like dirt?" Callum grinned when Bethoc fell into a fit of the giggles.

It was late by the time they sought their bedchambers. Bethoc allowed Callum to lead her along as she planned what she would say to him. She could not allow him to simply set her up as his mistress without some rules, some mutual understanding. It was wrong to let him do it at all, but she was weak and admitted it. Even now she was not ready to give up on Callum, or walk away. Foolish though it was, she kept thinking he simply did not know or was not sure of what he wanted and just needed time.

Once inside the room, Callum made a fire and then turned to her. "Uven tells me ye are upset I put ye in here."

"How would he ken that?" she asked as she sat on the bed.

"Saw it on your face when ye first entered the great hall."

"Weel, aye, 'tis a bit upsetting. With this ye have told everyone here that I am your mistress."

"Lover," he quickly corrected, and moved closer to her.

"What is the difference?"

"Usually money. A mistress may nay ask for coin like a tavern maid but she definitely expects rewards.

Jewels. Gowns. A fine horse and carriage to ride about in. A lover is just one who wishes to be with you." He sat down beside her and took her into his arms. "If it makes ye feel better ye could sleep elsewhere and we can just slip into each other's rooms."

"Which everyone will ken about verra quickly."

"Aye."

"There are no secrets in places like these, are there?"

"Nary a one."

Bethoc sighed. "I am just nay sure why ye brought me to Whytemont, and feared being in the room would ruin any chance of making a place for myself, if that is what ye sought, or of being accepted."

He kissed her. "Ye do as ye please and, I promise ye, ye will suffer naught for being my lover. We are nay so caring here of who is doing what to whom. Only when it comes to the bairns do they care if ye are e'en wedded. E'en I frown on adultery and we are nay committing that, either."

"So cease fretting, aye?"

"Aye." He began to unlace her gown. "Ye didnae tell me what I smell like."

"Oh." She giggled as he gave her a quick tickle before yanking off her gown. "Actually, I dinnae ken what to call it. 'Tis just ye. Just Callum. Mayhap one day I can name it. Although, right now, ye smell like cinnamon."

"Cinnamon?" He sat up and tugged off his boots, then reached for her shoes to remove them.

"I ken I have only smelled it once as 'tis so rare and expensive, but, aye. Cinnamon at certain times."

"What times?"

"Weel, like now."

"Ah, when I am feeling amorous. Do ye think everyone smells different at such times?"

"How would I ken that?" she asked, her words muffled

as he yanked off her chemise. "I have ne'er done it before ye, ne'er even kissed, and certainly ne'er seen any others doing it."

"Ah, of course. Still, 'tis an interesting thought. An intriguing question."

"One I believe I could go a verra long time without answering."

She realized their clothing was now scattered about the room. Callum got up to pull down the covers on the bed. Bethoc was so fascinated by watching his naked form as he moved, he was in bed and watching her while she still perched on top of the covers. Also naked, she realized in shock, and scrambled to get beneath the covers.

"Like watching me naked, eh?" Callum teased as he pulled her into his arms.

"Of course not. I am just continually astonished at your utter lack of modesty."

He laughed and kissed her. Bethoc clung to him as he skillfully stole her wits with his kiss. It was something she hoped he never discovered.

She stretched luxuriously as he kissed his way down her body. For a time he honored her breasts with his hands and mouth. She clutched at his shoulders when he took her nipple deep into his mouth and sucked, then lightly nipped it. The feel of that light pain shot straight to the core of her.

Bethoc lost herself in the pleasure he gave her, in the delight she felt as she caressed his back, the sides of his hips, and even his buttocks. The stroke of his hands warmed her. His kisses made her heart race and her body ache for him. The heady scent of cinnamon soon surrounded her.

Then his kisses reached that spot between her legs and she tensed. She reached down to grab his hair and pull him away but in the time it took her to do that, the shock that had briefly checked her passion faded and her desire rose so fast it left her dizzy. Bethoc wove her fingers into his hair and held him where he was.

She became aware of him running his hands over her legs. Strangely that touch soothed even as what he was doing with his mouth drove her wild. When he slid two fingers inside her, he then did something with his tongue that caused her raging desire to rapidly erupt and she cried out his name as pleasure swept her away.

Callum gave her no time to catch her breath. He kissed his way back up her body, his fingers still teasing her. Bethoc was stunned by how swiftly her passion stirred back to life. She was trembling with need by the time he touched his mouth to hers.

"Bethoc," he whispered as he kissed her cheek. "Mine."

"And are ye mine?" she asked quietly, amazed she was able to form words.

"I do believe I am," he said as he slowly joined their bodies. "So, are ye mine?"

Bethoc tensed briefly at his question then relaxed, wrapping her arms and legs around him. "Aye, I rather thought I said so by coming here." He was moving so leisurely she was astonished to feel her desire sparking into full life, especially after it had been satisfied so recently and thoroughly.

"Such bonnie breasts," he murmured before kissing them.

His soft flattery made her blush even as his hands and mouth roused the need she had thought had gone quiet. She slid her hands down to cup his buttocks, enjoying the feel of them flexing as he moved. Then he slipped his hand between their bodies and touched her, lightly stroked that part of her that made her crazed.

Callum watched as Bethoc struggled to hang on and then fell. He felt her body tighten around him and swiftly joined her in that blissful descent, his release so powerful it left him shaking. For a long moment he held himself steady over her, kissed her, and struggled to regain his senses. When he finally left her, he rolled onto his back and pulled her limp, panting body into his arms. He had lasted longer this time, he thought with a smile.

"Ah, lass, ye are going to make me old before my time," he teased and she laughed, warming his chest with her breath.

Bethoc kissed his chest and said, "Weel, at least ye will have a verra elegant walking stick."

He lightly slapped her bottom. "Wretch. So, how do ye like my rooms?"

Propping herself up on one arm and resting her chin on her hand, she looked around the room and then back at him. "They are quite grand."

"I thought so too, when I first came here. Had a moment of panic."

She laughed. "So did I." She looked around again. "So rich and large."

"Aye. So I thought. And when my grandfather died and I realized he had named me his heir"—he shook his head—"it took all I could muster nay to hide under this grand bed, hide from everyone who was now looking to me, to Callum the street brat, to be their laird."

"There is nay wrong with a street brat. 'Tis just a child tossed aside most times."

Callum took a deep breath. He had to tell her. She had a right to know what kind of man she was with, he thought as he slowly let that breath out, reaching for calm. There were times when it affected his behavior, though not as often as it used to. There were times when the dreams would come and he would wake to find himself trembling and hiding in some small, dark place. He still checked for places to hide or escape through whenever he visited a place. His rage could sometimes swamp him when he found a broken child, one who had suffered as he had.

Then there were the knives. She had not noticed yet because he was careful to remove them when there was even the smallest chance she would be close enough for her to know he had them. It was not normal to carry so many knives.

He grimaced. The ones who had beaten him had taken his knives but he had gotten most of them back. That was the moment he had started wearing them again.

"Bethoc, ye do ken I was a bit more than just a street rat, aye?" he said.

"I ken something bad happened after the mon ye mentioned, the bad one, took ye in."

"He liked young boys." The way she caught her breath, lifting her head even as her eyes widened, told him she had quickly grasped what he meant. "He got them when they were small, from the streets, from some trusting parents who thought to give their bairn a better life, and from an orphanage. Then he trained them to, weel, accept his ways. Punishment was harsh. E'en for his wife. And when they got too old, he often just killed them."

"That is why ye look hard at any who want one of your 'lambs' as Uven called them."

"Aye, verra hard. Some who come here have already suffered so I have to be verra careful placing them."

She stroked his cheek. "But ye got away."

"Aye, thanks to Kirstie and Payton Murray. They fought for us, for me, Robbie, Simon, and the others. It was a long hard fight, too. Then I found my grandfather and all this."

"Did they kill him?" she asked in a hard voice. "Did they kill the mon who hurt so many children?"

"Aye, we killed him. Actually Simon did. He was only twelve but we dinnae think he suffered much for it. The mon had killed his father, beaten him and threatened his wee sister—Brenda."

"Your cook?"

He grinned. "Aye. She loves cooking so I let her be ours when the old cook died."

"I am glad it all turned out weel but I am verra glad Simon killed the mon. I suspicion he would have smelled terrible. Probably like rotting meat."

"Aye. But, Bethoc, I am telling ye this because ye have the right to ken what kind of mon ye have accepted into your bed."

"What do ye mean?"

"Weel, I am soiled. I am nay all this but a feral child, abused and . . ." He halted when she clapped her hand over his mouth.

"What ye being right now is an idiot. Ye are Callum. Aye, ye were a street lad and all that other horror, but ye are nay now. Ye have become Callum who rescues the wee ones who need it, some women, too, and tries to find them homes and a good life. Ye are a laird and e'en in this short time I can see that the people here like ye in that place just fine. I grieve for that child ye were but ye are nay him now."

He moved her hand. "He slips back," he confessed softly. "I carry a lot of knives on me at all times. I can get blindly angry. I wake from dreams, nightmares of my time with him and am hiding in a small, dark place, trembling like a wee bairn. Not as much as I used to but it could still happen."

"Then when ye feel those dreams grab ye, ye just grab me and hold on."

He just stared at her. Her eyes held nothing but softness and, he thought, as much understanding as anyone who had not suffered as he had could have, and acceptance. Callum felt a stinging in his eyes that told him he was close to weeping like a woman and smiled.

"Aye, I will do that," he said, and hugged her.

Chapter Seventeen

Wiping the sweat from her face, Bethoc studied the garden she and the boys had finally finished. It was too late to plant anything but a good area was ready for the spring. She was just not sure if they would be at Whytemont then, or might be ready to leave it. The chill of fall was already in the air too often.

"'Tis a fine garden," said Liam as he sat down beside her. "'Tis a shame it cannae be planted yet. I am a wee bit surprised they didnae have one."

"It fell into disuse when the laird took ill. By the time he died, and the old cook soon followed him, it was gone, and no one had much interest in bringing it back when they could get all they needed in the village." She frowned. "I didnae think, but this could cost the villagers. They must be making a nice profit from the manor."

"And they still will," said Callum as he moved next to Bethoc and crouched down beside her. "We have a lot of mouths to feed. My cook, Brenda, is verra pleased to see this, and has a lot of ideas about what she would like to see planted."

After hasty excuses, the boys ran off to the kitchen

to speak to Brenda and Bethoc turned to Callum. "Are ye certain?"

"Oh, aye." He sat down beside her. "I suspicion by spring she will have more than enough for the boys to plant. 'Tis verra precise," he murmured, looking at the neatly raised garden beds with neat paths running between them. "They like doing this sort of thing, dinnae they."

"Aye, more than they have e'er liked working in the fields. 'Tis why I asked if we could do it. I could sense they missed the work. They like working in the dirt, making something, weel, pretty. They saw this at a monastery they snuck into and liked it. The monk that found them creeping about told them a lot, once he realized their interest. He e'en came to the house a few times to see what they were doing."

"Boys that like to make gardens," he murmured, and shook his head. "They want to be farmers?"

"I dinnae ken but I dinnae think so. As I said, they dinnae really like working in the big fields. Yet . . ." She frowned. "Liam smells like the earth a bit."

"Only a bit? What of the other lads?"

"Too young. I dinnae feel or smell anything about a person until they are an adult. Weel, unless there is something verra wrong with them." Then she noticed his legs. "Ye took Colin's boot off."

"Aye. Leg is fine, just a wee bit weak." He stretched his legs out. "Looks better though."

Bethoc took a minute to quickly check the area where his bone had been broken, then sat back down. "I believe it is healed but I suspicion 'tis a wee bit weak. Ye should still be cautious with it, I think."

"I am and will be. I just remind myself how I hated sitting round or trying to hobble about on one leg. Nay a thing I want to do again."

"Callum!" Simon hurried over. "That fool Graham is back wanting his grandson."

Callum cursed and got to his feet. He took Bethoc's hand and tugged her up after him. Not only did he not want Graham at Whytemont, the man had just ruined his plans to get Bethoc alone for a while. He marched off with Simon, belatedly realizing he was towing Bethoc with him. Just as he was about to apologize for that he recalled her strange ability and decided she might well prove a help.

Bethoc stared at the large man being held at sword point by two of Callum's guards. He was at least fifty, probably older, but his body held as much muscle as fat. His face was square with small eyes, or ones made so by the anger he made no effort to hide, and his mouth had a cruel twist to it. The look the man gave Callum chilled her for it told her he would like nothing more than running Cathan through with a sword. She stepped closer to Callum, a little afraid for him.

"Ye have nay right to keep my grandson from me," said the man, his voice coldly calm, which made Bethoc even more afraid.

"His mother is here with him," said Callum. "She is the one who has chosen to stay away from ye."

"Stupid cow," he snapped. "She kills my son . . ."

"Now, Graham, that is nay what I heard. Heard your son didnae want ye coming round to his cottage and ye beat him. T'was those kicks to the head ye gave him after he was down that killed him. Ye are lucky ye havenae been hanged. Ye would be if I had more than a little boy and a woman to speak out against ye."

"She made him say those things! She also lies. I didnae kick him in the head, either."

"Ah, my mistake. Ye stomped on his head all the while yelling how he wouldnae look like his mother anymore. When she tried to stop ye, ye knocked her into a wall. She and the boy ran to me. So, nay, ye will nay see the boy or his mother. If for no other reason than that she still grieves for your son. A true shame that. Ye actually had something good and ye killed it."

The man lunged at Callum only to be halted by the swords of his guards. "Ye may be the laird here but ye still have nay right to keep that boy from me."

"I do. His mother has sought shelter here and the boy is with her."

Graham stepped closer and Bethoc could not stop herself from softly gagging. Callum glanced her way but she had her hand over her mouth and nose. Her face revealed nothing that was telling concerning her emotions. This was not a situation that would leave her looking so placid.

Noticing that his guards were arguing with the man, Callum leaned closer to Bethoc and whispered, "A smell?"

"Like a rotting corpse but it could be that he is ill," she whispered back.

"Bad smell, bad mon."

"Aye, and I do, desperately, want to run away from him."

She huddled closer to him when he put his arm around her. Callum stood, frowning in thought, his gaze suddenly fixing on the stables. Bethoc looked that way to see what had caught his attention and could see what appeared to be a woman peering out. Callum moved his arm and, after a quick glance at Graham, made a shooing motion at the woman.

Bethoc looked back at Graham while Callum had a silent argument with the woman and Simon started to head over to her. At that moment the man abruptly overpowered the guard. She opened her mouth to say something only to see the man snatch up a sword from one of the guards and lunge for Callum.

"Nay!" Bethoc cried as she moved to shove Callum out of the way even as he started to turn.

Callum reached for Bethoc just as Graham finished his lunge, his sword penetrating Bethoc's side. He caught her in his arms as Simon stepped past them. Callum watched his friend take one swing of his sword, neatly separating Graham's head from his body.

"Bethoc!" Callum said, suddenly afraid he had misjudged the place where the sword struck her.

"I have been stabbed!" she said and, despite the weakness in her voice, she sounded outraged.

He picked her up, wincing when she cried out in pain. His hand was beneath the wound and he could feel her blood soaking through. "We will get ye fixed up first," he promised, sighing with relief when he saw several women rushing after him as he hurried up the stairs to his bedchamber.

"Oh, nay!" she cried, coming awake as he was about to lay her down on the bed. "I will bleed on it."

"Here, I have something to put under her." Brenda bustled over to lay down a thick layer of dark blankets. "Now set her down."

Callum did so and then frowned at Brenda. "Ye are the cook."

"I ken it but I was a healer for these people ere that. Worked with a good one before that, too." She sliced Bethoc's gown on her wounded side and parted the material. "Having any trouble breathing, Bethoc?" she asked.

"Nay." She took several breaths and let them out. "None."

"Then he didnae get your lung. Didnae poke your heart, either, or ye would be bleeding out right now."

"How do ye ken that?"

"Simon had the thought of going to war. Couldnae allow him to go alone, aye? Saw a lot of different wounds. Remembered them all. Now, afraid what comes next is going to hurt." Brenda stood up and went to wash her hands.

"Bethoc, what were ye thinking?" Callum asked as he sat on the edge of the bed and held her hand.

"That ye were about to be stabbed in the heart from behind?"

He glanced down at her wound. "Actually, I suspicion he was aiming lower. My liver, mayhap."

Brenda showed up beside Callum and nudged him away. "That wound would have taken your liver or cut into your innards. Bad wound. Bad death. Now, Bethoc, do ye want something to bite on?"

Bethoc glanced up at Callum who nodded, so she nodded at Brenda. A thick piece of leather was put between her teeth. She glanced at the band on her wrist and then at Callum as he sat down beside her. He smiled faintly and, as soon as Brenda urged her onto her side so her wound was facing upward, he clasped her hand. Then Brenda began to work and Bethoc was aware of nothing but the pain until she tumbled into darkness.

"Ah. Good. She has passed out. How did that old fool get a sword?" demanded Brenda as she began to stitch the wound.

"I dinnae ken. The guards were knocked down and then he was lunging for me, sword in hand. I was just turning and, if I had done so, if Bethoc hadnae knocked me out of the way, I could have been gutted. Then Simon arrived and lopped off the fool's head."

"Ah, mercy." Brenda sighed. "He had to kill again."

"He has been in a battle or two, Brenda."

"I ken it but 'tis different when ye are in the midst of men all fighting to survive."

He sighed. "Aye, true enough. But I dinnae think Simon will be too troubled by this. The mon did have a sword in his hand, had just stabbed Bethoc, and was still looking to stab me e'en as I sat on the ground with her in my arms."

"I hope ye are right." She tied off her stitches, bathed the wound again, and then bandaged it.

"Thank ye, Brenda."

"Fah, 'tis nay a bother. Fact is, had to near fight the other lassies to get here. She has a big heart, ye ken, and is free with it. When are ye going to wed with her?"

"I should, shouldnae I." With Brenda's help, he began to undress Bethoc.

"Ye dinnae love her?"

"I dinnae ken. What do I ken of love?" He shrugged and lightly stroked Bethoc's hand.

"Oh, Callum." She hurried over to the washbowl to clean her hands. "Ye ken a lot. Ye just dinnae ken it. Ye take in women and bairns, ye collect the lost children and find them good homes, and look at the people ye gather round you. Me, Simon, Uven, Robbie. We are nay here just because ye have a bonnie face." She walked back to the bed in time to help him tuck Bethoc in. "And then there is this lass. Her and her four lads, two back at her home. And that wee verra determined lass. Bethoc came with ye e'en though ye offered her naught but a bed."

"Weel, mayhap she really likes that bed."

She shook her head and patted him on the back. "Idiot male. Mayhap ye ought to visit with Payton and Kirstie. There are two people who ken a lot about love and loving."

Brenda headed to the door but stopped before

leaving, looking back at Callum. "Is Robbie e'er coming back?"

"I dinnae ken. There is this lass he fancies and he hopes to win," he replied, then started and turned to stare at her. "Ye werenae . . ."

"Nay! Oh, I do like him. He has always been there, hasnae he. Always saying 'I will go with ye,' always watching out for people. I just realized, if he doesnae come back, I will sorely miss him. Is she a good lass?"

"Oh, aye, but she was in prison when Bethoc was and the sheriff and his guards used her harshly."

"Poor lass. Is she bonnie? Big as he is, Robbie is a fine-looking mon. He deserves a bonnie lass."

Callum could not help it; he grinned. "Oh, aye, she is bonnie. The kind of bonnie to make a mon stupid. Just made Robbie determined to stay and try his wiles on her."

"Wiles? Robbie doesnae have any wiles."

"Nay, and, with this lass, that will work in his favor. Dinnae worry about him, Brenda. It was actually looking good for him before we left."

Brenda smiled and hurried out. Callum breathed a sigh of relief. For a moment there he had been very afraid Brenda had cared for Robbie as more than a friend. He was pleased to avoid that entanglement, more than pleased that Brenda's concern had been no more than that of a friend who wanted Robbie to be happy.

Bethoc made a noise and he took her hand in his again. She did not wake, though, and he studied her carefully. She was pale but that was to be expected. There had been a lot of blood loss but he was no judge as to whether it was too much or not. Callum just wished she was not so small, almost too delicate. He bent over and kissed her forehead.

He was wondering what to do with himself when the door opened and Margaret ran over to him. She climbed up on his lap and stared at Bethoc. Callum wondered just how much he should tell the child.

"Fix?" Margaret said, clutching his hand.

"Brenda fixed her, love. She is just sleeping now."

"Mon dead." She ran a finger across her throat and made a grotesque face complete with her tongue hanging out and to the side.

"Aye," he replied after forcing down the urge to laugh. "He was trying to stab me but Bethoc pushed me out of the way."

"Bethoc save ye."

"She did, aye."

"Good."

They sat quietly together watching Bethoc sleep. She asked no questions and he decided she knew all she felt she had to. A slight shift in Margaret's weight made him look down at her and he realized she had gone to sleep as well. After debating with himself for a while, he moved to settle the child on Bethoc's unwounded side. Sitting back down, he smiled faintly when Margaret curled up against Bethoc and, even though still sleeping, she put an arm around the child.

Bethoc woke slowly and the pain slipped in. She hissed but knew there was no way to turn to ease it. Then the whole incident of being stabbed filled her mind and she grimaced. The fool may not have hit her heart or lungs but it was still an incredibly inconvenient injury. It would be quite a while before she could turn or bend without some pain.

Cautiously, Bethoc eased herself up into a sitting position. It was painful but not too much so. She desperately needed to relieve herself, however, but had the sinking feeling she would not be able to get to the garderobe or chamber pot without help. Wounds stripped one of a lot more than the ability to move. Dignity disappeared as well, she thought morosely as Brenda arrived with a tray of food.

"Ah, ye are sitting up," said Brenda. "Need some help?"

"Aye," Bethoc said, fighting not to sound cross. "I have to get to the garderobe."

"Weel, we have a chamber pot for ye. And a screen for ye to hide behind. I will just set ye down on it and help ye off."

"Are ye sure the garderobe wouldnae be better? It is higher."

Brenda stared at her for a moment, her eyes wide, then she laughed. "Aye, ye are right. It would be better. Now we just have to see if ye can walk there." Brenda took her by both arms, ready to help her out of bed. "May need to give Callum a call if ye cannae make the walk."

That was a humiliation she was determined to avoid. Bethoc suspected Brenda knew that and was using it to encourage her. It worked. She was determined to get to the garderobe and back without calling for Callum. To her relief no one interrupted as they made a thankfully short walk to the garderobe. Brenda stood guard at the door and Bethoc endured the pain the simple act of sitting caused her. By the time Brenda helped her back to bed, Bethoc was trembling and sweaty.

"Now for some of my excellent broth." Brenda set the tray on Bethoc's lap. "Eat up."

Bethoc picked up the spoon and saw her hand shake. Grimacing, she put it down. "I think I had best wait a wee while."

"Nay, I will feed ye." Brenda spooned up some of the broth and put it in her mouth.

After she swallowed Bethoc had to say, "That is verra good."

"Thank ye. Boiled the meat for a verra long time along with a lot of vegetables. Decided that, if ye have to drink your meal when ye are ill or injured, it ought to be as full and rich as the food ye have to chew."

"Weel, I think ye have succeeded admirably. Just wish I wasnae so weak. Then I could shove it down my own gullet." She smiled a little when Brenda laughed.

"It was a deep wound, ye ken," said Brenda. "He may nay have struck anything important but he went deep and ye lost a lot of blood. I was surprised ye made it to the garderobe and back. But, ye are right. Much better ye go there then try to squat over a chamber pot. Just dinnae try going by yourself for a while."

Even though she hated the idea, the memory of how weak she had felt made her nod in agreement. At least she did not need anyone following her inside. After Bethoc finished with the hearty broth, Brenda gave her a small drink of cider. She found she wanted more but did not ask for any. For now, she wanted to try to avoid having to be helped to the garderobe too often. Then Brenda moved to help her lie flat on the bed again.

"I need to check your wound," said Brenda. "It will hurt but I need to ken ye have ceased bleeding, inside and out."

"Weel, let us get it done then."

Gritting her teeth, Bethoc watched Brenda leave the room. The moment the door shut behind the woman Bethoc began to softly swear and kept at it for several minutes. She suspected nothing she could say would

shock Brenda but felt that swearing like a fish-gutter
was not the way to show her appreciation for all the
woman's work. Brenda had been efficient and gentle.
It was not her fault it had hurt.

She carefully wiped the sweat from her face using
the arm on her uninjured side. There had been no
sign of bleeding inside or out, and Bethoc knew that
was a very good sign. The pain had not faded one little
bit though. The tight wrapping that was her bandage
did not help but she suspected Brenda was right about
it. For now, it was needed to make certain the new
stitches held firm and all the bleeding had completely
ceased.

This was going to drive her mad, however, she decided after staring up at the ceiling for a while. She was
accustomed to working, to doing something. It was
hard to imagine how Callum had stayed trapped in a
cave for so long with his broken leg, hiding from his
enemies instead of confronting them. He had remained
remarkably even-tempered throughout it all. She
doubted she would do the same if she did not think of
something to do with herself, something she could do
in bed and with a very limited use of one arm.

The door opened and Margaret walked in. Shortly
after her came the boys. When they gathered around
the bed, staring at her, she began to feel uneasy. Either
they wanted something or she looked far worse than
she had thought.

"I am fine, ye ken," she said, reaching out to stroke
Margaret's curls.

"Ye got in the way of the sword," said Liam, frowning
at her. "Saving him."

"Ah, weel, if I hadnae he would have been gutted."
When Liam winced she nodded. "An agonizing way to
die and it doesnae kill ye quickly." She touched her

bandage. "This hurts so bad I just had a hearty curse"—she shared a grin with him—"but it willnae kill me and it will heal and probably stop hurting so much verra soon."

"Then ye willnae be able to curse."

She laughed softly and winced. "Dinnae make me laugh."

"Weel, we had to come and see you. Brenda said ye were fine and so did Callum but we had to come and see that."

"I understand that. So, ye badgered Brenda with questions about me but did ye take the time to get any idea of what she would like in the garden?"

Gavin grinned and sat on the edge of the bed. "She wants a lot."

That started the boys talking. As Margaret crawled up to sit beside her, she listened to all the boys had to tell her. They had settled, she realized. They were making a place for themselves. Soon she would have to push Callum for more than what they had and either get that or leave, before the boys began to accept Whytemont as their home.

Chapter Eighteen

"There. I now declared ye healed." Brenda grinned as she threw the newly removed stitches away. "But, and isnae there always one of those, ye must be verra careful. The closed wound is so new ye could break it open again."

"Aye, I will be verra careful." Bethoc smiled. "'Tis what I keep telling Callum, so I had best heed my own advice."

"Good idea. And I must tell ye, those lads of yours are a treasure."

"A treasure, eh?" She grinned. "There are days I would heartily disagree with ye."

Brenda laughed as she went to wash her hands. "Och, they are lads when all is said and done." She walked back as she dried her hands. "What they ken about gardening is astonishing."

"I ken it. They love it. If I didnae ken how much they dislike working in the big fields, like a farmer, I would think they would become ones themselves. I dinnae ken if they e'en ken what they want to be yet. This, though, putting a kitchen garden together makes them happy and keeps them busy."

Callum suddenly strode into the room and the look on his face told Bethoc something had gone wrong. She was a little jealous when Brenda hurried over to him. She swung her legs over the edge of the bed and was about to stand up when Callum strode over to her and sat down beside her. He bent his head and rubbed his hands over his face. Bethoc looked at Brenda, who was looking very sad, and the woman just shook her head and left.

"What is wrong, Callum?" she asked, and gently rubbed his arm.

"Cathan's mother is dead."

She gasped. Although she had only met with the woman a few times, and thought her a bit silly, she had seen no taint of illness. Smelled no taint at all. Now she felt bad for thinking the woman a bit dim-witted but sweet. And then there was Cathan. He had just been in with the other boys to visit her and had been so happy. She felt so very bad for the boy.

Callum looked at her, his eyes dark with sadness. "None of us kenned it but she was in touch with this mon she kenned for a verra brief while after her husband was killed. He sent a message and arranged to meet with her. She slipped into the village to see him, they argued, and he beat her to death. I am nay sure we can clean her up enough to allow Cathan to see her. She was so broken up."

Bethoc rubbed his back. "Why? Why would she go to him secretly? She said once she left him because of what he was, was afraid of him."

"She said that to ye?"

"Aye. She was missing him and wondered out loud why she should be and then it came out." She sighed. "I should have told ye. Ye would have been able to keep a closer watch."

"Nay. Ye are nay at fault in even the smallest of ways. That was a confidence between lassies and ye just kept it to yourself as ye have always done, I suspicion. But it wouldnae have helped. If she was that eager to see the fool she would have slipped away somehow. We could ne'er get her to cease thinking she needed a husband, needed a father for her boy."

"She was saving him. Nay only from the ones who killed his da, either."

"Aye, and we thought we had gotten her to believe it, but I think now that she simply stopped saying it. She was surprisingly stealthy about the notes and going to see him."

"Did ye get him?"

"Oh, aye. Aye, and I was enraged. I doubt she gave him any fight at all so he was doing naught but beating on a helpless weeping woman. It angered me so much. Simon finally yanked me off the mon and I realized he was dead, didnae look much better than poor, wee Sarah." He turned and pulled her into his arms. "I warned ye. It was the rage."

"Did ye hit Simon when he pulled ye off?"

"Nay!" He pulled back enough to frown. "Why would I hurt him?"

"And there is the answer to your worry. Aye, ye go into a rage when ye see a child or a woman abused, and ye may need to get a rein on that, but ye are nay sense-less with it for all it might seem so. Nay a danger to everyone around ye. Ye visit that rage on the one who earned it."

Callum frowned and thought about what he said. He had known it was Simon who grabbed him, knew without looking that it was his friend. As he had stood there panting, his bloodied fists still held in front of him, he had never once thought of striking Simon.

Then regret swamped him. He had looked down at the mess he had made of the man and had been sickened by it.

"How can I tell Cathan I killed the mon? He seemed to like Donal. Talked of him now and then."

"Why do ye need to? Has he asked?"

"Aye. He worried the mon would come for him and I said he cannae because he is dead."

"And he didnae ask why, did he."

"Nay, but he might yet. He is still too upset o'er his mother."

"Then dinnae say it at all. Just say the mon was killed the same way he killed Sarah."

"Ah, that might work although it feels like a lie." He breathed a little easier for he had not wished the boy to learn of how, mad with rage, he had broken the man into pieces.

"Weel, mayhap a wee bit, but we both ken that, if the boy asks ye directly, ye will tell him the truth."

"Aye, 'tis true. I will."

Callum gently hugged her and rested his chin on top of her head. Her words were not just sympathy; they made sense. He worried for a moment that he believed that only because he needed to, then decided that was not it. She made sense and he simply could not ignore that. His rage was not a blind one, but it did need to be controlled. He could not just beat to death every man who raised his hand against a woman or a child, and not just because some of them were very high born and it would only get him hanged. It made him judge, jury, and executioner.

He needed to speak with Payton, he decided. It was time that Bethoc had a good talk with a Murray. She had met Brett but they had not realized she had one of those strange gifts that ran rampant in the family.

Now that he was aware of it, he believed she needed to talk to someone who had knowledge of such things. Bethoc handled it well but he thought it might be because she had thought everyone could do as she did. She had certainly blurted it out to him and Uven as if they would know exactly what she was talking about. If nothing else, she needed to understand the need to be secretive.

"We are going to visit Payton and Kirstie" he announced, and kissed her.

His kiss clouded her mind as it did too often and it took Bethoc a minute to grasp the import of what he had just said. "Why?"

"I need to talk with him and I think ye should as weel."

"Because I can smell a taint in people?"

"Aye. 'Tis a gift, lass."

"Kerr said it was witchery."

"Weel, many think so, but 'tis just like sight and hearing. Ye just have an added sense."

"That doesnae sound quite so bad."

"It isnae bad, love. 'Tis rather wondrous. Ye can tell who should nay be trusted, who should be avoided. Ye have an added weapon, an added defense against any threat."

Bethoc thought that sounded nice but was not sure. She had never thought what she could do was special but had never spoken of it because of Kerr's horrified reaction. At times she had thought it was a reaction born of jealousy because he was lacking in the ability many others must surely have. The way she had spoken of it to Callum and Uven, however, told her she might be in need of some advice on how to hide it. It would also be nice to know there were others out there who understood, who struggled with their own "gift."

"So when do we go?" she asked, resting against Callum's chest.

"I am nay sure. I must write him first to be sure he isnae traveling and that 'tis a good time to visit. Ye can bring Margaret."

"Oh, good. I was just trying to think of how to explain it all to her and nay looking forward to it."

He kissed her again, hungry for her but knowing it was too soon. "We will be gone at least a week, mayhap more for we will stop at your home since we ride right past it. Then, the time we spend at Payton's depends on a great many things." He stood up. "But now I must tend to the burial of poor Cathan's mother."

"Help me dress, please. I need to be with him when ye do."

Callum only hesitated a moment before helping her out of bed. He watched as she collected her clothes. It was going to be a true test of his willpower to help her dress. He wanted her but Brenda had warned him that her wound needed time to do more than just close.

To his relief, she did much of her dressing by herself and did it in a way that tempted him with few sights of bare skin. He realized living with Kerr and so many boys had probably taught her such skills. He helped with laces and then helped her don her shoes so that she did not need to bend down. Then, despite her protests, he brushed her hair out and neatly braided it.

"How did ye learn to do that?" Bethoc asked with a hint of suspicion as she patted the braid and looked at him over her shoulder.

"Horses' tails," he replied, and grinned.

"Wretch." She stood up and brushed down her skirts. "Let us go get the sad deed done. I pray poor Cathan's heart is nay too broken."

Taking her by the arm, he led her out of the room.

"I cannae say whether the lad is heartbroken though I suspicion he is, but I cannae believe it will last all that long. She was a sweet woman but nay so good as a mother. She was too caught up in her own sadness and wee Cathan looks a lot like his da."

"Yet she ran off to meet another mon?"

"I do wonder if she was one of those women who doesnae feel, weel, whole, unless she has a mon."

"Ye say it is his relatives trying to get his inheritance, so do ye think this mon was all part of that?"

"'Tis a possibility. Without her about they may think it will be easier to get the boy. I dinnae ken exactly who the mon was to her but she was ripe for seduction. Verra easily swayed. And the mon had the look of her husband. Good bait, I am thinking."

She shook her head. "I hate to speak ill of the dead, but she was, mayhap, a bit foolish."

"Oh, aye, and filled with romantic fancies. I now think she was sneaking out to see him for a while. So excitingly dangerous but, she assumed, the penalty would only be embarrassment. If she thought at all. 'Tis nay as if she was unaware of the danger. 'Tis why she came here, brought Cathan here."

"I am nay sure we can e'er ken what she was thinking."

"Nay," he agreed. "Ye and I would ne'er have done it. Now the poor lad is an orphan."

"Does that put him in more danger?" Bethoc asked, worried about the child.

"Aye, I think it might, but then I wonder if this trick means it willnae be a direct threat. He may have been trying to get her to bring Cathan out when she came to him and that was what the argument was about. This implies they willnae act openly against me. Cathan willnae leave here either. So he should be safe."

"He willnae be able to be given to any family, will

he?" She felt sad that Cathan would not be able to have a family of his own.

"Nay. It would be too dangerous. I have someone watching that cursed family of her husband's but he clearly missed this plot."

They arrived at the small graveyard just beyond the walls of the manor. Two guards stood near Cathan but so did all her boys. Liam stood the closest, his arm around young Cathan's shoulders. Cathan had only been with them a short time but it was clear they considered him one of them.

"I do think I may be right and he willnae stay heartbroken for long," whispered Callum as they moved closer. "He is not alone."

"Nay, he isnae." Bethoc stepped next to the boy and Cathan clutched her around the legs and buried his face in her skirts. She stroked his head as Callum began the service for the poor woman. "She is with the angels now, Cathan," said Bethoc.

"Will the angels make her happy?" he asked.

"Oh, aye. Angels are verra good with that."

"Good. She hasnae been happy since my da died."

Bethoc thought about that and then smothered a sigh. The woman had had a bright, handsome little boy, a son to be proud of. Clearly that had not been enough. The woman had been ripe for a sly seduction. Her enemies had probably searched for some fool who had looked a lot like her husband. A few meetings, a few love notes, and she was his. She did wonder if he had been ordered to kill her or if there had been some argument. Perhaps Callum was right and her lover had asked Sarah to bring the boy but she had retained enough sense not to do that and it had cost Sarah her life.

Then she decided the way did not matter as much as

the result. Sarah had been killed and it made it easier, or so their enemy thought, to get to the boy. She put her arm around him and held him close as the priest spoke over the woman's coffin. The enemy was wrong. Cathan was not alone.

She led him over to the grave when the priest signaled and gently led him through the ritual of tossing dirt and a flower in the grave. He looked so small and lost Bethoc had to swallow hard to keep back the tears. Then, as the service trailed to an end, she saw Margaret march up to stand next to Cathan and take his hand in hers. She went up on her tiptoes and kissed his cheek. Then she stood close to him and pressed her cheek against his arm. Bethoc silently cursed when she felt the sting of tears again and then realized Liam was now standing on her other side. She turned to look at him.

"Lass has a way of kenning what is needed," Liam said.

"Aye. Aye, she does," Bethoc said as she fought down her urge to cry.

Callum stepped up behind her and put his hands on her shoulders. "She is a clever, fierce, demanding wee angel with a verra big heart," he whispered in her ear. "Now we need to get ye back to bed."

Bethoc turned to Cathan and carefully crouched down in front of him. There were tears but he was not sobbing. As she looked at his face, something there told her he was fully aware that his mother was gone and would never return. She brushed his curls back from his face and kissed his forehead.

"Ye ken ye will always have a place with me, Margaret, and the lads, aye?"

"Aye."

Nodding, she let Callum help her up and they started back to the house. As they drew near the gates she heard the sound of horses approaching and felt Callum tense. She turned with him but he nudged her until she stood behind him. Facing him were four rough men. They did not have their swords drawn but they did not look as if they were friendly, either.

"We have come for the laddie," said one of the men.

"What laddie? I have quite a few running about."

"Oh, I think ye ken weel which laddie. Cathan. His kin want him back."

"They have made that clear. E'en killed the poor lad's mother but she had already given me the rights o'er the care of her child."

"Sarah is dead?"

"Aye, we just had the burial."

"Weel, she had no right to give over the right to the boy."

"Nay? She was the lad's mother. The mon who has paid ye killed the lad's father. Now he has hired some fool who beat her to death. So what do ye plan to do?"

"We have been paid naught," the man snapped. "We are just here to collect the boy and take him home."

"Ye do ken the one after the boy has already let five of his hirelings die. Then sent the last on a hunt he kenned he would lose, and he did. So, six dead and the one who actually benefits from all this deadly nonsense has yet to reveal himself. Ye, I think, are working for a coward."

"We are nay working for anyone."

The man just stared at Callum for a moment then exchanged long looks with each of the other men riding with him. Callum waited patiently, knowing they were considering all he had said. He just had to hope these men were smarter than the last ones. He needed this hunt ended.

Something made him suspect the man was telling the truth, that these were not hirelings, might even be men from Cathan's own clan. "If one pauses to think, killing isnae needed," he said. "There is a good fourteen years ere the boy would be ready to lay claim to anything."

"Ye keep talking of killing," the man began.

"And why shouldnae I? I just buried the child's mother. Since I got the boy there have been several attempts to kill me. His father was murdered."

"Nay, he wasnae." The man shook his head and Callum began to be certain he was actually speaking to relations of Cathan's father. "Weel, aye, he was, but t'was by her. And I figure she must have had help. Mayhap the mon who just killed her."

"Weel met, Cousin Duncan."

Callum quickly grasped hold of Cathan's hand as the boy stepped close to his kinsmen. He was beginning to question what he had been told and his own assumptions concerning Cathan's kinsmen but he was not ready to trust any one of them near the boy. It was interesting to see that Cathan had no fear at all of the man he called Cousin Duncan.

"Weel met, Cathan, me lad. I have come to take ye back to your uncle Wallace."

Cathan shuddered then vigorously shook his head and kept shaking it as he climbed up Callum's body. "Nay! Callum said he would keep me here. Aye, ye did. I cannae go back there. I dinnae want to die like my da!"

"What do ye mean, Cathan?" Callum asked as the boy buried his face in his neck.

"Uncle Wallace came to see Da and they were fighting then he hit him and hit him and hit him." Cathan started crying. "He kicked him too. A lot. So did the other men."

"Where were ye, love?" asked Bethoc as she stepped closer to rub the boy on the back.

"Hiding in a wee hidey-hole, *Maman* called it, over near the fireplace. I left Tippy there."

"Tippy?"

"My toy. It was supposed to be a dog. It was my favorite toy too, because *Maman* made it for me. But the men looked for us so we had to stay hiding then we ran and ran until we came here. *Maman* said we would be safe here but she died because she left. Aye?"

"I fear so, love. But ye willnae do that, will ye?" Cathan vigorously shook his head.

"What did those other men look like, Cathan?" asked Duncan.

Callum looked at the man and almost smiled. He, as well as his companions, looked coldly furious. These were definitely kinsmen and ones who kenned nothing about what the current laird had done or had planned to do. He was certain they intended to deal with it and he wished them luck.

"If ye would be so kind as to tell your men to nay skewer me the moment I step down, I would like to have a word or two with the lad," said Duncan, but his attempt to keep his voice pleasant was not good, the hard tone of his anger leaching into it.

"Nay too far from us," Callum said as he signaled his men, who then let the man dismount but disarmed him.

"Agreed."

"Are ye certain?" asked Bethoc quietly as she watched the man walk Cathan a few feet away before crouching in front of him to talk.

"Aye. These men are his kin and they didnae ken the truth. They didnae like it either. I suspicion he is trying to get more information, such as what the other men looked like. I will ken what was said soon enough."

"How?" She looked where he nodded and sighed as she saw all her boys and Margaret standing close to the man. "Oh." She grimaced as Margaret marched over and took Cathan by the hand.

"My wee spies." He kissed her cheek, causing her to blush since there were so many people seeing him do it.

Several moments later the man delivered Cathan and Margaret back to Callum. His face was stern but there was laughter in his eyes. "Nay verra private."

"Ye could have shooed them away," Callum said.

He glanced at Margaret and then at the boys. "Och, nay, I dinnae think so. I will let ye ken how it falls out," he said as he collected his sword and remounted. "Ye should hear from me within a fortnight. If nay, then ye can assume it didnae go weel and continue to guard the lad. And watch that wee lass. She will be trouble," he called back as he and his men rode away.

Callum glanced at the fierce face Margaret was making as she stood next to Cathan and just laughed.

"What did he mean?" Bethoc asked as she watched the men ride off.

"About Margaret?"

"Nay, that was just rude." She ignored him when he laughed.

"That if I dinnae hear from him in a fortnight, the men who wish to hurt Cathan will still live."

"Oh. And he will probably be dead. Aye?"

"Aye, but I suspicion we soon hear that young Cathan is free." He took her by the hand.

"And then ye will let them take him home?"

"Then we shall see what Cathan wants to do," he said and she nodded. "Now let me get ye back to your bed. Ye are beginning to look weary."

She felt it too so did not argue. It would be good when Cathan was no longer in danger but she hoped he would ask to stay. In such a short time with them, he already felt like part of her family. Men fostered their sons out all the time. They would just offer to foster Cathan, she thought, and inwardly nodded, pleased she had that settled. Now all she had to do was get her own life settled, she thought with a peek at Callum. Unfortunately, she knew it would not be so easy.

Chapter Nineteen

"Are ye sure about this, Callum?"

"Verra sure. Ye are healed, we got word that the kinsman responsible for trying to kill Cathan is quite thoroughly dead as are several of those who worked with him. They even sent Tippy back to Cathan. Ye need to speak with a Murray, Bethoc. Payton said Gillyanne might be visiting too. Ye can learn a lot about your gift."

Bethoc smothered a sigh as she rode beside him through the streets of the town with Margaret settled comfortably in front of her. She was not sure why he thought she needed to learn about her gift. It was something she had always had and she understood it as well as anyone could. She also usually had enough sense to not tell anyone about it. Something she had slowly learned, especially when she had spoken so freely about it in front of him and Uven, but Kerr's horrified reaction had started her on the path of caution. Uven and Callum had had good reactions but had told her quite clearly that that was decidedly unusual.

She glanced at Callum and started worrying again, just as she had consistently since her stitches had been taken out. That had been almost three weeks ago and he still had not made love to her. Bethoc was increasingly afraid he had lost all desire for her. She knew it could be that his hesitation was all due to her being stabbed but that excuse did not hold back the hurt any longer. There was only one other reason for him to not make love to her. He was done with her but did not know how to say so.

It was the hardest thing she thought she had ever done but she pushed that unhappiness aside as they halted before a big town house. It had a surprisingly large piece of land around it. She would find out whatever Callum felt she needed to know about what he called her gift and then they could go back to Whytemont via her home so that she could see Colin and Bean and perhaps even Robbie and Laurel.

Margaret patted her hands and Bethoc suspected she was clenching them. Her body had gotten taut as well. Bethoc took a couple of deep breaths and let them out slowly. It helped only a little as Callum came to help her and Margaret down. He took her by the hand and led her up to the door only to have it open before he knocked. A young man stood there grinning at him.

"*Jesu*, David, cease growing," said Callum as the two hugged.

He laughed then turned to look at her and Margaret. Callum took Bethoc by the hand and brought her closer. "This is David. He was one of us rescued by Kirstie and is now Payton's man, Strong Ian's and his wife, Wee Alice's son. David, this is Bethoc Matheson and her sister, Margaret."

Bethoc shook the young man's hand and watched as he shook Margaret's hand, delighting her with the adult treatment. Then they were escorted inside. She was impressed. It was not overtly rich but it was elegant. When they entered the great hall all of her nervousness returned.

The man at the head of the table stood up, his reddish-gold hair gleaming. There was interest in his golden-brown eyes and she had an urge to hit Callum for not telling her what the man looked like. The other man who rose was also breathtaking, big, blond, blue-eyed, and harshly handsome. The two women were a definite contrast. The one next to the man at the head of the table was of a build like hers, slender and short, but she had thick black hair and gray eyes. The other had hair that was a reddish brown and eyes that did not match. She, too, was a small woman, made to look even smaller by the size of the man beside her.

Introductions came next and Bethoc began to relax. Gillyanne was the one with the large, blond husband and she knew that that woman was the one Callum felt could tell her the most about her strange skill. Then she met Payton and his wife, Kirstie. She could see where Callum got his strength and wished she could openly thank the man for all he had done for Callum the boy. The way they all greeted Margaret in much the same way they did Callum pleased her almost as much as it did Margaret.

Once food was served, she listened as Callum told Payton all that had happened to him. Gillyanne hurried to Callum's side and insisted on checking on his leg. Before she did so, she looked at Bethoc. Bethoc readily nodded for she still worried she had committed some error, that Callum might not be telling her about some ache or pain he had.

"'Tis fully healed," said Gillyanne, smiling at Bethoc as she stood up. "Ye did a fine job."

"I told ye it was fine," said Callum.

"Aye, but 'tis good to have it confirmed as men can be, weel shy about admitting something hurts."

"Och, I always tell Gillyanne when something hurts," Connor said, then shrugged when everyone looked at him. "Why shouldnae I? She fixes it. Of course, I whisper it and only when we are alone."

Bethoc joined the other women in laughing. A few moments later, Gillyanne stood and gently encouraged the women to come with her. Although uneasy, Bethoc collected Margaret and followed Gillyanne and Kirstie into the gardens. Margaret pulled free of her hand to explore and then she sat on a bench next to Kirstie. It was then that Bethoc suddenly realized the woman was with child.

"Oh, Lady Kirstie, congratulations," she said.

Kirstie smoothed down her gown, which made the rounding of her stomach even more noticeable. "Our last, I am thinking. I am also praying it will be a girl."

It was faint but Bethoc could smell lavender. She had discovered that, if a woman was with child, a scent of lavender meant a girl. It was difficult to say nothing, but she kept quiet. This might not be the right time to reveal herself.

"What is it, Bethoc?" asked Gillyanne.

"'Tis naught. Really."

"Callum told me what ye can do. I have my own wee gift, ye ken, as do many in my clan, though I think smelling a person and being able to tell something about them is one I havenae heard about. So, what did ye smell on Kirstie? Naught bad, I hope."

"Nay! I just smelled a hint of lavender. It is there, beneath her normal scent."

"What is her normal scent?"

"The ocean. I smell the ocean. I fear I dinnae ken what that means though as 'tis new to me." She frowned. "I have only e'er smelled it with Uven, Callum's cousin."

"The ocean? The water? Is that what ye mean?" asked Kirstie.

Bethoc sighed. "This is where I have trouble. Think of what the ocean smells like if ye were on a cliff above it. A fresh, clean smell yet distinctive."

"Weel, that isnae bad then. I wonder what it means?"

"I have only come to understand a few, mostly bad. 'Tis a struggle. Sir Connor smells like the earth. I have figured that one out. It means he is a good mon, that he will always stand firm. Strong and steadfast."

"That is my Connor," Gillyanne said, and smiled. "What does Payton smell like?"

Bethoc grimaced. "I am nay sure. 'Tis nice, verra nice, and nay flowers yet I am nay sure what it is. Just that it is nice. Ye simply want to stand there and breathe it in." She could not help but smile when Kirstie began giggling. "I am sorry I cannae give ye a name for it. 'Tis probably just something I have ne'er had a sniff of."

"We will just call it Payton," she said, and grinned. "Fool had too many women who just wanted to stand and breathe him in so it probably warrants being given his name. The smell of Payton." She laughed again but then abruptly grew serious. "So what is this hint of lavender ye smell under my ocean scent?"

It felt oddly freeing to speak so openly about what she could do, yet she hesitated for a moment. "I was rarely amongst people outside of home, ye ken, so I am nay skilled in this. And the mon I called Father hated it, called it witchery and a curse."

"Tell me what ye do ken or can guess."

"The few times I have scented it beneath another

like this was when a woman carried a girl child." Kirstie's face lit up and she hugged her belly. "I am just nay sure ye can trust me in this."

"How do ye stop?" asked Gillyanne.

"Stop?"

"How do ye stop smelling people? I can sense what a person feels or e'en thinks. At times I can e'en hear snatches of what someone thinks but I dinnae have to. So, how do ye stop smelling?"

"I am nay certain. I do think of stopping and it often happens but mostly 'tis just that I ignore it, make it simply part of what is around me."

"Then ye are shutting it off. Ye just need to try and ken how ye are doing it."

"I shall really have to study the matter. It would be good to ken how to do it exactly when I wish to."

"What does Callum smell like?" asked Gillyanne quietly.

"Oh, I am not sure. He is much like Payton in that. But sometimes he smells like cinnamon."

"Cinnamon?" Gillyanne grinned when Bethoc blushed. "Oh-ho! I understand. 'Tis a wondrous thing ye can do. And aye, I suspicion the bad smells are horrifying but what it tells ye is verra useful."

"I suppose. I certainly ken who I must avoid."

"Ye may nay be able to shut out the bad. 'Tis a warning, aye? I cannae always shut out the bad thoughts I catch, no matter how much I may wish to."

Kirstie looked at the two women and shook her head. "I think I may be glad I am nay one of that bloodline. What does Payton do? I havenae noticed any odd gift in him nor has he spoken of one."

"The men in the family are nay always so blessed," drawled Gillyanne. "They may have a wee one, like seeing danger. I always thought Payton's was the way he drew the ladies. But I think 'tis a charm he has, an ability to win people o'er. People, especially children, just trust him, e'en before they truly ken who he is."

"Aye, they do," said Kirstie, "although Callum took a few days."

Bethoc suddenly saw Margaret walk by clutching a handful of flowers. "Oh, nay, Margaret." She caught hold of the little girl's skirts and tugged her close. "Those were nay yours to pick."

"For mon. Pretty mon."

Gillyanne choked on a laugh and Kirstie said, "'Tis all right, child. I dinnae mind."

Bethoc let go of the child, who started back into the house. Gillyanne grabbed Kirstie by the hand and tugged her to her feet. "I must see this."

Following the women, Bethoc watched from the doorway with them. Margaret marched over to Payton and tugged on his sleeve. He turned to smile down at her and she held out her flowers, nearly hitting him in the face with the small bouquet.

"For me?" he asked, and when she nodded, said, "Thank ye, Margaret."

She reached up to touch his cheek. "Pretty." Then she touched the flowers. "Pretty, too."

Gillyanne laughed as she sat next to Connor. Kirstie's smile was wide as she returned to her seat by Payton's side. Bethoc found she could not resist smiling as she collected Margaret and sat down.

"Ye are a wee flirt," she said to Margaret who giggled and reached for a honey cake.

"She is a wee darling," Payton said, smiling at Margaret before looking at Bethoc. "Did ye talk to Gillyanne about gifts and all that?"

"Aye, and she told me a great deal."

"So what is it?" When Bethoc stared at him in confusion, he added, "Your wee intuition, gift, thing ye must hide from all others."

"She can smell people," said Gillyanne as she refilled her tankard.

Bethoc found herself trying to explain all over again. It was not easy but it warmed her to see no hint of disbelief, fear, or disgust. Here was acceptance and she reveled in it as they talked until she felt a weight settle against her side. She looked down to see that Margaret had gone to sleep.

"Let me show ye to your rooms," said Kirstie as she left her seat.

Bethoc picked up Margaret and followed Kirstie. The room she showed her to was beautiful. The small room connected to it with a little bed for Margaret was even better. She allowed Kirstie to put the child to bed and then went back to the larger room to wash up. When she turned around it was to find Kirstie laying out a night shift for her.

"Oh, ye didnae need to do that," she protested.

"Nay trouble and I wished to speak to ye, away from *pretty mon.*" She smiled. "Margaret is adorable." Kirstie sat on the edge of the bed and patted the space beside her. "Come, sit."

Sitting down Bethoc tried to push aside her sudden tension. Kirstie was a sweet lady. There was nothing to feel nervous about, she assured herself.

"What do ye wish to talk about, m'lady?" Bethoc asked.

"How much do ye ken about the life Callum suffered through ere he came to us?"

"It was horrible and the mon who made it so deserved to die. Many times over."

"Ah, so he told ye." Kirstie smiled faintly. "That is interesting."

"M'lady, I dinnae mean to be rude but I am nay good with subtlety and such as that. Mayhap it would be best to just say, or ask, what ye want to."

"Then I will be direct. I dinnae ken exactly what is going on with ye and him but dinnae hurt him."

"Hurt Callum? I would ne'er hurt Callum."

Kirstie patted her hands and Bethoc realized she had clenched them together in her lap. "I didnae really think so but Callum is verra dear to me and I felt a deep need to say that." She sighed and her eyes darkened with memory. "Ye didnae ken him as a child, how hurt he was, how broken in so many ways. And, aye, he would be most angry with me for speaking with ye but I couldnae stop myself." She laughed softly. "Mayhap protecting him is a habit I cannae shake free of."

"Ye didnae need to explain. My lads havenae suffered as he did but they were worked hard and beaten. They get old enough to run after lassies and I will feel the same. 'Tis hard to shake that need to protect once it sets in hard. All I can say is, I have no intention of hurting Callum in any way. Of course, I am nay sure I am the one ye should worry about."

"Oh, Bethoc, I dinnae think so. I think I was worrying about exactly the right one."

Bethoc watched the woman leave and shook her head. She wished she could have said something to the woman to calm her fears. Trouble was, she had no idea what was going on between her and Callum. She was his lover and, despite her growing hope, no more.

Sighing, Bethoc stood up and got ready for bed, washing up and donning the night shift Kirstie had laid out. She realized it was not her own but, not wishing to be rude and refuse a gift, she put it on. It took a while as it had a surprising number of laces down the front. When she walked she realized her legs were revealed for it had slits up both sides to just below her hips. An odd garment, she decided, and went to check on Margaret.

Margaret, her hair neatly braided, was curled up in the small bed and clutching what looked to be a doll of some kind. As Bethoc tucked the covers around the child she realized her little night shift was delicately embroidered with flowers. She wondered if it was something made for that girl child Kirstie wanted so badly.

Then she gently pulled the door closed and went to her own bed. It was a wonder with its soft pillows and clean, lavender-scented sheets. Closing her eyes she realized she missed Callum next to her. They had not been lovers all that long but she was already accustomed to having him at her side. As she closed her eyes, she wondered if he would join her even though she knew it would be wrong.

His head still reeling with all the advice Payton had offered on how to woo a woman, Callum was caught by surprise when Payton asked, "Do ye love her?"

Callum rubbed his hands over his face as he struggled to answer and then looked at Payton. "I dinnae ken." He sighed. "I dinnae ken what I feel. After I spoke with Brenda I gave it some thought . . ."

"Dinnae think, lad. That leads to trouble. I thought a lot about what I was feeling about Kirstie and it got me nowhere, just confused. *Feel* it. What do ye *feel*?"

"I dinnae ken!" Callum dragged his hands through

his hair. "I keep finding reasons for her to stay at my side but really dinnae ken why."

"Lad, ye are in a sorer state than I e'er was," said Connor.

Looking at the man, Callum asked, "What do ye mean?"

"Ye are thinking o'er everything, to nay use, like pretty mon says." Connor ignored Payton's scowl. "I at least had a good reason to do so much thinking. Couldnae appear weak, ye ken."

"Aye, of course." Callum was not quite sure it all had to do with appearing weak but he had learned a long time ago not to even try to argue with Connor. "I dinnae worry o'er that."

"I ken it. Ye just worry about why am I doing this, or why am I doing that. Useless. Ye are doing it because ye have to. Accept that. Ye took her with ye because ye wanted to. Ye keep her with ye because ye want to. Ye just have to figure out why ye want to though it seems plain to me." He poured himself some ale.

"That is what I am doing. Trying to decide why I am doing such things."

Connor sighed. "I just told ye why. Ye want to. Tell me, when she got stabbed, how did ye feel?"

"Terrified," he answered without hesitation.

"There ye go then."

Callum rested his hand against the back of the chair, ignored a grinning Payton, and sighed. "And where am I going?"

Connor caught Callum's stare and held it. "Mon doesnae get terrified over naught. Doesnae get terrified because a bed warmer got hurt nay matter how likable she is. Doesnae get terrified over a lass who saved his life."

One did not and he should have understood what that meant. Before he could say anything, however,

Payton cursed and tossed an empty tankard at Connor. Connor smiled and calmly dodged it, then returned to drinking his ale.

"Before the two of ye get into one of your long, winding arguments," said Callum, "I believe I will retire. I have a woman to woo."

"Havenae done that yet?" asked Connor. "Ne'er thought ye a slow lad."

Laughing, Callum headed to the bedchamber. He would hear Payton and Connor trading jovial insults behind him. When he entered the bedchamber given him he sighed with satisfaction because Bethoc was tucked up in the bed. He suspected she had no idea they were sharing a room but hoped she would not be unpleasantly surprised.

He was certain she was fully healed now. Just the thought of that was enough to make him hard and he silently cursed as he shed his clothes and washed up. Hastily turning back to the bed, he saw that she still slept and he smiled faintly, slipping under the covers as quietly as he was able before reaching for her.

Bethoc woke to the slow rise of desire in her belly. There was no fear of the hands running over her body because the air was scented with cinnamon. She turned in his arms and put her arms around his neck as she kissed him. Bethoc sank into the sweet, hot passion of his kiss.

Callum slowly untied the laces on her night shift, kissing each newly bared patch of soft skin. He had already found the high slits on the sides allowed easy access to her slim legs. Whoever had made this night shift deserved a knighthood, he decided. Then Bethoc's small hands slid over his belly and she curled the fingers of one hand around his erection.

The feel of that soft hand intimately stroking him was like a kick in the gut and had his passion increasing in one giant lunge. If he did not escape that tormenting hold soon he would be spent before he even got inside her. Then he smiled against her breast. He knew one way to get away from that teasing touch without making her think she had done something wrong.

Bethoc sighed with delight as he kissed his way down her body. She made a soft sound of disappointment when he slipped out of her reach but moved her hands to his back, then his hair. When he kissed the inside of her thighs she shivered with a mixture of desire and anticipation. Her cry when he finally kissed her where she so badly needed it was a mixture of shock and welcome. It was a shocking intimacy yet she welcomed it with only the briefest of hesitations. Passion ruled her and she let it.

She was soon clutching at his arms, trying to pull him into hers. The ache of need was making her frantic with its demands and she wanted him joined with her. He kissed his way slowly back up her body until he was kissing her neck. She wrapped her legs around him, silently urging him to join with her. Then he did, so slowly she thought she would scream. He propped himself up on his arms and looked at her.

"'Tis like coming home," he said, barely moving, savoring the heated welcome of her body as long as he could.

"I wasnae saying nay," she said, surprised she was still able to talk.

"Brenda did and ye dinnae argue with Brenda when it comes to healing. So I waited."

"And are waiting now."

"Trying to go slow. Been trying since I met ye," he added in a disgruntled mumble.

"Weel, ye are being annoyingly slow now."

His laughter cut off quickly when she scraped her nails over his backside then slid a hand between their bodies to stroke him just above where they were joined. She quickly wrapped her arms around him when he finally began to move. Bethoc clung to him, sharing greedy kisses, until they both found their release.

As he left her, rolling to his side and pulling her into his arms, he said, "Still cannae do slow, make it last."

She rested her cheek against his chest as she struggled to catch her breath and idly stroked his chest. "I dinnae understand why ye think it so verra important."

"Ye will when I finally succeed."

She wondered why that sounded as much a threat as it did a promise.

Chapter Twenty

"Ye do ken that ye must be verra careful who ye let ken about your gift, aye?"

Bethoc looked at Gillyanne as they walked out to where the horses waited and idly wondered if the Murray clan had any plain people among its members. "Aye. As I said, I told Kerr about it when I was still a small child and thought it something everyone could do and he reacted badly." She grimaced. "Backed away as if I was a leper and said it was witchery. My mother was sensible that day and intervened saying it was a gift from the Murrays. I didnae ken what she meant then but he did. He knocked her down and then told me to never mention it to him again. I didnae.

"I did try to understand why he was so upset from time to time and decided it was because he couldnae do it. It took me a long time to understand it was nay something everyone could do but then I was rarely out of the cottage. I think t'was the fact that nay one of the children said a word about how he smelled like soured milk."

Gillyanne laughed. "And they would have. But the way Kerr acted is, I fear, how many would act. 'Tis fear.

Fear is a verra dangerous thing to cause in people as weel. So just be verra cautious."

"Oh, I shall be. There are times that I wish I didnae have this *gift*."

"When ye meet bad people?"

"Aye." Bethoc laughed. "The things they smell like are verra hard to endure. 'Tis also, weel, e'en though I ken it helps me to ken who I should avoid, it is upsetting to meet someone and abruptly realize he is wrong, deep down wrong."

"I can only imagine. 'Tis right up your nose. I dinnae ken how ye can nay reveal yourself."

"Weel, if ye e'er see me place my hand o'er my nose and mouth 'tis because whoe'er is near me is verra bad."

"How do ye do that without them kenning that ye are smelling something bad and asking what it is?"

"Practice. I practiced it so that it just looks as if I make some wee feminine gesture that is of no consequence." She smiled when Gillyanne laughed.

"Ah, Callum looks ready to leave, and allow me to apologize for Kirstie nay coming to see ye off. She has difficulty in the morning and also gets very tired. I cannae think she truly believes Payton doesnae ken that. Oh dear, my husband is tormenting Payton again. I best go get him to be quiet." She started toward Connor.

Bethoc saw Margaret leave Callum's side and hurry over to protect Sir Payton so she reached out to catch Gillyanne by the hand. "Nay. Wait. Margaret appears to have gone to protect Sir Payton." She exchanged a grin with Gillyanne.

Margaret put on her fierce face and shook her finger at Connor. "Nay! Bad mon. Bad, bad." She then turned to Payton, took his hand in hers, and patted it, but when Connor tried to say something, she glared at him again and bellowed, "Hush!"

Gillyanne was leaning against Bethoc, laughing so hard all the while struggling to be quiet about it. Bethoc had to struggle not to join her. She made a point of not looking at Callum who had turned as if to adjust his saddle, his shoulders shaking with laughter.

"That child has no fear," said Gillyanne, and wiped tears of laughter from her eyes.

That Margaret had come out of the home run by Kerr Matheson and his fists with such boldness delighted Bethoc but she said, "And no manners." She started after Margaret who was merrily chattering with Payton.

"Ye must nay bellow at adults, Margaret," she said as she picked the child up. "We must leave now, love."

"Kiss!" Margaret flung herself toward Payton, nearly unbalancing Bethoc.

After Margaret kissed his cheek, Bethoc gave her a quick scold for grabbing the poor man by the ear and the nose to hold his cheek in place for that kiss. After reassuring her that no harm was done, she turned to find Connor presenting his cheek to Margaret. She had to choke back a laugh when the little girl sighed and then kissed him. Despite the somewhat insulting behavior of the child Connor was grinning as Bethoc hurried over to join Callum.

They were soon on their way and Bethoc felt Margaret relax in sleep against her. Checking closely to be certain she was asleep and doubting it, she said to Callum, "I am pleased beyond words that there is such spirit in the child, that she was not with Kerr long enough to be cowed, but I believe the good manners lessons must begin, beyond the 'please' and 'thank you.'"

Callum laughed. "Dinnae be too strict. Connor and

Payton are likely still laughing, especially over Connor being bellowed at. And at Payton having such a tiny, fierce protector."

"Pay—ton," said Margaret sleepily, not bothering to open her eyes even though she smiled in Callum's direction. "Pretty mon."

"Aye, lass. Verra pretty. The lassies have always liked Payton."

"Is that why Connor goads him?"

"Nay." He laughed. "Connor just finds amusement in irritating Payton. Does it whene'er he can. 'Tis an old game with them."

Bethoc rolled her eyes. "Men's games."

"Aye, and verra enjoyable they can be." He chuckled then asked quietly, "Was Gillyanne any help to ye?"

"Oh, aye, she was, though she also had a good laugh. Seems she cannae think of another who has my gift. She did warn me of the need to be careful who I let ken about it, even explained why 'tis fear that makes it all so dangerous. That I understood. That was what I saw in Kerr's face. It is frightening when ye ken it is something about ye that put that look of fear there." She sighed and then frowned as she tried to think of how to explain her unease. "'Tis nay pleasant to be something that causes people to feel fear."

"Ye dinnae cause them fear, love. Their own blind stupidity does. 'Tis naught but a different skill ye have and I believe such things are God-given."

"I ken it. 'Tis just verra bothersome but I shall sort it out. How long a ride is it from here to my home?"

"Be there on the morrow. Probably by late afternoon."

Bethoc nodded and tried not to think on how much riding she would have to do. She glanced down at Margaret and bit back a sigh. It would not be a romantic night under the stars for her. She suspected there would not even be a chance for them to slip away and steal some time for themselves. Although she loved Margaret dearly, loved all the boys as well, she found she was increasingly wanting them to somehow miraculously disappear for a while. It was a selfish thought yet she could not really feel ashamed for having it.

Then she thought of Colin and Bean. It had been weeks since she had seen them and she was looking forward to that. She was curious to see if they had made any changes to the old house. They had often talked of things that could be changed, surprisingly clever ideas that would have made the house more like Laurel's, a bit more elegant and comfortable. Considering it was harvest time though, she doubted they would have accomplished much at all yet.

Perhaps she should just stay there and let Callum return to Whytemont on his own, she suddenly thought, and resisted the urge to rub at the ache in her heart such a thought caused. She desperately wanted to stay at his side. She was not sure, however, if that was the right thing to do. There had been no change in their relationship in all the time they had been together, no deepening of his feelings as far as she could tell, and no talk of what future he may have thought of for them.

It was not her good name she was worried about. She was not a part of the society that would condemn her, had no need of them. It was her heart that she feared for. Bethoc knew she had already given it to him but she increasingly needed him to give back. Each day that passed that lack ate at her. She feared all they did share would soon end simply because she was too hurt and bitter to keep waiting for something he was not giving her. It would be much better to end it all before that could happen and taint all of her memories of their time together.

Then she thought of the boys and realized she could not just stay at home and let him go. She had to go back and gather up her boys. By the time they were ready to leave her home she had to make up her mind, if for no other reason than to let Colin and Bean know she would be coming back. A part of her was ridiculously eager to stay with Callum but, too often, she could see the devastation she would suffer when he decided to leave her. She was not so naïve she did not know how easily a lover could be discarded. Kerr's love of gossip had given her enough tales to see that hard truth. She knew, deep in her heart, it would be a good thing to leave him while everything was still good rather than linger until he lost all interest and cast her aside. At least with the former she would be able to cling to her pride, although it was not something that would keep her warm at night.

Bethoc then forced all such thoughts from her head and turned her attention to where they were going. For someone who had rarely left her home except to escape to her cave, the journey was exciting even if the riding grew tedious. At least when she left him, she thought, she would know a lot more about the world than she had when she had dragged him out of the river. One day she might actually see that as a fair trade for the heartache she knew would come.

Glancing up at the sky, Bethoc realized it was very late in the day. She quickly covered a yawn. The inn they had spent the night in had been noisy and full. That and all she had been thinking on concerning her and Callum had kept her awake for most of the night. She had almost suggested they sleep outside somewhere for, at least then, she could have stared up at the stars while she thought. Then, just as she had been preparing to make the suggestion, the rain had started. So they had been stuck in a tiny room at the top of the narrow inn stairs, and the only one she suspected had slept well was Margaret, where she had been cozily tucked up between them.

She was growing eager to see Colin and Bean. They had been the closest to her in age and they had always been the ones she had to talk with. They were her friends, not just her family.

Her hope was that she would also see Laurel, Magnus, and Robbie. Knowing what Laurel had suffered in the jail, she wanted to see the woman happy, even settled, and knew Robbie would be a very good choice. She had passed the forty days of mourning so the gossips would be satisfied. It was time Laurel had a chance at a good life.

"Almost there," said Callum.

"I ken it. I just saw the crooked tree." She glanced toward the wind-contorted tree. "I hope there are no ill feelings because I left them for so long."

"Nay, not them. Verra practical boys they are."

"Aye. I just hate to think I may have hurt them."

Callum reached over and touched her arm. "Never. Ye will see."

Suddenly, as he drew near to touch her arm, Bethoc knew exactly what he smelled like, even wondered how she could have not known before as it was something she was so familiar with. Callum smelled like an oak tree, a big old oak tree with roots that ran deep and had wide branches that could shelter or shade a lot of people. It suited him well, she decided, and smiled back at him.

"Ye suddenly look verra pleased," he said.

"I just realized what ye smell like."

"What?"

"A sturdy old oak tree. Deep roots, wide branches." She pointed to the one they were about to pass. "Just like that one."

"An oak. That isnae so bad. An old gnarled one or a nice straight proud one, standing tall."

"The latter, of course." She rolled her eyes over his training. "A sturdy big oak and nay sure about the age. And I willnae go about sniffing them in order to make sure which kind matches your scent."

He laughed. "Mayhap ye just need to sniff a lot of things."

She was about to tell him just what she thought of that, when it struck her that it was not such a stupid idea. It actually made sense. There was no need to be obvious, something that would undoubtedly have people thinking she was insane. Yet, she could still take the time to breathe in the scent of things as she came across them. She had thought on it before but never actually gotten around to doing anything about it in any serious way. It might mean pausing now and then, but it would help her to better use what she could do. What a person smelled like meant something and she needed to widen her knowledge so that she could better judge what certain smells meant. Bethoc decided Callum did not need to know all that, however.

"Boys? See boys?"

Bethoc looked down at a now wide-awake Margaret and smiled. "Aye, Margaret. We are going to see Colin and Bean and maybe Magnus."

"Good."

Stroking Margaret's hair, Bethoc frowned. The child used a lot more words than she used to yet she was beginning to fear what others had occasionally implied might be true. There was no doubt in her mind that Margaret understood a great deal of what was said to her, if not all; it had been shown time and time again. Although there had been a lot of ugliness in her life, Bethoc had done her best not to let much of it touch Margaret. Now she wondered if she had not done as good a job as she had thought.

"Something wrong?" asked Callum when he noticed how Bethoc was frowning down at the child in her arms, a child who was pretending to be asleep.

"I was just worrying over her lack of speaking," Bethoc admitted. "I ken she understands most of what we say so why doesnae she use more words?"

"Mayhap she still holds tight to the lesson of being quiet."

"But at so young an age?"

"Aye. Bairns can learn how to keep the bad away verra early. She has nay trouble understanding and she says more every day now that . . ."

"Kerr is dead and gone," she said. "Then I shall try nay to fret o'er it."

He reached over to stroke her cheek. "Aye, ye should. And, there lies your home."

Bethoc stared at her home. It had just come fully into view and she had to fight down the urge to race toward it. For once, she was eager to get home. She needed to see how Colin and Bean fared and make certain that she had done the right thing for Magnus.

Robbie stood in the door as they dismounted. "So how are Payton and Kirstie?" he asked.

"Excellent health," replied Callum, stepping up to clap Robbie on the back. "Kirstie is with child again.

The lads are growing fast and David, too. Didnae see Moira but seems she is with child and near her time."

"I still cannae believe she wed Alan. T'was a good match though. Ye could see it."

"Aye. Where are the lads?"

"In the fields. Harvest coming in. Still a wee bit slow but gaining fast. Looks like there will be a lot to take to market."

"And for once they can decide what is done with the money," said Bethoc.

"Och, aye, they are looking forward to that," said Robbie as they all walked inside.

Bethoc gasped and looked around. The floor had been fixed and scrubbed so clean she had briefly thought it a new floor. Her father's bed was gone and her nook appeared to have been made into a place to sit. The rough steps up to the loft had been replaced by a sturdier stairway and, she realized, it disappeared into a proper opening. Someone had finished closing off the upstairs making a full second floor instead of just a rough loft.

"Someone has been busy," she said, fighting the urge to run up the stairs and see what else had been done.

"Aye," replied Robbie as he set some cider and tankards on the table, "I am nay good in the fields except for helping to move rocks or the like. Dinnae like it, either. But I could do something about all the ideas they had about what to do to the house. That I could do, like to do. Like to build things."

As they moved to sit at the table, Callum said, "Aye, Moira still talks of her kitchen as if it was a gift from the gods." He poured some cider not for himself, Bethoc, and Moira.

"Weel, Alan made the chimney. Did a fine job, too," said Robbie as he sat down and poured himself some cider.

Seeing the framing on the back of the house, Bethoc asked, "Is that what ye plan to do here?"

"Aye, but ye already have the chimney to use." He winked at her. "Will get that closed in ere the winter comes and can do the rest during the cold time."

"So, are ye nay coming back to Whytemont then?" asked Callum.

"I dinnae think so," he answered, and sighed. "Nay certain. She and Magnus live at her house and I stay here. 'Tis probably best for now but e'en my patient nature is being tested by it. Building helps."

"Where are the boys?"

"In the fields, sweetling, but they are due to come home or I would have gone out to tell them ye are here." He glanced at the front door. "Laurel and Magnus should come soon. She insists on feeding us." He grinned. "Told her I can do it myself and the boys said they kenned a lot but she wouldnae hear of it."

Margaret heard the boys before Bethoc did and raced out the back to greet them. A laughing Colin entered with her clinging to him. Bethoc took her as he and Bean washed up and saw that they had grown some. They were turning into two very handsome young men. It was not until they were all seated at the table, the boys talking about the harvest, that she realized they had also changed in temperament. Gone was the precise recitation of facts, replaced by a vigorous discussion of the harvest.

They could now truly enjoy pride in what they did, she decided. Their work was both appreciated and complimented on by Robbie and Callum but they also knew the money it would bring would truly be theirs.

It was their home now, she thought, and felt both pleased for them and worried about what she would face when she was alone again.

A knock came at the door and everyone grew silent. Robbie frowned as he stood up and went toward the door. Bethoc looked at frowning Colin and cocked one brow.

"Should be Laurel and Magnus bringing our meal," Colin said, "but she ne'er knocks. As Robbie's lady she just walks in, ye ken."

"Robbie's lady?"

"Aye, although I am thinking she doesnae ken it yet." He grinned.

Bethoc grinned back and looked toward the door even as Laurel and Magnus entered. She smiled at the woman as Magnus rushed over to hug her in greeting. Laurel looked so much better than she had when Bethoc had left. There was life in her face, the sadness and anger gone, or at least had retreated. The moment Magnus let her go and went to sit next to Colin, she got up to see if she could help Laurel.

"*Jesu*, woman," said Robbie as he took the pot from her to hang it over the fire. "This must weigh more than I do. Mayhap when we are done with the meal ye can help me shift a few boulders in the back."

Laurel laughed and slapped him on the arm. Bethoc helped her set out the bowls, spoons, and bread as Laurel explained that she had knocked because she had not realized who the horses had belonged to. It was a hearty meal and there was more than enough for all of them.

Conversation was mainly about the changes to the house. Bethoc listened in fascination to all the boys had to say and then to what Robbie discussed with Callum about what it would take to make the change.

The boys were being treated as equals and she could see that they loved it.

The boys cleaned up with no complaint after they were done with the meal, especially since Robbie and Callum helped. Bethoc finally found herself alone with Laurel. They slipped outside into the fading light of day and began to stroll through the garden.

"It seems to me that ye are much improved." Bethoc said. "In spirit."

"I am. I have my moments when I recall too much and am either afraid or very angry but they already become less as time slips by and life goes on. Odd thing is, the end of my mourning helped. I was free, not only of prison and those animals but my husband." She glanced toward the house. "I now fret o'er what step to take next."

"I wondered. Do ye like the mon, Laurel?"

"Aye, in truth I think 'tis more than like." She smiled faintly. "He is so calm. I feel safe when I am with him and all the dark thoughts prison gave me fade. They nay disappear, just grow distant. Robbie said ye told him he smelled like a grave."

Bethoc gasped, horrified. "I ne'er said that. He smells like the earth. Just the earth. Oh." She tensed. "He told ye about me."

"Aye. Dinnae worry. I dinnae understand it but I am nay one to fear what I dinnae understand. I would be afeared all the time if I did. But I think I nay longer trust myself. My husband was a poor choice. What if I am about to make another one?"

"Nay with Robbie. He is what ye see. Aye, he smells of the earth, good, fertile earth. It means he is steady and when he decides, he stands firm on that decision. 'Tis a good smell. You can trust in it, in him, and lean on it."

"'Tisnae that I dinnae ken that, 'tis that I fear I can ne'er be a proper wife, one a mon like that needs."

"The only way to ken that for certain is to try, but only if ye really wish to. And, mayhap let him ken your fears."

Laurel frowned for a moment and then smiled. "'Tis good advice and I dinnae say that just because it was the same thing I was thinking." She laughed with Bethoc. "'Tis really the only thing to do."

"But only if ye care for him."

"Oh, I do. I swear it." She sighed. "I just pray he cares for me." She stared at Bethoc who started laughing. "What is it?"

"Oh, Laurel, why do ye think he is here?"

Bethoc crawled into her bed and discovered it now had a much better mattress, then got distracted when Callum crawled in beside her. "I dinnae think this bed was made for two."

"Then we shall have to sleep really close," he murmured, pulling her up next to him.

"Should we nay worry about Robbie coming back?" She slipped her arms around his neck.

He laughed softly. "Nay. When he left to escort Laurel home he wasnae intending to come back here till the morning."

"Dinnae forget what Laurel suffered in prison. She may nay let him stay, or just cannae let him."

"Nay, I dinnae think so."

"What makes ye so certain? And why would Robbie be so certain?"

"Magnus is sleeping upstairs with the lads."

"Oh." She wondered how she had missed that, then shivered with pleasure as Callum slid his hands under her night shift and up to caress her breasts. "That doesnae really mean she will keep Robbie all night. If she gets, weel, scared by something, he could be coming back a lot earlier." Her last words were smothered by his dragging her shift over her head.

"He willnae come back." He sighed and kissed her between her breasts as he slid his hand between her legs. "He told me he will stay e'en if all he can do is hold her close all night."

For a moment Bethoc was so touched by that that her desire eased back. "Oh, that is so sweet. Laurel has to accept him. I think he is the kind of mon she deserves."

He kissed the hollow at the base of her throat. "I really dinnae want to talk about Robbie."

She laughed but her humor ended when he kissed her. Her desire for him returned in a rush, fed and nurtured by his. The stroking of his tongue in her mouth matched the movement of the two fingers he had slipped inside her. She was breathless and shaking a little by the time he ended the kiss. Bethoc clung to him as he kissed his way down her body, lingering for a short while at her breasts.

A pang of disappointment cut through her desire when he kissed his way down her leg. It was wonderful, the little nips he gave her soothed quickly by the strokes of his tongue, but it was not what she had expected him to do. She realized she was no longer shy or shocked by such intimacy, she was eager for it. A restless need overtook her, her legs shifting as he kissed his way back up her other leg. Then he finally gave her the intimate kiss she had been craving and Bethoc called out his name.

Her desire rose fast and she fought its demand, wanting the pleasure he gave her to last. When she knew she could not hold back any longer she tried to pull him up, to make him join their bodies but he continued to push her with his kiss. Then she shattered and, as she began to come down from the heights, he drove into her. Bethoc hung on to him as he took them both over the edge.

She was still struggling to catch her breath as he settled himself more comfortably in the bed and pulled her into his arms. Resting her cheek on his chest she wished for words of love but he said nothing. Bethoc knew she could not keep living with the lack for long.

Chapter Twenty-One

Sunlight woke her and Bethoc tried to ease her body away from Callum's, not an easy thing to do when they were spooned together. He groaned and rolled onto his back, one arm flung over his face. She sat up and drew on her shift then reached for her hose. For a moment she paused and stared out at the room, not really seeing it as she became lost in her thoughts.

They had made love, spent the night sleeping in each other's arms, yet there was still no talk of love or a future. Callum was obviously content with the way things were. They were lovers, mayhap even friends, and that was apparently enough for him. Bethoc knew it could not be enough for her but she did not want to leave him either.

Her eyes stung and she realized she was making herself sad. She quickly forced her wandering mind back to the mundane matter of getting dressed. Just as she was reaching for her shoes, Callum wrapped his arm around her waist, tugged her back up against him, and kissed the back of her neck.

"The boys are waking up," she warned just before he kissed her.

Callum was disappointed by that news for it meant he could not make love to her again but he savored the short kiss they shared before reaching for his clothes. He had let another night slip by without speaking. It appeared his cowardice ran deeper than he had thought. It was surprising that she stayed with him yet he could see a look in her eyes, a sadness that told him his luck would not hold for long. If for no other reason than to take that look of sadness from her eyes, he had to work up the courage to tell her what was in his heart.

He did not understand where his lack of courage came from. Yet just thinking of Bethoc not returning in kind anything he had to say to get her to stay was, to his dismay, terrifying. Callum told himself that he owed it to her. He could not just continue to find reasons or ways to keep her close without offering her more. Bethoc deserved better than that.

It was as they readied breakfast that Robbie and Laurel returned. There was a faint color in Laurel's cheeks and she kept exchanging looks with Robbie. Bethoc was eager to talk with the woman before she left for Whytemont and finally grabbed the chance when they went into the garden to dump the wash water on the plants.

"I am going to marry that mon," Laurel announced before Bethoc had a chance to even think of what question to ask her.

"Ye love him?"

"Oh, aye, but 'tis more than that. He kens what happened to me."

"Weel, aye, he was with the ones who saved us and things were said . . ."

"Nay, I mean he *kens* it, understands it, kens the wounds it leaves on mind and heart. He was one of the children saved by Payton and Kirstie." She nodded when Bethoc gasped and put her hand over her mouth for she had not given a thought to what that had meant. "He was beaten near to death yet still got away to stay by his sister's side. He still carries the scars from that," she whispered. "So he understands when I say I cannae bear a mon on top of me." Laurel abruptly grinned. "He showed me one didnae have to be on top."

Bethoc took Laurel's hands in hers. "That is good news. And does he love ye?"

"Aye and I didnae e'en have to pry it out of him. He freely told me. And I can tell by the sadness clouding your eyes that ye wish for such words to come from Callum."

"I do but ne'er think that I am nay happy for ye."

"I ken it. My opinion? I fear ye may have to open your heart to him ere he gets the courage to speak."

She sighed for she had begun to think the same. "I dinnae ken why he needs courage. Mon has that in abundance."

"Mayhap nay when it comes to something that matters to him, someone he needs to gain something from—like love or acceptance. Dinnae e'er forget what his childhood was like. I dinnae ken how much he has told ye but it was bad, Bethoc, verra bad. He is a wounded mon e'en if he thinks he is fully recovered. To, weel, expose himself so may be too hard."

"Aye, I ken what ye are saying. Do ye ken, I thought of just staying here but I left the boys at Whytemont. Then I fear if I do that he still willnae say anything and I will be left alone. For the moment, I just stay and pray he will eventually give me the more I want, I need. 'Tis nay a good situation and certainly nay a good solution."

Hooking her arm through Bethoc's, Laurel said, "Then I best tell ye that I am moving here. I will sell my house or mayhap get some tenants so that we will still have a place when the lads get older. The lads asked if I would move in ere Robbie did. 'Tis their house, aye? But, if ye wish me to wait . . ."

"Nay, dinnae wait on what I will do. Aye, this is Colin's and Bean's house now. I dinnae think Kerr left anything saying just that but I believe he would have named them his heirs if only to keep his land from falling into the hands of a girl child. All the work that has been done is theirs."

"T'was your mother's parent who bought it."

"Aye, to be rid of the embarrassment their daughter had become. Nay, do what ye will. If I decide, or Callum does, that I should leave him, I have a father and I suspicion he may have a cottage I could use if needed."

"And that wouldnae trouble ye?"

"Only a little but if I take it as just another tenant, nay. All I ask is an empty house he would have given to some other tenant. 'Tis nay so much to ask of the mon who fathered me."

"Nay, it isnae. I could wait until ye ken for sure ye need one and then rent ye mine."

"Nay. If ye can find someone to take it, I suspicion ye could use the money."

"Weel, I wish ye luck."

"Oh, weel, I dinnae doubt Sir Murray . . ."

"Nay, I mean with getting Callum to tell ye exactly what he wants, what he feels, too. From the tales Robbie told me of what happened when they were lads, it willnae be easy. I truly think he may fear ye will reject him."

"Robbie wasnae afraid."

"Robbie is a mon who kens what he wants and doesnae let anything stand in his way. He wasnae calm, nay at all, but kenned he had to speak his heart if he was to win me."

"And he did."

"Aye, he did, and we will marry next month. I expect ye to attend."

Bethoc readily agreed. When they reached the house it was obvious Robbie had told the boys. Their pleasure decided Bethoc; she would consider the house out of her reach now. It was not until she stood outside waiting for Callum to ready the horses that she remembered to ask Laurel about Lorraine.

"She is to wed Walter next week," she said as she stood holding Robbie's hand.

"Ah, that is good, I hope." She watched Robbie kiss Laurel on the cheek and then go join Callum.

"'Tis. She told me she doesnae ken when their childhood friendship changed but it had. I think some of Walter's guilt has eased as weel. No one blames him for the women who were hanged but they did blame the sheriff and his men. They have all been hanged, ye ken, and Walter did all he could to make sure what was done to me was kept a secret. I went to the hangings but although a part of me was eased, I didnae get any joy out of it. It was all rather sad."

"Aye, 'tis. I hope Walter continues to lose his guilt as he doesnae deserve to suffer."

"Nay. And he spoke up to Lorraine quickly," Laurel said with a pointed look at Bethoc. "Ye need to be firm and brave, my friend."

"Dinnae nag," Bethoc murmured, and briefly grinned. "I will think most seriously about it."

"Are ye going to marry that lass?" asked Robbie as he reached Callum's side.

Callum sighed. "I should, shouldnae I."

"Aye, and I dinnae understand why ye are so slow to do something. The lass loves ye, if that is what holds ye back."

"And just how do ye ken that?"

"She is with ye. She is nay a wanton lass yet she is your lover. Ye give her no hint of how ye feel about her yet she stays. And then there is the way she looks at ye."

"Oh."

"Of course, lately, she has a sad look when she looks at ye. I think she is starting to wonder if she is wasting her time."

"I have seen it," he whispered. "I dinnae ken what to do about it."

"Say something. Speak your heart to her. Ye best do it soon or ye will find she is gone."

Callum knew that was true. He could almost see it coming. What he was not sure of was whether he had the courage to speak the kind of words that would stop it.

Bethoc pulled Margaret away from the boys and went to the horses when she saw that Callum was ready to leave. Callum held the child until Bethoc had mounted and gotten settled then handed her the child. Once he mounted they started on their way. Despite her efforts not to, Bethoc felt her eyes sting with tears. This part of her life was over and she had to accept it. Laurel and Robbie would care well for the boys, she knew, and only felt sorry that she would now see little of them. She made a silent promise that she would not allow them to lose touch.

"I am sorry about Robbie," she said, suddenly realizing that Callum had lost someone who had been at his side since he had been a child, someone who knew what he had suffered, had shared that horror. "He willnae come back to Whytemont now."

"Nay. And, aye, 'tis something that saddens me, but I am also verra happy for him. He has found the life he wants," Callum said, and smiled at her. "That is nae small thing."

"Nay, it isnae. Laurel loves him."

"Good. That's good. Robbie deserves it."

"He does. And Colin and Bean are pleased. They ken they are too young to live alone at the house, that they would be easy prey for anyone thinking to take it, and, I think, they like the promise of being part of a family again."

"And by the time Robbie is finished they will have a verra fine house indeed."

Bethoc laughed and nodded. They fell into an easy silence yet she caught him sneaking looks at her often enough to make her a little nervous. She wondered if Robbie and Laurel's announcement had made him think about their own situation. It would be wonderful if it had but she forced herself not to hope. He had had weeks to do or say something to change their situation and had not. Bethoc would not allow herself to think that he would do so now.

The sun was almost down when they crossed onto MacMillan lands. Callum asked if Bethoc could ride a little farther for Whytemont was only an hour or two away and she agreed even though her backside was already numb. But with the choice of sleeping outside or in a nice soft bed, she was more than willing to endure another hour or so on a horse.

When Whytemont finally came into view, Bethoc would have done a dance for joy if she was not so uncertain her legs would actually hold her up when she

finally tried to stand on them. She waited until Callum
took Margaret then slowly dismounted, clinging to the
saddle when her feet touched the ground for she knew
her legs would fold if she tried to have them carry her
weight. The boy who had come to take her horse was
fighting a grin. She scowled at him and he looked away,
although she doubted he ceased to be amused. Then
Callum clasped her hand gripping the saddle horn and
wrapped his arm around her waist.

"Come along, lass, I will get ye inside," he said.

"What about Margaret?"

"She is with the lads. They will watch her for now."
Since she had begun to walk properly, if very slowly,
Callum simply hooked his arm through hers to lead
her up to his bedchamber.

Once inside his room he nudged her toward the
bed but noticed she made no move to sit on it. Callum
called a maid and ordered a bath for her. Bethoc
opened her mouth to protest then shut it. A hot bath
was just what she needed. She would apologize later
for causing the women so much extra work. As the
bath arrived and was being filled, Callum knelt at her
feet and unlaced her boots. When he stood up and
began to unlace her gown, she placed her hands over
his to halt him as she looked for the maids, only to find
them now gone.

"I can undress myself," she said, and frowned at him
when he grinned.

"Now, allow a poor mon to help prepare his lass for
her bath." He nudged her hands out of the way and
took her gown off. "I am going to take care of ye."

Bethoc thought on protesting again but gave it up.
Considering all that had passed between them a show
of modesty now would be foolish. She also wanted
desperately to get into that bath. When he tossed the

last of her clothing aside, he helped her into the tub. She quickly sank beneath the water and sighed with pleasure as the warmth surrounded her. Closing her eyes she let that warmth work its magic on all her aches and pains.

Her eyes flew open when Callum stepped into the tub. The man had shed his clothes quickly. He grinned as he arranged his body around hers. Bethoc narrowed her eyes and, beneath the water, reached out to tickle his foot. She grinned as he yelped and gave an involuntary laugh then pulled his feet back until his legs were bent with his knees nearly up to his chin.

"Evil lass," he said, and gathered up the washing cloth, dipping a corner of it into the pot of soap. "Turn round and I will wash your back then ye can do mine."

She did as he asked and sighed with pleasure as he gently scrubbed her back. Bethoc was just about to turn to scrub his back when he wrapped his arms around her. He placed his soapy hands on her breasts, his washing of them more of a caress than a hearty cleaning. She slowly leaned back against him, seduced into letting him have his way. Through half-closed eyes she watched his elegant long-fingered hands move down her body, pausing now and then to wash her, until he slipped his hand between her legs. She closed her eyes as he stroked her, finding his touch both arousing and soothing. When her release came it caught her completely by surprise. She had felt her desire growing but it had been so slow she had missed the moment when it had gone from pleasure to demanding need.

Once she caught her breath, she sat up and turned around. "I was supposed to wash your back."

Ignoring his aching need to be inside her, Callum turned. He enjoyed the feel of her small hands on his back. She not only washed him but nicely kneaded the muscles weary from such a long ride. Then her hands were on his chest and he had the feeling he was about to pay in kind for his play. By the time her hand curled around his erection he was desperate enough for her that he doubted he would be able to enjoy her touch for long.

When she slipped her other hand down to caress his sack, he lost the ability to wait. He turned, picked her up in his arms, and quickly joined their bodies. She gasped and clutched at his shoulders. Callum moved her and savored the look of passion on her face. When she took over the movement, he held her and kissed her breasts.

For a while the lovemaking was slow, sensual, the need tightly held back so the pleasure would last. Callum desperately wanted it to last, wanted her to see that it could be a long, enjoyable wallow in pleasure. Then she gave a little twist of her body and clenched her inner muscles. The last tenuous thread on his control snapped. He grabbed her by the hips even as he straightened up and kissed her. The finish came quickly then, both of them crying out as the pleasure swept over them and took them down.

"The water is growing cold," Bethoc muttered against Callum's chest when she finally regained enough breath to speak coherently.

"Mayhap ye could carry me to bed."

"Drag ye more like and ye will end up with splinters in places ye dinnae wish them to be."

Callum laughed and sat up straight. "Suspicion I best learn to walk again then."

He got out of the tub and then helped her step out. It was not hard to see that she was suddenly uncomfortable with her nudity for her cheeks were flushed a bright red and she could not look at him. As he dried himself off, he watched her wrap a drying cloth around herself and use another to dry off her arms and legs. He wrapped his around his waist as she moved to her bags that had been brought in by the maids and pulled out a clean shift and braies. She then managed to get them both on and discard the drying cloth without revealing anything in what he decided was a clever sleight of hand.

"I best go see what Margaret is getting into," she said as she finished lacing up her gown and reached for her shoes.

"Probably just running her wee legs off after being trapped on a horse all day." Callum donned his shirt and started to put his plaid on, inwardly cursing himself for the knot of words caught in his throat, words he could not seem to spit out even in the throes of passion. "Ye worry about her."

"Aye. She is just fearless enough to get herself in trouble or hurt. The boys are too young to protect her from everything." She moved toward him, picking up his clan badge from the small table near the bed. "'Tis a hard path one must walk with Margaret. Ye have to keep her safe yet ye dinnae want to dim that courage she has, make her fearful." She paused in front of him to carefully pin the brooch in place.

Callum tugged her close and kissed her, trying desperately to let her know how he felt even though he knew it was not enough. She looked pleasingly flushed when he let her go but only smiled and left to go find Margaret. Callum cursed, and followed a moment later.

Bethoc sat on the grassy hillside and watched Margaret race around with the boys. Liam was at that age where he could occasionally think himself too old to play with the younger ones but chasing a ball around suited him. He had magnanimously partnered with Margaret and Cathan against Georgie and Gavin plus some young boy from Whytemont. Bethoc could see that Margaret and Cathan were beginning to falter, however. She smiled as a moment later Liam ordered the game over and started to bring the two little ones over to her.

"Thank ye. I was going to call them soon anyway." Bethoc kissed Margaret's cheek. "'Tis time to eat. I just heard the bell rung calling us in to sup." She stood up and brushed off her skirts. "And the light is nearly gone."

"Days are growing shorter," Liam said as he carried Cathan and walked beside Bethoc. "How fare Bean and Colin?"

Bethoc told him everything she had learned and seen, including about the coming marriage of Robbie and Laurel. Just talking of the two lovers gave her a pang. She was very happy for them but could not fully suppress a stab of envy. Somehow, if she wanted even a small chance for having what Laurel had found with Robbie, she needed to build up the courage to tell Callum how she felt and what she wanted.

It was past time she did a little pushing, Bethoc thought as they entered the great hall. She had been all that was amiable, following him around without complaint or demand. In truth, she had been amiable about everything. At some point she should have spoken up, she thought. Once Angus had been taken off and there was no longer any danger to her, so why had she let him take her with him?

Sitting down next to him, Bethoc tried not to sulk as she continued to ponder what she did or did not have with Callum. They were lovers but she had no proof, nothing to cling to in order to reassure herself, to say she was any more than that. She believed they were friends and felt confident in that. He had told her about his childhood although he had been careful not to be blunt, but she suspected that care was taken simply because she was a woman. Despite all women dealt with day to day, men still believed they could not hear the bad things.

It was not enough, she decided. She could no longer be just his lover. Nor could she continue to stay around until he decided he was tired of her. That was a humiliation she did not even want to think about.

By the time the meal was done, she had given herself an aching head. She excused herself and took Margaret up to bed. Tucking the child into bed after changing her into a small night shift, she told her a story. She smiled when the child fell asleep before she was even half the way done. She kissed the little girl then went to ready herself for bed.

Even as she changed into her night shift she wondered if it was the right thing to do. If Callum did not say what she needed to hear, it would be awkward to get up and get dressed before leaving. Then she shook her head as she climbed into bed. No matter what happened she intended to have one last night with him. Crossing her arms beneath her head she stared up at the ceiling and prayed he did not linger down in the great hall for too long. The last thing she needed was to lose the courage she had spent the day building.

Chapter Twenty-Two

Callum found himself alone with Simon and Uven shortly after Bethoc left. He sighed and realized he missed Robbie more than he had thought he would. Before, there had been some small chance Robbie would return, but there was no chance at all now. He wished the man well but would have preferred he had found a lady at Whytemont to love.

"Here's to Robbie," said Simon, raising his tankard of ale. "Going to miss the big oaf."

They all knocked their tankards together and then drank before Callum said, "She is a beautiful lass. Ye might not have seen that when she was in the prison. She also loves him. The lads he was watching o'er are verra happy he is staying with them, him and Laurel and young Magnus, at least until they are older. He is improving their house while they work in the fields and a big harvest is promised this season so they shall have money enough."

"He has found his place."

"Aye, Simon, he has. He has found himself a whole family."

"So, when do ye follow his lead, my friend?"

Callum sighed and took a deep drink. "Who says I want to?" Both men laughed and Callum frowned at them as he refilled his tankard. "What is so cursed funny?"

"Ye are," said Simon. "'Tis either laugh or berate ye for being an idiot." Simon studied Callum's face before looking at Uven and saying, "I believe 'tis the latter choice. Sad."

Uven smiled briefly then studied Callum. Callum began to shift in his seat, uneasy under that steady stare. It was as if Uven was seeing deep inside him, seeing what he kept hidden from himself and others. Uven had been able to do it since they had been boys and Callum had hated it from the start. He did not want someone seeing too much, seeing the dark places that still lingered, and if he did not love the man like family, he might have sent him away. Being part Murray, Uven had a small gift and Callum always had to resist the urge to ask him what he saw.

"Ye have to do something, Callum. Ye give her no reason to stay otherwise," said Uven.

"I will do something. And what do ye mean I give her nay reason to stay?"

"A reason aside from your skill beneath the sheets," drawled Simon, "which I dinnae believe is as vast as ye sometimes claim."

"Vaster than yours."

"I but keep my experience most secret."

"'Tis nay hard to keep secret one or two bouts."

"Boys," said Uven in a good imitation of a stern father, "I believe ye have wandered off into a pointless argument. We were discussing Callum's current lady and what he should do."

"There is naught to discuss," said Callum, but he doubted either man would listen to him.

"Oh aye, my friend, there is. Ye need to either wed her or let her go."

"And why would ye say those are my only choices? Where is the *let things stay as they are* choice?"

"In the midden heap where it belongs," Uven snapped. "Ye cannae keep treating her like your mistress. That is what ye are doing, as if ye didnae see it yourself. Ye just tote her around with ye yet ne'er go beyond that."

"How do ye ken I havenae?"

"I ken ye. Most people would look into their own hearts and see that they need to speak out but ye are hiding all feeling as ye always do. Turning away from it in any way ye can. Weel, except the lusting. That lack is the cause for the sadness in her eyes from time to time." When Callum just frowned, Uven sighed. "Something ye have also seen and yet ye still say nothing, offer nay soft words, or cut her loose."

"For what? She cannae go home now. Robbie and Laurel are there."

"And so ye have another reason to tell yourself why ye are keeping her close." Uven shook his head. "Ye need to give the poor lass a home. *Jesu*, Callum, can ye nay see how unkind ye are being?"

"I have ne'er been unkind to her." Callum could hear the lack of force and conviction behind his words and inwardly winced.

"Ye are treating her as if all ye do for her is a favor and the fact that ye are lovers is just a pleasant benefit. She loves ye and ye just ignore it."

"Ye cannae be sure . . ." He fell silent when Uven made a slashing movement with his hand that cut off his words.

"We dinnae happen to be idiots. 'Tis there to see if one just looks. E'en the people here have taken to calling her m'lady, though she keeps correcting them, for they see and assume, because ye keep her with ye, that ye ken it, that ye will soon make her the lady of Whytemont. She has walked away from two lads who were like family to her to stay with ye. Her home, too. I think, if she didnae have the four children with her, she would walk away from ye as weel soon. A lass can only give her all to a mon for so long with nay return before she realizes she begins to shame herself. Ye need to marry the lass, ye fool."

"Ye marry a lass when ye love her and I am nae sure if I do."

"Weel, ye are e'en more witless than I thought," said Simon.

"I await the day the confusion comes to ye, Simon. However, I do think I should consider what Connor told me. He asked how I felt when she got stabbed. Terrified, I said. He said a mon doesnae get terrified o'er naught. It sounded so brilliant when he said it but the more I thought . . ." He looked at his friends in surprise when they both cursed.

"Stop thinking so much," Simon snapped. "That is where your problem lies. Ye think o'er everything too much. Some things just are and they dinnae always make sense or follow a straight path. Ye have found reasons to drag her around with ye, keep her at your side, for months now. Aye, it proved helpful in several cases but there really was no need. But ye always thought of one, didnae ye. Always came up with some good reason why she had to stay with ye. And then there is what Connor said though I cannae believe I agree with him. A mon doesnae get terrified o'er naught. Stop thinking it to death. There is only one thing ye need to decide."

"And what is that, oh wise one?"

"Do ye want her to stay with ye?"

* * *

Callum was still mulling that over when he entered his bedchamber. Simon was right. He teased Bethoc about fretting too much but he overthought everything. Maybe there were things that you just could not think out clearly no matter how hard you tried. Emotions got in the way.

He walked over to the bed and began to shed his clothes. Looking at a sleeping Bethoc he had an answer to the question Simon said was the only one he had to ask. He wanted her to stay with him. He could not think of a future without her by his side.

After taking a moment to wash up, he slid into bed and pulled her into his arms. This was where she belonged. It was the one thing he had no doubt about. He had not even looked at a woman since he had met her. He suddenly recalled an incident with Payton as they walked the streets of the town and he caught the man looking at a pretty, buxom lass walking past them. When he had reminded the man he had Kirstie and should not be looking, Payton had laughed and said a man cannot help appreciating the scenery, that the proof of his love for Kirstie was that he only looked, never touched or even tried to.

It made sense even then. He had not even looked at the moment because he was still completely caught up in what he had with Bethoc, and in trying to decide exactly what that was. Callum idly promised himself to remember that moment with Payton later, when he did catch himself enjoying the scenery. It was not wise to do so if one's woman was close at hand.

He kissed the top of her head and began to lightly explore her body with his hands. The night shift was an irritant but he did not yet dare to remove it. If she woke now, he would, but he was hesitant to do so too abruptly. They had had a long day and she was undoubtedly exhausted.

Bethoc woke to the thrill of warm hands sliding beneath her night shift. Even before she was fully awake she knew it was Callum. The smell of an old oak tree wrapped around her. She sleepily lifted her arms to wrap them around his neck and pull him close. If she was only going to have one more night with him she did not wish to waste it sleeping. She had a few daring ideas of what she wanted to do and wanted to be certain to have the time to do them.

"Recovered from all that riding?" he asked as he eased her night shift over her head.

"Aye. The hot bath helped."

"Sorry I woke you."

"Nay, ye are not."

Hearing the laughter in her words, he grinned. "Nay, I am not. Ye did look sweet sleeping there."

"Sweet?" He pulled her close and Bethoc reveled in the touch of their skin, the warmth of his body sinking into hers.

"Peaceful then." He sighed with pleasure when she gently pushed him onto his back and sprawled on top of him. "Sweetly peaceful and, aye, I did feel a tiny touch of guilt for disturbing ye." He ran his hands up and down her back as she teased him with small, soft kisses.

Then he kissed her, lost for the moment in the hot sweetness of it. When it ended she moved her kisses to his neck and he murmured his delight. It was not until he realized she was not stopping there that he became tense with anticipation. She kissed her way down his chest, pausing now and then to give him a little nip and soothe the sting of it with her tongue.

Bethoc was not certain about what she was doing but did feel sure she would know if she erred. After all the times he had kissed her so intimately she had to believe he would like it in return. As she kissed his strong thighs, taking the occasional little bite and laving the spot with her tongue, she slipped her hand over to his erection and lightly, slowly stroked it. His groan and the faint jerk of his body told her he liked that.

When she finally kissed him there, his whole body tensed beneath her. Afraid she had made a mistake, that it was one of those things considered fine for a man to do but not a woman, she lifted her head to say something. He curled his fingers in her hair and gently pushed her head back down. Bethoc took that as a sign of welcome and went back to driving him wild with her tongue.

Then she took him into her mouth and he cried out. The sound was one of pleasure and welcome so she continued, pleased that she had found something that gave him such delight. It amazed her that, as she roused his passion, her own grew and she knew she could not continue the play for long.

Callum was both surprised and delighted at Bethoc's boldness. He gritted his teeth and tried to enjoy what she was doing for as long as he could. It was a hard battle and he was only able to enjoy her intimate attentions for a little while before he dragged her up his body and then joined them. As she rode him he grasped her breasts to squeeze and stroke. When he lifted his head to kiss them, he felt her tighten around him and let go of his own control to go over the edge with her.

Their cries blended and then Bethoc collapsed in

his arms. For a while they just held each other, panting softly as they struggled to catch their breath. Callum had never felt so replete. He knew he would not find such a feeling with any other woman.

"Ah, Bethoc, I really think I might love ye."

The moment he heard his own words, he softly cursed. That was not what he had meant to say. He was not surprised when she got off him quickly and stared down at him with an expression that was a strange mixture of delight and aggravation. It had been a totally ignorant thing to say.

"Ye *think* ye *might* love me?" While her heart was pounding with hope and happiness, her mind said it was not what she needed.

"That was foolish," he muttered, and ran his hands through his hair. "I meant to say I think I love ye."

"Why are ye e'en saying it if ye arenae sure?"

"Because I dinnae want ye to leave me."

Bethoc stared at him. She was now disappointed yet not crushed or heartbroken. What she had, she decided, was a man who did not know what he felt. She could not stop herself from thinking that he did love her but just did not feel certain. Not only did it sound vain to think it, but she knew she might be grasping at false hope but could not shake the feeling.

"Love is nay a maybe, Callum. Ye either do or ye don't. I love ye and have nay a doubt about it." She pushed against his chest when he tried to take her into his arms. "Why is it that ye think ye might love me?"

"Weel, I look into the future and ye are always there. Each thing I plan, I wonder how it will suit ye." He frowned for he had never listed the reasons before and was not sure how to say what needed saying. "I dinnae look at another woman," he said, and wondered why she was not delighted by that.

"Weel, that is verra nice but doesnae mean ye love me, really. Ye have been a wee bit busy of late and nae in a place where women have been plentiful. And, to be honest, I dinnae think it will last. Wheesht, nae sure I would want it to because then I couldnae look at a mon and when ye have ones like Payton and Connor about, a woman would have to be on her deathbed to nae look at them and e'en then they would probably try."

Callum looked at her and suddenly grinned, recalling what Payton had said. "Fair enough. What do ye think tells ye whether ye are in love or nae?"

"Worry when they are out of your sight or in trouble, delight when they come home nay matter how short the trip or how far they went, this"—she waved her hand at the two of them in bed—"mayhap having trouble sleeping when the other isnae with ye, feeling it when they are hurt or sad and wanting to fix it fast, and wanting to do things just because ye think they may like it or wondering if ye should do something because ye worry they may nae like it. 'Tis nae so easy to describe. When ye get good or bad news they are the first one ye think of to tell. That and feeling guilty if ye try to keep a secret from them." She shrugged.

"Or being bone-deep terrified because they just got hurt, e'en though ye can see it isnae a mortal wound."

"Exactly."

He frowned and said carefully, "Or being afraid that if ye admit it, it might nae be returned." He felt lighter in heart for saying that and began to know that that had been his real fear, one that had been set so deep he had not really recognized it.

"Most certainly that. That would mean heartache and nay rational person courts that."

He stared at her. She sat with the linen sheet covering her lap and her hair draped over her breasts. He thought her the most beautiful thing he had seen. She loved him and he could only marvel at the fact that she did. His inept words had not sent her storming from the room either, and he began to think that was because she understood him better than he did himself.

"Then I love ye, Bethoc Matheson, and I want ye to marry me." He felt a cold grip his innards as he spoke the words and waited for her answer.

"Oh, aye, Callum. Aye."

She flung herself into his arms and hugged him tightly. Callum breathed a hearty sigh of relief. It was odd how he had ignored his own fear but he was relieved it had not cost him Bethoc. When she lifted her head to look at him, he kissed her.

"I have four children," she warned after the kiss ended.

"I collect them and quite often have more than four."

"Are ye certain, Callum? I couldnae bear having ye change your mind later and find myself wed to ye but ye nae bound to me."

"Actually, aye, I am verra sure." He touched a kiss to her nose. "I realized as we talked that my doubts were born of fear. I am nae clean and have often doubted why anyone would have anything to do with me. I didnae heed my grandfather's words of affection for a long time because of that."

"Ye are nae unclean, Callum. That is utter nonsense. Do ye think Laurel unclean and unworthy of Robbie's love?"

"Weel, nay. Of course not. Sadly, too many women

suffer the horror of rape, e'en from their own husbands. How could one fault them for that?"

"And how could one fault a child for the same thing?"

"That's what Payton always said."

"Weel, ye obviously didnae listen. Would ye have thought me unclean if ye hadnae arrived in time at the jail and the sheriff and his men had done as they were intending?"

"Nay, but I would have killed them and that would have caused a problem or two."

He sighed and nodded. "I understand. I do. 'Tis just hard to recall it from time to time. I will try harder to do so."

"Good, because it twists up your thoughts, I think."

He laughed. "Aye, it does."

"So when would ye like to be married? In the spring?"

"Nay, that is too long to wait. Soon. I want ye to be the lady here as soon as possible." He slid his hands down to caress her buttocks.

"I dinnae need anything fancy so whene'er ye choose is fine with me. Maybe before all the flowers are gone though. I think a wee basket of petals to throw about would please Margaret."

"I was thinking we would wed as soon as I can get a priest here."

She grinned. "Then find your priest. I will be ready."

He kissed her and began to make love to her. Slow and languid, he dragged out every caress and kiss to savor the pleasure. When they finally found release as one, he held her close as she fell asleep. Once he was sure she was sound asleep he slipped out of bed and donned his plaid. He intended to get the vows said as soon as possible and for that he needed someone to fetch him a priest.

Once in the room that Simon and Uven shared, he

nudged Simon awake, knowing without looking that Uven had already woken up and was watching him. The man had that ability to sense when someone approached. If he had been a threat he would already be bleeding out on the floor.

"I need a priest as soon as one can be found," he told Simon.

"So ye finally came to your senses," Simon said, and yawned widely.

"Aye, though it was a long road and I said stupid things. Fortunately, she is a forgiving lass and a lot smarter about such things than I am. And I think she kens me better than I do myself. But I dinnae want to wait long in case she comes to her senses." He glared at Uven who just laughed.

"So ye wish us to be up early and go search out a priest?"

"Aye."

"She is happy enough with such a hurried wedding?" asked Uven.

"She said aye."

"Might I ask just what made ye so slow? I ken ye think about things too much but nae sure that explains it all."

Callum sighed and dragged his hand through his hair. "It was stupid and something Payton often lectured me on. I kenned it the moment I asked her to marry me and my innards froze in fear she would say nay. I ne'er fully accepted his lesson that I am nae to blame."

"Ah. That whole 'unclean' problem. Fool."

"Weel, she didnae call me that but I think she thought me a fool." He grinned. "Then asked me a couple of questions concerning Laurel and what might have been her if I was not in time and something just fell into place for me. Nae sure what it was and why it didnae work with Payton, but there it is."

"Probably because Payton didnae have someone ye kenned that he could point to and ask ye if ye thought them unclean. Aye, there were the other lads, but too close, too much like ye were. Who kens. Things like that are hard to understand and what fixes them even harder. But glad ye finally came to your senses. It would have been bad if ye had lost her."

Callum stood up. "Aye, there is nay doubting that. So I will see ye two when ye return with a priest, aye?"

"Aye. Might be a day or two or e'en longer. If we cannae get one close at hand I ken where to find one."

"Thank ye. Best get back to bed in case she wakes and wonders where I have run off to."

Uven watched Callum leave and looked at Simon. "I had wondered if he still had that old fear but it isnae something ye can ask him about verra often."

"Nay. Ye dinnae wish to bring up old, sad memories either. Then there's how cocky and strong he is and ye forget there might still be scars on his heart. Weel, except for that anger that can show at times."

"True. Weel, 'tis just ye and I left, old mon."

"I am nae about to run out and get wed just because Callum and Robbie feel the urge. I have a lot of living yet to do. A lot of lassies yet to enjoy."

"Certainly and I am sure they are all lined up eagerly waiting for ye to come and enjoy them."

Simon cursed and tossed his pillow at Uven.

Callum slipped back into bed and tugged Bethoc into his arms. She settled herself against his chest and he smiled. This was what he wanted. He could not believe he had been such a fool as to not see it clearly.

He felt an odd lightness in his chest. Then he realized it was because he had recognized and tossed aside an old fear. He had finally accepted that what had been done to him when he was a child had not been his fault, had never been his fault. Most of the time he had believed he had ceased thinking that but, facing Bethoc, opening his heart to her, had shown him that he had just buried it deep, not gotten rid of it. Some part of him had still clung to that useless guilt and shame.

"Callum?"

"What, love?"

"Why are your feet cold?"

"Ah, I went to see Simon and Uven to be sure they left early to find us a priest."

She sleepily kissed his chest, snuggled closer, and went back to sleep. Callum smiled and closed his eyes. He wondered if his nightmares were gone too, and had a feeling they would not return. After all, he could reach for Bethoc now and he knew she would always be there.

Epilogue

One year later

Payton stood next to Callum as they watched Robbie and Laurel arrive. "Robbie looks happy."

"Oh, aye, he is. As happy as a pig in mud, he says. He has a fine wife, a fine son, and three foster children who would do any mon proud," answered Callum.

"And now ye are a settled wedded mon."

Callum grinned. "Aye. Have a son, too."

"And five foster children, one of them a hellion of a little girl as a sister by law."

"More fool me for thinking she would calm just because she can talk so well now."

Payton laughed. "Aye, that one will ne'er calm. Brett should be along soon. They were almost ready to leave when we left their home. Ah, let us see what Robbie has produced."

When Robbie introduced Laurel to Payton, she hugged him hard and kissed his cheek. She stepped back and held his hands in hers. "Thank ye, Sir Payton, for raising up such a fine mon," she said.

"Ye did notice that he is a stubborn fellow, didnae

ye?" Payton said, but Callum could see that the man was both pleased and embarrassed by her thanks.

"'Tis hard not to," she said, and laughed.

"My son, Quentin," Robbie said, and tickled the small child's neck as he showed him to Payton. "Just old enough to bring him out on such a journey."

"A fine lad. He will make a fine playmate for your son one day, Callum."

"Aye, that he will. Go on in, Robbie. Bethoc has been eager to see Laurel."

The moment Robbie and his family went inside, Payton said, "That is a verra beautiful woman. Must admit, at first I wondered how our Robbie got her and then I saw how well they suited each other."

"Aye," Callum answered as he and Payton made their way inside. "He decided he would try for her and ye ken how stubborn he can be. He also obviously has the patience of a saint. But, it worked for him. I think they will move back into her house in a year as Colin will be eighteen then and mon enough to hold the house."

Once inside, Callum found himself swept up in the crowd of visitors. Then Brett arrived and he watched Payton and Brett fall into a deep discussion. The brothers did not see each other as often as they probably would have liked. Callum then went and joined his friends.

"So, the family gathers," said Uven.

"Aye, new babies often bring them out. 'Tis a good excuse to make a journey and be away from what work ye need to do for a while." Callum frowned as he watched Bethoc hitch their small son on her hip while talking to Laurel and Kirstie. "I should probably see if she wants to be relieved of the bairn."

"She will tell ye if she does," said Simon and he suddenly looked around. "Where is Margaret? She should be here. So much company is just what she likes."

"Aye, ye are right."

As Callum started to go back outside he realized his two friends were following. Just as he stepped outside he caught sight of Margaret, or what looked like it might be her. It was the muddiest child he had ever seen and it did not look as if much of the mud was being removed by the water she was trying to wash it away with.

"Margaret?" he asked as he walked up and she looked at him with wide green eyes. "What happened?"

"I was trying to get a puppy out of the mud but I fell in."

"I dinnae think this water is helping much, sweetling. Mayhap we should just go in and get ye into a new gown."

"Bethoc will be mad."

"Ye didnae do it on purpose, did ye?"

"Nay. I fell and the puppy ran out and got away."

"Then let us go and get this gown off and wash ye up."

Keeping the child a safe distance from the rest of them, he took her inside. He then found himself holding his small son as Bethoc hurried Margaret up the stairs to change. He looked down at the boy who stared up at him solemnly with wide green eyes. Looking around he noticed his friends had quietly fled. Laurel walked up to him and smiled.

"Margaret is still getting into trouble, I see," said Laurel.

"I think trouble and Margaret will always be close friends. Happy, are ye, Laurel?"

"Verra happy. I have what I tried to get the first time I got married and found only misery. I have scars and so does he but we seem to smooth them away when we are together. That isnae such a bad thing."

"Nay, it certainly isnae. I am pleased ye saw the worth in our Robbie."

"Ye miss him, dinnae ye."

"Aye, but I wouldnae wish him anywhere but where he is. Miss him though I do, I also wish him to be happy." He smiled when she blushed. "And, may I say, that was a verra kind thing ye said to Payton."

"T'was the simple truth." She placed a hand on his arm. "And are ye happy, Callum?"

"Oh, aye, verra happy. Were ye worried about that?"

"Some, aye." She stroked the child's head. "She gave ye a fine son."

"Aye, Bhaltair was a nice surprise. I am glad we didnae ken he was on his way ere I asked her to wed me though."

For a while they talked about the house Robbie still worked on and the harvest, what was being planted this year, and even the bairns. Then she was called away to tend to her son who was clearly hungry. Callum walked outside with his son and ran into Brett and Payton. He reluctantly allowed Brett to hold the boy for a while.

"A grandson, Brett. Best get your walking stick," teased Payton.

"Ye had more to do with raising the father than I did with raising the mother so 'tis ye who best get the walking stick."

Payton laughed and then studied Callum for a minute. "Ye are doing fine. There is a lightness about ye that wasnae there before."

Glancing at Brett, Callum sighed. "I faced a truth that I hadn't faced before nay matter what ye said. I buried it instead. Buried it deep. Then I asked Bethoc to wed me and when she said aye, I kenned it was there for it left me. She accepted me."

"Ah, I see. Ye always were the one who didnae listen.

I thought ye had but I can see what ye mean. There was a darkness, aye? And now ye are rid of it. Good. Ye were ne'er to blame."

"I ken it. Now." He saw Bethoc looking for him and waved her over.

"A fine son, Daughter," said Brett, and grinned. "I suppose I should tell Triona that she was right although I hate to."

Bethoc laughed and took her son when he lunged toward her. She kissed her father on the cheek, hooked her arm through his, and walked back to the keep. Callum watched the two of them talk and was glad that she and Brett were beginning to grow together.

"So ye are all settled and the darkness gone?" asked Payton, once they were alone.

"I think so. I havenae had my temper tested yet though. Not a single nightmare since I married though. They try but, as Bethoc told me, I just grab on to her and hold her and they fade."

"I am glad ye and Robbie found such good women. Ones who could heal those last scars. And nay, I am nae fool enough to think they are all gone and gone forever, but growing distant is good. Keep holding on, Callum."

It was late by the time Callum found himself tucked up in bed with his wife. He held her close as she grew sleepy and smiled as he thought of what Payton had said. He kissed the top of Bethoc's head, rubbing his nose in her sweet-smelling hair, and smiled again. *Keep holding on,* Payton had said. He had no intention of letting go.

Books by Bestselling Author
Fern Michaels

___ **The Jury**	0-8217-7878-1	$6.99US/$9.99CAN
___ **Sweet Revenge**	0-8217-7879-X	$6.99US/$9.99CAN
___ **Lethal Justice**	0-8217-7880-3	$6.99US/$9.99CAN
___ **Free Fall**	0-8217-7881-1	$6.99US/$9.99CAN
___ **Fool Me Once**	0-8217-8071-9	$7.99US/$10.99CAN
___ **Vegas Rich**	0-8217-8112-X	$7.99US/$10.99CAN
___ **Hide and Seek**	1-4201-0184-6	$6.99US/$9.99CAN
___ **Hokus Pokus**	1-4201-0185-4	$6.99US/$9.99CAN
___ **Fast Track**	1-4201-0186-2	$6.99US/$9.99CAN
___ **Collateral Damage**	1-4201-0187-0	$6.99US/$9.99CAN
___ **Final Justice**	1-4201-0188-9	$6.99US/$9.99CAN
___ **Up Close and Personal**	0-8217-7956-7	$7.99US/$9.99CAN
___ **Under the Radar**	1-4201-0683-X	$6.99US/$9.99CAN
___ **Razor Sharp**	1-4201-0684-8	$7.99US/$10.99CAN
___ **Yesterday**	1-4201-1494-8	$5.99US/$6.99CAN
___ **Vanishing Act**	1-4201-0685-6	$7.99US/$10.99CAN
___ **Sara's Song**	1-4201-1493-X	$5.99US/$6.99CAN
___ **Deadly Deals**	1-4201-0686-4	$7.99US/$10.99CAN
___ **Game Over**	1-4201-0687-2	$7.99US/$10.99CAN
___ **Sins of Omission**	1-4201-1153-1	$7.99US/$10.99CAN
___ **Sins of the Flesh**	1-4201-1154-X	$7.99US/$10.99CAN
___ **Cross Roads**	1-4201-1192-2	$7.99US/$10.99CAN

Available Wherever Books Are Sold!
Check out our website at www.kensingtonbooks.com

More by Bestselling Author
Hannah Howell